DEAD LAWYER ON AISLE 11

JOHN ELLSWORTH

COPYRIGHT

1

Linda was married to a husband with a roving eye. But their children kept him centered at home. Then the kids went away to college. She sensed him becoming restless. No matter what she tried, he was uneasy and arriving home after work later and later.

Then her mother moved into Linda's townhouse—dementia. Why move her into your own home? There was no more insurance left.

The husband hated the new setup; he hated having his mother-in-law around upsetting their lives. He wouldn't ever admit that, but Linda knew.

Dementia took over every corner of the townhouse. Six months inched past. Long, long days; longer nights. The mother went for her semi-annual physical with her gerontologist. Perfect physical health. Which Linda's husband, Congressman Peter Chaisson, took as his cue for renting a townhouse in Georgetown and leaving Linda and her mother in Bethesda. Caring for mom now fell to Linda alone. Though Linda was sure dementia couldn't get any worse, it did. Her mother cried for hours. She shattered the TV with a TV tray. She turned on all the stove burners and branded her hand. She lost her uppers down the garbage disposal, which Linda didn't know until the next time she ran it and teeth came whirring out. Linda was exhausted, but she didn't waver.

Linda learned that her husband had taken up with his administrative assistant. He even moved her into his townhouse. Linda was heart-broken and dispirited. She went numbly through her days with no one to talk to except mom. Having their two children away at college added to her feelings of abandonment.

Dementia wasn't pretty. There were wet and soiled sheets and blan-kets to change—the washer/dryer thrummed day and night. Then there were medications to administer—medications the fifty-seven-year-old woman detested and fought off with flailing arms and curse words Linda had never heard from the gentlewoman who'd raised her.

Nighttimes posed the most thorny problem. Mom was a runner: she'd wait until Linda wasn't looking, pass quietly out the front door of the house, and run down the street, stripping the clothes from her body and casting them aside as she bounded along, exhilarated at breaking free. The police were routinely called to help locate her. Linda finally hired a company to install a siren on the outside doors. It played *Take Me Out to the Ballgame* whenever a door opened without the three-digit keypad code. At least now Linda could catch a little sleep without worrying her mom was quietly getting out to streak.

As for herself, Linda was thirty-eight with finely-chiseled cheekbones and nose, pale skin, and violet eyes—men got weak in the knees on meeting her for the first time. She was average height, tending toward a plumpness from added pounds now that Peter was gone and she constantly ate to medicate her feelings. No health club, no yoga, no Pilates, no Zumba could help her drop the weight. Nor did she have the kind of time a regular exercise routine required. A saving grace: supported by bras from the Bra Whisperer, her figure still attracted male eyes.

She learned everything there was to know about loneliness. Lips that forgot how to kiss—except for her son who got an air kiss when he took out the garbage while home on school break. Aching for love, real love. She remembered from long ago the gentle words of a man next to her in bed when she would no longer be scared of anything in the world because he had just helped her believe in herself again. A real man.

But that didn't happen. Her dance card was already full up with mom. She had no time for dating, no time to devote to a real relationship with a man. Realizing that one day after mom was gone Linda might look around and find she no longer attracted the kind of men she liked, there would come times—mostly at night—when she would get panicky at watching her life being poured out on a mental illness that didn't care. There were times when her mother knew her —maybe once a week. But Linda knew the ravages of time and stress would take their toll and then what? She was afraid to ask.

Still, in her mind, she refused to believe she wouldn't love again. Some part of her remained hopeful. Not much, but a tiny spark.

As time crept by and she began talking to herself in the bathroom mirror, Linda realized she had developed her own kind of crazy. Try as she might, she couldn't blame her husband for leaving. Sure, it made her beat herself up when Linda saw younger women in their svelte twenties wooing away men like Congressman Chaisson. But— despite what her friend Harriet Stoner told her—she didn't blame the man. Young women excited men her husband's age. Those men were watching their own lamps dimming out. "That's part of your problem," chided Harriet. "You're too damn forgiving. That rat bastard deserves to have his weenie snipped off."

"Please, Harriet," Linda pleaded with her friend, "I hate that kind of talk. Maybe he does deserve it, and maybe he doesn't. Either way, I don't think like that, and I'm not about to become hateful and bitter now. If I allow myself to become that way, he's won. And I won't let him win. I'm going to become my better self each day. It will be his loss."

Linda optimistically paid her bar association dues semi-annually. Someday—when mom was gone—maybe she would return to the practice of law. That was her ace in the hole. But as long as the old woman was alive, Linda was prevented from joining a law firm. Night after night with her calculator and pencil she just couldn't make the money work. Nursing homes wanted as much as she might earn at a law firm. So she put it out of her mind as best she could.

One day, Linda's mother pulled the phone out of the kitchen wall. Linda called the phone company. They came, and the man quickly fixed it right back up. When leaving, he paused. He had noticed no phone books. Would Linda like the Yellow Pages from his van? Sure, she said, so the man went out and returned with a five-pound book of Yellow Pages—advertisements. Mom was napping. Linda made a cup of tea and began leafing aimlessly through the book. Which was when she saw it: ADVERTISE HERE. She turned the page. Legal ads appeared no matter how far back she turned pages. Lawyers every-where: 88 pages of them. Which meant the ads must be working. Without giving it much thought, Linda dialed the 1-800 number and said she wanted to buy a Yellow Page ad. The salesman came out that very afternoon. The cheapest display advertisement they offered was a listing under CRIMINAL LAW. The first month was free.

Linda needed something hopeful in her life. She signed up.

Two months later, the phone rang. A man with a heavy accent had been arrested for drunk driving and was looking for a lawyer. Linda nearly told him he had a wrong number, then she realized: he was calling her. The Yellow Pages must have come out!

So Linda did something she never in her wildest dreams thought she would ever see herself doing: she started a law practice on her dining room table. The dining table law office was open for calls between nine and eleven. During this time, Visiting Nurses collected up mom and took her outside the home for a couple of hours.

Still, the washer and dryer thrummed on, but now Linda would sometimes remember with a start that she hadn't heard the dryer buzz. Engrossed in a shoplifting case, she had missed the machine's demand for love.

Two years flew past. Linda was divorced from Congressman Peter Chaisson. Let him get to know the misery of marrying a woman twenty-years his junior; she had finally decided. Because those romances seldom end well, especially when the young wife surfaces for air and begins looking around at younger men.

Linda even had a man in her life. A police officer named Harry Burrows had asked her to coffee after she had destroyed him on the witness stand. She thought that admirable of him and agreed to go once the case concluded. They sipped coffee and talked. Harry had contacts all over town. He was forty-six and knew all of the prosecutors and even knew the U.S. Attorney, Niles Boudreaux.

One day, Harry was talking across the desk with Niles at the U.S. Attorney's office in Washington, D.C. Niles was complaining that he forever needed experienced help to prosecute an ever-enlarging caseload now that terrorism cases required a third of his staff on those alone. Harry got him to promise to call Linda. "At least interview her. She's a terrific lawyer, and it would be a personal favor to me."

It was on a Friday morning at nine-thirty when Linda received a call from a man whose name she recognized. At first, she held the phone away from her ear and stared at it in disbelief. Then she replaced it and listened. Niles Boudreaux said her friend, Sergeant Harry Burrows, had given him Linda's number. Linda held her breath and asked how she could help him.

"I'm looking for a prosecutor," Boudreaux said. "Are you working now?"

"A little," Linda said. "I'm working from home. You see, Mr. Boudreaux, I'm divorced, and my mother requires constant care for her health problems. My situation keeps me pretty much housebound."

"Sorry to hear that. I've heard great things about you from Harry Burrows. Let me think. You know what? I believe we have a rider on our insurance policy that covers family members who need full-time care. Maybe it would cover a nursing home. Would that work?"

"That would be fantastic." She kept her voice even to keep from shouting how interested she immediately was.

"I'll get our civil division to check the coverage. If it covers would you be interested in an interview? I can't promise anything."

"Yes."

"Good, because Harry tells me you're the owner of a great mind and a great work ethic."

"I don't know about all that. But I did graduate first in my class at law school. I outworked everybody back then."

"First in your class? Would you send a résumé?"

"Of course I will. Is this afternoon okay?"

"Sure. Tell you what. Be here at one. Bring your résumé; we'll order sandwiches and eat at my desk while we talk. Does that work for you?"

"It does."

"See you then, Ms. Chaisson,"

"Linda is fine."

"Okay, Linda. See you at one o'clock, my office."

Harry came off duty at noon. He took a shower and changed clothes at Linda's. He now had two clothing drawers of his own and a small third of the only closet. But it was enough.

Linda told him about the call from Niles Boudreaux. Harry seemed pleased enough—but not as she had anticipated.

"I thought you'd be jumping up and down like me," she said. "I can't thank you enough!"

"Let me give you the straight scoop, Linda. These are the most powerful guys in Washington. The Speaker of the House isn't the most powerful. The Senate Majority Leader isn't the most powerful. Not even the president is the most powerful—though he's close. The real power belongs to the U.S. Attorney because this guy can put any of those guys in prison if he decides. He has the FBI, the DEA, the ATF, the Metro Police—he can get anything on anyone if he wants. So I want you to be careful there if you take the job I know he's going to offer you."

"Be careful how?"

"Power corrupts. I don't want the job or the men in the office to change you."

A tiny red stoplight went off in her head.

"Men change me? How would they do that?"

"Oh, forget I said it. It's probably my imagination running away with me."

"No, seriously, how would men corrupt me?"

He stopped lacing his navy belt through his clean khakis. He looked at her for several long seconds.

"You're a beautiful woman."

"I'm old, Harry! O-L-D!"

"You don't look old. You look young. These guys are going to take to you. Trust me on this. Now forget I even mentioned it."

She laughed. "You're very flattering, but you're also off your rocker." She would have said more, said that men were beginning not to notice her, but she didn't.

"I'm sorry I even mentioned it."

A half-hour later she was being shown into Niles Boudreaux's office.

2

Every killing season, Niles Boudreaux hunted deer along the Kaibab Plateau in northern Arizona. From the age of eight until the day he left for Columbia University he never missed his kill.

The hunting came naturally, passed down from father to son. His father was a lineman with Arizona Public Service and reserved two weeks off every deer season to get his buck. His first week, he took young Niles to their cabin out in the Kaibab National Forest, and they hunted together every day, all day. Niles became immune to his initial shock at the death of innocent animals. By his early teens, he was every bit as much the hunter when the Autumn came, and the aspen went yellow, and the deer disappeared on the first day of the season. He and Kenny—his father—swaddled themselves in camo fatigues and hats and slathered camo paint on their faces and began the search for droppings and tracks. It was on; by his middle-teens Niles was bagging large animals without a pang of guilt at the magnificence some would say was being destroyed in the killing. Kenny called his gun "The meat-gittin gun," and he called Niles' gun, "Sudden death." When the meat-getter and sudden death set out on a crisp autumn day they were of one mind: kill, kill, kill.

As a young man at Harvard Law, hunting seasons on the Plateau passed him by. School was his pursuit. So he studied and progressed and torturously stayed in the top three of his law school class, receiving an offer from the U.S. Attorney's office in Washington, D.C., his final semester. He accepted. He arrived in D.C. on a sweltering July first, ready to join the other neophytes in the third-floor library where every day they would prepare for the bar exam and plan weekend parties.

Every last one of the eleven bar candidates passed the exam on the first try. Niles was sworn in with the others and then found himself assigned to Counterterrorism. It fit him like a glove, his first assignment. He excelled among excellence (the others were that), and promotions and eye-catching salaries reflected his place in the USAO.

On Niles' thirtieth birthday, Kenny died. That autumn, Niles' Uncle Quentin phoned him from Kingman to invite him to hunt deer. Niles jumped right in; it was an honorary hunt in his father's name, as Niles saw it, and there was almost a spiritual overtone now to killing, gutting, and skinning bucks. As always, Niles felt nothing upon bringing down a beautiful animal. Killing had become easy.

He continued with the yearly hunt for twenty years.

Then it all changed. Niles' boss promoted him to senior assistant united states attorney, just one step below the U.S. Attorney himself. The new position saw him flooded with administrative tasks as well as attorney assignments prosecuting terrorists. He married his law school sweetheart along the way and fathered three smart kids. But his days and nights were spent at the office. His wife grew bored. Soon she was meeting the husband of her best friend, after the friend died, for coffee, then drinks, then dinners. One night she found herself in bed—and in love—with the widower. Two weeks later she walked out on twenty-five years of her life and moved to Phoenix with her new man. Niles was devastated—and he wasn't. There had been very little to keep them together after the kids were grown and gone;

in a way, he was even relieved. Now he could do his job without guilt. With his new freedom came greater effort at work and more extended hours and he excelled in his career.

But he was short-staffed. The U.S. Attorney's Counterterrorism team was always understaffed, and Niles forever had to cover some last-minute court appearance because a team member was called away on a more pressing case.

Then Harry Burrows stayed late with him one evening as they worked up a case. Niles mentioned how short-handed his team was.

Harry mentioned his girlfriend, Linda Chaisson.

The next day, at one p.m., she was shown into his office. Her beautiful, white smile made his heart melt. He thought her magnificent. Even the eyes—he had seen the eyes of many female deer up close. Her eyes—wide, trusting—reminded him of that natural beauty. She was hired even before she sat down. What was left was to go through the motions before he could tell her she had the job.

So they talked.

SHE WENT to work at the United States Attorney's Office the following Monday. Handpicked by Boudreaux to join his Counterterrorism team, Linda became accustomed to seeing her boss on a daily basis at least once, maybe more. There were lunches in the office lunchroom; later on, there were lunches at his desk, just the two of them. Then there were lunches away from the office. She told Harry about the rest of it, but she didn't tell him about the lunches away from the office. She'd always thought the means were part of the job, but she knew Harry wouldn't understand. Nor would he let it slide. He'd have an opinion, maybe even try to circumscribe her freedom at work. Which put her in a quandary: why was she keeping a secret from the man who'd asked her to marry? Then it came to her. She would accept his proposal, and that would put him at ease. He would know that she belonged to him and no one else. So they got a license and rings and had a civil ceremony.

It worked, too. For six months. Then ever so slowly a new jealousy reared its head.

"Where did you have lunch today?"

"With some friends."

"With Boudreaux?"

"Honestly, I don't know why you would even ask. You know I belong to you and you alone, Harry."

"Tell me this one time, and I won't ask again. Was it Boudreaux?"

"Yes."

"I knew it! All right, I'm asking as your husband not to go out to lunch with him again. Eat at the office, please. And don't stay late with him. That kind of stuff rips my heart out."

"All right!"

"I'm asking you—no, I'm telling you. No wife of mine is going out to lunch with another man. It just isn't gonna be that way, Linda."

Linda's small deceit kept on for another six months. One night after too much wine, she made the mistake of telling him—confiding, after love-making—that she'd kept on lunching alone with Boudreaux. It was always to discuss work, she promised. It was only a block from the office. He'd never been inappropriate with her—all true. So, she felt innocent and safe in telling Harry.

She couldn't have been more wrong. Harry straddled her in their bed and forced his pillow down onto her face.

"Do you hear me under there? No more lunches! No more Boudreaux! I want you to work somewhere else!"

Then he withdrew the pillow, and she reached up and slapped him. He backhanded her. As it always must, her love died then and there.

She moved him out of her house the next day—setting all his things outside in the driveway while he was at work, and filing for divorce and the restraining order that would keep him at a distance.

Harry, the police officer, knew better than to violate the restraining order. He stayed away. But that didn't stop him from sending flowers. Roses, to be sure. And the cards: Hallmark's most gushy and most expensive. Her heart melted, and she let him back into the house. But she didn't dismiss the divorce case.

Two weeks later it happened again. Harry figured his probationary period had shown her how much he had changed. But he hadn't. When she admitted she and Boudreaux were working closely together on several cases, Harry lost it. This time it was no backhand; he doubled up his fist and hit her squarely in the jaw. Teeth cracked, and the jaw got huge. She went to the ER.

"Are you safe at home?" the ER doctor pleasantly asked.

"I will be," Linda said.

She was finished.

Harry moved his things back to his apartment while Linda was away at the ER. If he hadn't, he knew he would come home the next day after work and again find everything in the driveway.

But he didn't give up.

Harry continued to obsess over Linda. He tried flowers again. They were refused. He tried long letters to her. They were returned unopened. He called her cell and left long messages full of the words that had worked before with her. They were erased without listening. She didn't respond. The divorce became final. She was done with him.

He got counseling. He went twice and then quit. No one could convince him it was over. He never referred to Linda as his ex-wife; she was and always would be his wife. He was carrying a torch, and professional counselors couldn't get him to let go.

"Your obsession rewards you how, Harry?"

"Makes me feel in touch with her."

"But you aren't in touch with her. Are you?"

"Not really."

"Not really? Or not at all."

"I'm just not ready to give her up."

He was obsessed, and it kept them connected—in his mind.

And it gave him hope.

3

For Niles and Linda, it was only natural. They were divorced but looking—Niles thought they were looking, anyway. They had the office and the prosecution cases in common. Kids were not an issue—Linda's had graduated and were off in the world. He was attractive, but even more, he was engaging and charming. She didn't rush right in, however; the arms-length courtship went on for months. Then she let down her guard.

It happened late one night at the office retreat in New York. After too much wine, Linda found herself in bed with her boss. Then they made love, and she was basking in the afterglow, propped up against the headboard while the wine made the room spin. She was rocked back to the real world when she heard him repeat himself, heard him ask her again if she was ready to enter into a committed relationship. She sucked in her breath and shut her eyes. Was it just a bad dream? Was it Harry all over again—the need to own her after she was finally free of kids, sick mother, and obsessive husband? Had he listened to nothing she had shared with him? But he continued laying out his plans for her.

Linda heard him out, then giggled. From a wine-fog, she watched

Niles throw himself at her. She laughed, propped up against the headboard of the Hilton Hotel bed when Niles confessed he was in love with her, that he wanted her to marry him. He even went so far as to say he wanted to stepfather her children. Stepfather my grown children? She thought. It sounded preposterous, even half-drunk. Despite knowing better—the wine had removed all inhibition—Linda laughed long and hard. Niles slumped back against his pillow. He turned his head away from her. She didn't notice, shocked as she was by his confession of love: he had just proposed.

"That's what I call premature ejaculation," she joked through the wine. "The words just came pouring out when no one expected."

"Not funny, Linda." His voice was small and distant. He had withdrawn.

She heard him talking to himself when he went into the bathroom minutes later and shut the door. She couldn't make it out, but it was intense, and it sounded like immense anger shouted into a wadded towel.

She knocked on the bathroom door and said softly, "Niles, please come out. I'm sorry."

"Just get dressed and leave, please."

"No, I want to tell you I'm sorry. I wouldn't hurt you for anything."

The door opened. He stood there and looked at her quizzically. "You wouldn't?"

"Of course not." She looped an arm around his neck and pulled him closer, keeping her lips pressed against his.

"It's okay," he said. "It was stupid for me to go there. I just misread everything. I thought we had something special."

She pulled back and turned to dress. The outing was way too intense. She was going home.

"Niles, you know there's no special for me. It's all a big game, all this grunting, and rutting we do. After Harry, I can't go there with you. Not yet anyway."

"Not yet? I can still hope?"

"It's way, way too soon for me to get married again. I just need time to flit around and have fun, Niles."

It would have been all right with Linda if it had ended right there between them.

But it didn't. Niles asked her for an afternoon later that same week. Begged her. But she declined. "I don't think we're good together," she said sadly. "I think we're done."

"You think we're done?" Niles spat the words through his rage. "Just like that, you're in charge of our time together?"

"Of course I am. So are you. When one of us says it's over, it's over. You knew that going in."

"I didn't. You didn't tell me that. Instead, you whispered you loved me. You whispered you'd never been with another man like me. You whispered and cried out that I satisfied you like no other man ever. Were those all lies?"

She wasn't sure how to answer. She decided the truth was the best policy. "You're not saying you meant all those nice things you said about me, are you? Niles, that's just sex talk. It means nothing."

The rage seized him, and he shook. He had been used and tossed away. Used. It was a smothering realization, and he wished he had never met Linda. He thought about firing her but knew that would result in a massive sexual harassment lawsuit. So he—and his office —were stuck with Linda Burrows. He would have to see her and pretend with her the rest of his professional life. Or until she resigned and went elsewhere. Or until she died.

A year later a new president came into office. The U.S. Attorney's politics were all wrong so he was asked to leave. The new president appointed Niles Boudreaux U.S. Attorney. Boudreaux's first act was to call Linda into his office and request her resignation. She smiled and waggled a finger at him. "Niles, Niles. Are you serious? Don't you know this is the best job a woman can ever have? I could even be U.S. Attorney myself someday. All I have to do is outlast you. Which I'm planning to do and then some. Just let it go, Niles. We had something once for a few weeks; it was fun, then it was over. It's way back in my rearview mirror, and it should be way back behind in yours, too."

He said nothing more to her that time. He just raised his hand, indicating she should leave his office. Which she did. With a long sigh and a flounce of the curls he'd once buried his face in, she was gone. It was final this time. He was done with her.

Slowly, then, over his first several months as he saw her day after day, a plan began to form in Niles' mind. For openers, he knew Harry still carried a torch for her—a fact Harry never tried to hide at those times when Niles and Harry chatted after working on a case together. He knew Harry must harbor murderous feelings to think his Linda was seeing other men. A plan began forming in Niles' mind.

He lived with this partially-formed plan for several months. Then, out of the blue, Linda asked to see him. They met in his office just as the staff was leaving for the day. Before he had even taken his seat behind his desk, she reached out and pulled him near. "I've missed you," she whispered. The man had no resistance. She had him in the first thirty seconds they were alone. And so it began again.

But this time it ended much sooner. Harry had tracked them down in the hotel and walked in on them. He had confronted them—which Linda thought was ridiculous since they were no longer married. She waited for Niles to eject her ex from the room. But he didn't eject Harry. He capitulated, which turned Linda's stomach. He hadn't fought for her and he should have.

Linda ended it one night in his office after hours.

"I'm pregnant, Niles. You're the baby's father because I haven't been with anyone else. It's your baby."

Niles' first reaction was horror, but then his long-ago words came rushing back: "I don't care, I'm glad you're pregnant. We can become a family, Linda, don't you see it? I can support you and take care of you, so you never have to work again. Our kids will attend Redskins games with me when they're older. You and our daughters can go to DAR because I qualify. All you have to do is say 'yes' this time."

She stood up from her chair and placed her hands on her hips. Her eyes narrowed. He was going to try to use the pregnancy to reel her in. That wasn't about to happen.

"Seriously, Niles? You seriously think this changes anything for us?"

"Then—then—what do you want from me?"

"I think you should pay for the abortion, that's all. I could easily pay for it, but it's the principle. You impregnated me; you should do your part by paying. It's twenty-five-hundred dollars. Please get me a check or cash by Friday."

"And if I don't?"

"Then I'll sue you for sexual harassment. You'll be the first witness I call."

He crumpled beneath that. His hands shook, and his mouth went dry. Sexual harassment? He'd lose his appointment as U.S. Attorney if she made a case against him for sexual harassment! In fact, he'd likely never get another job—anywhere. The silk stocking firms didn't hire known sexual predators. Something about too much risk going in. His mouth moved, but nothing came out. She glared at him and then slowly shook her head. "Pathetic," she muttered.

She turned and walked backward away from him, bearing his unborn child in her belly as she turned and stomped out.

He watched her go. He was bathed in a cold sweat, the likes of which he hadn't felt since the last time she screwed him over. And now she was going to murder his child? Was she serious? Did she honestly believe he would let her murder his child?

Never.

But he would let Harry murder them both.

Harry just needed to know why.

So he screwed up his courage and called the police officer into his office for a private meeting.

"It's about your Linda," Niles told the grave police sergeant. "She's bouncing from man to man in my office. If you're trying to get back together, she's cheating on you. I can't have it, but I can't stop it because she'll sue me for sexual harassment. And here's the worst thing of all: your ex-wife is pregnant by a man here in my office. That's a huge scandal, and I can't have that. Please take care of this, Harry. Please take care of Linda and help me avoid a scandal that would even put you in a bad light at your job. Her treachery has put us all in jeopardy. I'm begging you. Put an end to it now."

Harry sat there stunned. Pregnant? His wife pregnant by another man?

That was all it took. All of the humiliation, all of the nights of sleeping alone. In a blink, Harry knew what was expected. And he would have the blessing of the most influential prosecutor in the District. The older man needed to say no more. Harry was struck down, leaving him blind with rage.

Linda was about to become everyone's memory.

4

Neither the grocery store's customers nor employees noticed the blue latex gloves worn by the man dressed as a police officer when he entered the Foggy Bottom Grocery. Neither could they describe the man, for he wore bronzer, fake eyebrows, mustache, and sideburns, a police hat, and Ray-Bans. He wore the uniform of the Washington, D.C. Metro Police Department. No one among them noticed his SUV just outside, hidden between a Toyota Tundra and a Ford F-150. He might have well been invisible when he walked up aisle 11, an unregistered .38 Police Special in his gloved hand. He seemed to study the foodstuff on the shelves as he came. His target: a fortyish woman dressed in a pink summer dress—short hemline—sandals, wearing sunglasses perched on her head. It was just after 11:30 on a Sunday morning, and she was relaxing on her weekend off from the U.S. Attorney's office. Her name was Linda Burrows.

Linda smiled as the uniformed man approached. "What are you doing here?" she asked, but then her smile turned to horror as the man swept his arm out, placing the muzzle of the gun squarely against her forehead. He squeezed the trigger, just like cops and military are taught to shoot. The ballistic round entered her head and did its work before exiting out the back of her skull. The explosion pasted brain matter and blood down a stack of Del Monte Peaches. Her knees crumpled; she fell onto her side. Her feet twitched. Just for good measure, the uniformed man fired two more rounds into the side of her head before turning and striding out of the store. He took the gun with him.

Linda Burrows hadn't drawn on anyone before being shot. In fact, she didn't even own a gun. However, if the dead could speak, she would have told the detectives exactly why the man shot her that Sunday morning in the Foggy Bottom Grocery. As an assistant U.S. Attorney, she had introduced some evil people into the federal penal system; there had been threats on her life. Later in her career, she had moved into business crimes. As a prosecutor dedicated to white collar crime cases, threats on her life would have been unexpected. Tax cheats don't usually murder the AUSA who sends them to the penitentiary to serve their eighteen months and mow fairways.

The shoppers and employees froze in place as the uniformed man walked out the front door. For several seconds after he was gone no one said a word. Then all hell broke loose with crying, sobbing, cell phones dialing 911, and managers creeping up to aisle 11 to investigate the three gunshots. Of course, they trampled through the scene of the shooting, one of them hysterically calling for a cleanup of the aisle, another, a senior manager, canceling his call, demanding that all employees leave aisle 11 so the police would have a pristine scene.

As for the uniformed man, he jogged out to his SUV, slid in on the driver's side, and proceeded to remove all traces of makeup, fake hair, and the rest of it. Then he jumped out. He worked one of the blue gloves over his rear license plate and the other over his front plate. Then he reached inside and inserted the key and turned it clockwise until the police scanner jumped to life. When the "all units" came over the speaker, directing all officers in the region to the grocery store, he checked his mirror and backed out of the parking slot. He knew he had a good three minutes before squad cars arrived. He didn't waste any time getting his car up to speed and exiting the strip mall. Gone in less than one minute. He was miles away, chewing beef jerky lifted from aisle 11 when the first police officer roared into the parking lot.

Additional police units arrived. Officers crowded through the front door, weapons drawn, spreading to search for the killer if he still lingered in the store. Finding nothing after surging throughout the store and crying out, "Clear!" they all gathered on aisle 11. EMTs came charging inside and examined the woman sprawled in aisle 11. After taking vitals and checking for breathing, they pronounced her dead. A newly arrived officer cordoned off the scene with yellow police tape. Other officers hopped to and moved the gawkers away. CSI came, and the evidence-gathering began.

But after all was said and done, Linda Burrows was no closer to avoiding the bullets than before the photographs, measurements, evidence bags, and donuts. At long last the body was placed on a gurney, beginning its trip to the M.E. for processing through autopsy and disposal.

Detectives wrote witness names and numbers into police reports. Questions and answers followed. A promise was made that police contacts would follow and in-depth statements recorded.

Near the end, the store's cleanup crew heard over the PA, "Cleanup on aisle eleven." They proceeded with mops, astringents, and waxing machines to make short shrift of the bloody floor. There was a brief discussion between the chief of cleanup and the assistant manager as to the disposal of the cans of vegetables and fruit that had been blood-spattered. In the end, the products were carted into the washing room at the rear of the store and sprayed with a water hose. They were then wheeled back out to the shelves and restocked.

While all of this was underway, the store was open to shoppers. In fact, sales took a particular bump that day of 115%, causing the produce manager to remark, "Maybe we should host a homicide every day if it's going to skyrocket sales."

A nearby assistant manager heard this and immediately ordered the speaker to spray the crookneck squash.

5

Annie and I arrived at the memorial service for Linda Burrows by taxi. Annie was my adopted daughter, just entering her teen years. Her family massacred by a madman, I had taken her in. She was a consternation to some: low verbal and socially non-existent, but a savant capable of miracles. She worked part-time at the U.S. Attorney's office, where I was working, and she profiled suspects from crime scene evidence and likely demographics. There was your miracle: she never failed us. I loved her like my own and tried to do as much with her as possible.

Annie took my hand as we entered the funeral home. Annie almost never held my hand—or anyone else's hand, for that matter. Then it occurred to me: it was her first funeral. She was frightened. I bent down to her and whispered sotto voce, "Don't worry. I promise we won't look inside the casket."

She pulled free of me. "That doesn't bother me, Michael. It's just that I hate crowds."

And it was, indeed, very crowded in the small memorial room. I could see many of Linda's—our—colleagues from the U.S. Attorney's office. In the center of the room, in front of the rows of chairs, Niles Boudreaux, the U.S. Attorney himself, an after-hours weightlifter, strutted like a buff rooster. Thick neck, handsome face, a nose once-broken—I think he mentioned college football—hands impossibly big even for his sausage body, and a shock of enough white hair to make the clouds jealous. He spoke to others and, as he did, he watched over their shoulders for the next encounter and the next. A man who worked the room like a master. I predicted he would speak to everyone in attendance before finally leaving the funeral home and climbing into his U.S. marshals-chauffeured Lincoln. Office etiquette required that we say hello, so I steered Annie in Niles' direction. We reached him just as he turned away from an FBI agent I vaguely knew.

"Michael!" he greeted me. "And you've brought Annie along. How are you, dear?"

Annie had gone on autopilot and wouldn't be speaking while we were there. Many of our staff recognized the vacuous look on her face and didn't push.

"She's speaking very little this morning," I told Boudreaux.

"My God, Mike"—people who know me well don't call me 'Mike'—"it's a terrible thing that a great prosecutor like Linda could be gunned down in a grocery store in broad daylight. Terrible thing."

"Agree," I said. "But I fear that this was anything but random. I am afraid that Linda died because she was a prosecutor with the U.S. Attorney's office. That puts everyone in the office at risk."

He reached to touch my shoulder. "Please come see me later at the office. I'm assigning this case to you."

"Linda's killer?"

"Yes, you and Annie. She's received court clearance to work?"

"She's cleared to work half-time." Obtaining judicial approval for

Annie to work at thirteen had been touch-and-go as many didn't want to see her out of school. But we were finally able to convince a forward-thinking juvenile court judge that working was more therapeutic for Annie than school would ever be. The key to our success was Ramona S. Tilling, Psy.D, who supported me in my decision to have her work rather than waste time in school staring at the floor. Which—the lack of engagement—she had done for the three previous years. Dr. Tilling educated the judge to the fact that Annie would never engage in regular classwork and master subjects like algebra, chemistry, and so forth. Her brain, said Dr. Tilling, just wasn't wired that way. Her hours were limited: she was allowed to work four hours a day, and that was it. Which was enough.

Staff at the USAO all asked me the same thing about Annie: was she autistic? The answer was a simple no. She didn't fit that profile. Dr. Tilling only told me that Annie was a low-verbal savant. I hated terms like that and tried to put them out of mind. Annie was just Annie, at least to me.

So far, Annie had been a success at the U.S. Attorney's office. More and more staff and FBI dropped by her cubicle to run things by her. And she was always happy to help because criminal profiling was about data accumulation and interpretation of data—both of which fit the schema in Annie's mind that wanted to absorb facts off the Internet and out of police reports and then make conclusions based on what she had learned.

Annie had access to all law enforcement databases. Armed with the additional facts she gleaned from the police databases, she was accommodating to anyone who asked for help. All in all, it was a good fit, Annie and the USAO. Which was therapeutic and uplifting for her, and relief for me, her adoptive father, who wanted nothing for Annie except her happiness. Whatever it took, I was up for it. Annie was my special girl, and I adored her.

So, U.S. Attorney Boudreaux told me that he was assigning the Linda Burrows case to Annie and me. That morning, I suddenly found I was a man of two minds. For my lawyer part, I'd probably use the grand jury to begin acquiring evidence and witness statements and police reports and turn these items over to Annie for her to start building a profile of the subject. I again took Annie's hand and backed away. No need: Boudreaux had already disengaged with us and was speaking to the next mourner.

We moved off from the U.S. Attorney and immediately ran into Antonia Xiang—my supervisor. She was wearing a black dress, a pearl necklace, very little makeup, and no earrings. I greeted her, and in her eyes, I could see a flash of fury over Linda. Antonia was quiet, greeting us with a nod. I knew she was having trouble keeping an emotional distance from her cases, and it was coming out as a kind of shrillness in her voice that wasn't there before. It pained me. Antonia was overwhelmed.

"Hello, Michael, good morning, Annie. Isn't this horrible? I can't stop crying. Linda and I often had lunch together. She wanted so much to transfer to my team and was about to make the switch. It's so sad."

"I couldn't agree more. I didn't know Linda very well, but she was one of us. It makes me want to wrap my hands around someone's throat and make justice happen. This is all too close to home for any of us."

"Michael, whatever in God's name would motivate someone to do this?"

I shrugged, but that raised what I had heard more than once about Linda: she was having an affair with Niles Boudreaux himself. Additionally, I'd heard from Antonia that maybe Linda was involved with another man in the office at one time. And perhaps even another. I decided I was going to ignore the suggestion Linda might have gotten around with a couple of other men. While we at the USAO put bad guys in jail, we were all human, all teeming with human foibles. Doing good didn't make us good—far from it. Our staffers might have engaged in office flings and dalliances. But we all knew better than to point fingers. We knew we were guilty of being failed saints.

I responded to Antonia's question, "What would motivate someone to shoot her? Maybe something as simple as an angry ex-husband."

"True that. Oh, God, I so need a drink. Boudreaux pulled me aside and asked if your caseload could handle this case. I told him definitely, that I'd never had the sense you were overwhelmed by the cases piled a foot deep on your desk like everyone else in the office. I encouraged him to assign you."

"Thank you. You know I'm motivated. You know I want to see someone pay for this."

At that point, we were turning and finding seats for the service as a hush had fallen over the room. I turned and saw that the funeral director had entered the room, signaling it was about to begin.

Six men sat like statues facing the lectern on the right side of the room, reminding me of a misdemeanor jury. In the foreground, the casket's shiny metal gleamed under the fluorescent light, which cast a bluish tint upon the steel that held our Linda. One by one the speakers arose from the pew on the left and took up positions behind the lectern where they recalled a loving woman, a doting mother, and an extremely competent assistant U.S. Attorney. We were the best possible audience: we were already convinced.

Niles Boudreaux came the closest to telling the real truth about Linda as he recalled her as someone who enjoyed life one-hundred-and-ten percent and, on the other hand, someone who was restless and forever searching for ways to make her world a happier one. Shorthand for saying he'd had a romance with her and we all knew it, and he knew better than to ignore it at such a solemn moment. The more Boudreaux spoke, the more I became convinced he had been in love with the woman—just the words he used, the tears, the positive feelings. When he finished, I liked Linda even more and Boudreaux even less. Why? Because he came off as a man who had feelings but also had a certain amount of pride in bedding Linda and didn't care who knew it. For men like that, they believe that it adds to their allure. For me, sitting there feeling maybe Linda had been used, I found myself suddenly disliking Boudreaux for that alone. Did I include myself in that group because I was living with a woman I hadn't married? Not at all: Verona had turned aside my marriage proposals on two occasions. I was batting zero, but at least I was batting.

Linda's group manager, a woman named Marjorie Letelle, remembered her with genuine fondness and respect. Linda's ability to woo a jury, and turn their heads away from the alternate universes created in her courtrooms by slippery defense attorneys, was touted. "She took them all on," Marjorie said in the best-intentioned sense of "took them all on," then she added, "and she prevailed. I've never seen a more tenacious prosecutor in my twenty-five years in this office." We'd all heard how Linda excelled at her job and we were all quick to give her credit for that. Marjorie was another admirer of our co-worker.

But then came Harry Burrows, Linda's ex-husband. I would hear later that Harry had insisted on speaking at Linda's memorial despite her family's resistance. Harry was a police officer, a uniform who spent his shifts behind the wheel of a D.C. Metro PD squad car with its red bars cascading down the sides. We all understood his pain over Linda's death and his bewilderment in trying to honor her that day. Their two children were in the front row of our small room, bookended by Linda's parents.

"I loved Linda with all my heart," Harry choked out, followed by a long gasp for air that flooded our ears over the sound system. For that moment, he had us all in his corner immediately. Then he held onto the lectern and stared out the back windows of our room, small rectangular blots of light just below the ceiling line.

Harry wore a worn blue suit with a tie ten-years-old knotted amateurishly at his throat. We knew that Harry knew, that morning as he dressed, that he faced an impossible task before it even started. How would he paint himself as someone who loved Linda when we all knew why she had divorced him? The police-issue crew-cut and the bullish upper body worked against him. His was a black-and-white world and Linda was lost to him across a darkness that she had never pierced once his crazies set in: Harry was a hitter.

"We had our differences," he grossly understated—remember, he had knocked teeth out of her head with his fist. "Sometimes didn't see eye-to-eye, but we always loved each other. Sometimes we argued and fought, but we always got beyond our annoyances with each other. I would have done anything in the world for Linda. I would have moved mountains for Linda. And sometimes she required me to do just that. I'm trying to be honest here. I'm trying to say it wasn't all cookies and flowers with us."

Hear, hear.

Harry then withdrew a Bible from his pocket and began reading passages he thought appropriate. My thoughts drifted as he droned on like they always do when someone reads that book to me where I haven't asked for it. I wondered at the real Harry Burrows inside the Harry Burrows at the lectern, the Harry Burrows who must have been so terribly enraged to have hurt her so. That Harry must have been capable of murder.

Which brought me up short. I realized that I had just then decided that, in investigating Linda's murder, I could do much worse than to start with Harry.

I prayed that he owned an unimpeachable alibi the day she died. "Please let it be," I prayed to all the saints in Harry's Bible. His kids had suffered enough already.

LATER, riding home with Annie, I answered her questions. But my even disposition was a ruse; deep down I was grief-stricken about Linda and my part in her life, too. Maybe part of it was because my children had lost their mother, too, and I knew what a lousy substitute mother I had been to them. I was anxious to have my partner,

Verona, hold me while I cried it out. The office would be skeleton-staffed that afternoon while we took time away to process the loss of one of us. It was a dark time, and I was not alone in my sorrow for Linda and her family. Verona's warmth and love for me had never felt so necessary in my life as just then. We all need our supporters; me as much as anyone else.

And maybe, just maybe, I was Verona's serial suitor because I wanted my kids to have a replacement mother—someone who wouldn't ever leave them. Maybe there was more than just her love that I needed.

Maybe this had something to do with Verona turning me down twice before.

6

We never saw it coming, Verona and I.

After dinner, Dania and Mikey headed for their rooms. They were my kids by their mother, Danny, who was dead. Dania said she was off to work on her homework; Mikey wanted to play a video game. As for Annie, she went to her room and settled down on her bed, her back propped against the headboard, her laptop open and her fingers flying.

When they were asleep, Verona and I crept into our bedroom and undressed. I was very weary, but I was ready for comfort sex. We climbed in bed, and Verona had me turn over, so my back was to her. She reached around and spooned me. My eyes closed and then fluttered and then closed again and I was asleep.

Several hours later, Verona sat up in bed.

"Listen," she whispered, bringing me upright in bed.

"What?"

"Listen!"

I listened and heard the sound. Someone was crying. We pulled on robes and went to investigate, checking the little kids first then pausing outside Annie's closed bedroom door.

The crying—moaning—was inside. Without asking, we entered the dark room. Verona switched on the overhead light, and we found Annie lying on her side, her face and arms bathed in sweat. She twisted back and forth in pain. A series of moans came again and again.

"Michael, call nine-one-one, please."

"You think?"

"Don't argue with me. Her face is drained of color, I feel a wicked fever on her forehead, and she's bathed in sweat. It might be an appendix; it might be something else. But we shouldn't move her, and she needs to go to the ER without delay."

I ran to my bedside table and made the call. Within just minutes we could hear a siren approaching. The EMT's—there were three of them—came clamoring through the front door while their ambulance was left running, red and blue strobe lights flashing. I pulled my head back inside and followed them to Annie's room, guiding them as we went. A woman—who we would find was a trauma nurse—went to Annie and asked her what hurt. Annie, of course, didn't answer.

"She's low-verbal," I told the woman, whose yellow hair glinted in the glare of the bedroom's overhead lights. "But I can tell you this is new. She's never done this before."

"She's your daughter?" the first man who had come through the door asked.

"She is. Adopted. I don't know that much about her history. We have a PCP, but she's only done a physical and seen her for earaches and flu. That kind of stuff."

"Please," said Verona, "let's get her to the ER."

"Let us get vitals and call the hospital, and we're on our way," said the trauma nurse, attaching a BP cuff and pulse/oximeter all at once. She poked an instrument into Annie's ear and got her temperature then asked the girl if she could roll onto her back. Annie didn't respond verbally but slowly turned onto her back. As she turned, she kept her knees drawn to her chest.

"Definitely her gut," said the nurse. "Has she eaten anything out of the ordinary?"

"Nope. Red rice and pork chops for supper, green beans. No dessert," said Verona.

The nurse nodded and spoke into her shoulder mic, evidently talking to an ER doctor on the other end. It was decided to transport Annie to the hospital and examine her there.

A gurney was unfolded, and Annie was helped on. She again kept her legs drawn up and continued moaning.

"I'm coming with you in the ambulance, sweetheart," I said to her, and our eyes briefly met. She nodded ever so slightly. I took her hand and gave it a squeeze.

"I'll get help with the younger children," Verona said. "See you soon."

They loaded her into the ambulance. I climbed aboard and sat across from her, touching her shoulder with my hand and gently massaging. She pulled a hand away from her belly and reached up and momentarily laid her hand over mine.

"It's okay, honey, I've got you now," I said. "We're going to take excellent care of you."

We were taken straight to an examination suite. Under the direction of Dr. William Patent, X-rays were taken. He returned to our suite fifteen minutes after shooting the films. His look wasn't encouraging.

"Mr. Gresham, Annie has swallowed a coin."

"Is that serious?" I asked.

"Not normally, but let me tell you the rest of it."

"Please."

"We're able to count at least six coins, and they fit the diameter of quarters. All lodged within the stomach. Ordinarily, a single coin could be expected to pass through her digestive tract harmlessly in about three days. But six coins makes for a whole different case. We've just moved from a simple case to a complex one."

"So what can be done?" I asked.

"How old is Annie?"

"She's thirteen now."

"Has she ever done this before?"

"I adopted her at age twelve," I said. "So I'm not sure of her prior history with swallowing."

"Well, for one, I'd like a psychiatric consult. A child this age shouldn't be swallowing foreign objects. That's my first inclination. Second, I'm calling in a GI doc. He's going to want to do an endoscopy to remove the coins. Like I said, one coin, no problem. We just monitor stools for three days and wait for it to pass. But six coins is a whole other ballgame."

"Annie's a savant," I said. "You need to know that."

"I see. Savants quite commonly swallow foreign objects in the mistaken belief that they're eating food. They have a tough time distinguishing. You're lucky this hasn't happened before."

"I didn't know," I said. "Nobody ever mentioned it."

"Oh yes, we see lots of savants in here who've eaten breakfasts consisting of coins, tacks, keys, and what have you. It's more common than people realize. But I'd still like the psych consult."

"Okay. We'll do whatever you recommend."

"I called the GI department on the way back here. Dr. Gendum will be here shortly."

Which happened in the next minute. Dr. Gendum was a she and very young and very professional.

"I've seen the films," she said after introductions. "I want to put her under and yank those quarters out. Six is just too risky for nature to take its course."

"All right, then," I said. "When can you do this?"

"Right now. I've called, and the suite is ready."

Annie, who had been squirming and moaning on the examination table, seemed to hear none of what was being planned for her. So I turned to her and explained her situation. She reached and squeezed my hand without saying a word.

"She's ready to go," I said to Dr. Gendum.

Verona arrived. It had probably been thirty minutes or more since we said goodbye at home. She'd called the kids' nanny, and she was with them now, freeing Verona to speed to the hospital.

The nurse in attendance removed Verona and me to a waiting room down the hall from the GI suite, and we plopped down to wait. Four a.m. straight up. Morning Joe was two hours away, so I sat back and closed my eyes. Verona snuggled up beside me and lowered my head onto her shoulder. Within minutes, I was asleep.

Then I was awake as Verona prodded me upright on the couch. Dr. Gendum was standing there smiling at us.

"You're a buck-fifty richer," she said, and she held up a small plastic bottle containing six quarters.

"Lucky us," I groaned. "She's okay?"

"She's fine. I put her into a twilight and easily removed all six coins. She's been moved into an ICU suite where we'll watch her for the next twelve hours. Then she can go home."

"What about the psych consult?"

"I understand that's been scheduled. Ask Dr. Patent about that since it's his case."

"Okay. Thank you from the bottom of my heart," I heard myself say as I was suddenly overcome with emotion as tears washed into my eyes. "God, what a scare."

"The procedure went without a hitch. Annie's going to make a complete and speedy recovery."

"Thank God. And thank you, Doctor Gendum."

"I'm off now. They'll page me if anything develops. But I'm guessing you won't see me again. Not unless it happens again, that is."

She left us there after telling us a nurse would take us to Annie's ICU suite any minute.

The psychiatrist popped her head into Annie's ICU suite just after eight o'clock that morning. We smiled at her, and she came right inside. For her part, Annie was sitting up in bed watching—or at least staring at—the TV.

"I'm Greta Washoe," said a youngish, white-coated woman with a stethoscope coiled in the pocket of her lab coat and a long ponytail pulled back and held in place by a silver clasp. She wore clear plastic eyeglasses which kept slipping down on her nose, requiring constant attention as the doctor pushed them back up on her nose again and again. But she was smiling and warm and kept her eyes on Annie as she sauntered up to her bed. She bent down, catching Annie's eye. "Hey," she said gently. "How we doing this morning?"

Annie appeared not to hear, keeping her eyes on the TV.

"Are you Annie?"

No recognition.

"I'm Greta, and I'm here to see if you need anything. Are they treating you okay in here?"

Annie turned her head ever so slightly. I knew from experience that this meant that something had broken through her bubble.

Annie gathered herself to speak. "I'm okay."

"Do you know what happened?" Dr. Washoe asked.

"Sick."

"Do you know why you got sick?"

"No."

"Well, you ate some money. Did you know that?"

"No."

"Do you know what money looks like?"

"No."

"Do you—"

"Michael! Who is she?"

I stepped forward. "This is Doctor Washoe. She wants to help you. She wants to help you not come here again. Is that what you want, too?"

"Take me to my room, Michael."

"I can take you home around noon today."

"Noon."

Dr. Washoe turned to me. "Can we speak outside?"

"I'll stay here with Annie," said Verona.

The doctor and I trekked into the hallway, where she leaned against the wall and nodded.

"I understand she's been diagnosed as a savant. I have no reason to doubt that. Now, did you know, Michael, that savants often cannot distinguish between food and non-food items?"

"I don't remember hearing that."

"It's very common. And very dangerous. So here's what I propose. When you get her home, talk to her about what happened. And see if you can get her to agree that nothing goes into her mouth unless it's handed to her by you or your wife."

"I don't know if she'll agree."

"She might not—at first. But it's all we have. Otherwise, she might ingest something that can make her extremely sick, require major surgery, or maybe even kill her."

"I understand," I said and I did understand.

"Getting her to commit to eating only what you or your wife gives her is huge."

"I think I can do it. I don't think she'll understand the why of it, but I think I can get her to agree."

"Okay. And if I can help, please call me. Here's my card."

She pulled a card out of her lab coat and wrote on the back. "My cell number too. Call me if I can help, Michael. She's a beautiful child, and I'd hate to see anything bad happen."

"Oh, she's my special girl. I'll do everything I can."

"By the way, have you figured out why she talks to you and not others?"

"I think it had something to do with her feeling my pain from the loss of my wife. She was feeling the same thing from the loss of her father. That's as close as I get to understanding."

"Savants can be almost prescient about those things. Well, whatever it is, keep doing what you're doing."

"All I'm doing is standing in there with her."

"That's a lot. Savants can be a huge challenge. Many of them wind up in special needs facilities."

"I know that. But Annie won't. Not while I'm around."

She smiled. "I know that. If you want to talk more about her and how to help, call me."

She held the card out to me. "Thanks," I said

I pocketed her card and watched her walk off down the hall.

Six hours later, we were taking Annie home, where I had my first discussion with her about taking food only from Verona or me. She said she would agree, that she understood. I wasn't convinced she understood. And I wasn't convinced she would follow the rule.

With Annie, you just never knew. Which made me commit to redouble my efforts to protect her.

She deserved no less.

7

Niles Boudreaux's office was everything you'd expect a U.S. Attorney to have. Expansive desk, a dozen or more framed diplomas, news articles, and certificates of belonging and CLE courses he had taken—or even taught. The glory wall. Then there was the credenza behind him, resplendent in its photographs of family and friends, prize fish from his many fishing expeditions to the Sea of Cortez, as well as all manner of tchotchkes. A sailfish and a javelina's head adorned the eastern wall, and heavy curtains that could be drawn and block out listening devices were open on the west side, flooding the room with good sunlight and views of the government buildings beyond.

When I entered, Niles didn't look up from a file, saying only, "Michael. Grab a chair and give me two ticks."

I didn't respond but selected the chair on my right and pulled it closer to his desk. We were alone, and the only sound was the tick-tock of the grandfather clock, arranged across the front of his desk in the form of a miniature Capitol Building. I sat back and drew a deep breath. We were going to discuss the Linda Burrows murder case, I assumed since he had brought it up at the memorial service.

He finally set aside the file he'd been reading, leaned back and cracked his knuckles and looked me over. As he smiled at me, his thick neck and handsome face made me think of a Chicago line-backer of years ago, and I was impressed. His age was maybe late forties, although his dense white hair added ten years to my guess. I had noticed that whenever he faced people, he maneuvered around just right so that his Harvard Law class ring couldn't be missed. A proud graduate of what the school itself claimed was the world's most excellent law school. Maybe it was; I was a Georgetown grad and wouldn't know.

"Liking it here so far?" he asked.

"I like it just fine. In fact, I'm excited to come to work every day."

"Good, good. Excellent to hear. Well, Linda's case is all over the *Post* and TV, and the president expects a quick arrest."

"The president's talked to you about it?"

"William Sinclair makes himself out to be the great friend of the people. But he's also a politician, bottom line. Murder in a govern-ment office as high profile as ours is a big deal. He wants somebody brought to justice ASAP. He is demanding an arrest."

"Everything is politics at his level, I would imagine."

"Which is why I've asked you to come here, Mike. I want you to catch whoever did this. I'm reassigning your caseload to other members of your team. I want you to pick out FBI agents from those you've worked with, as well as a few MPD cops. Try to keep your team light and agile, so you don't get bogged down in administrative. I want you to attend police interviews and ride-along whenever possible to keep our investigators from doing something stupid that might result in a search and seizure or a witness statement being tossed out of court for violating someone's constitutional rights. I'm counting heavily on you for this. I absolutely cannot afford any snafus. I like my job; you like yours. Let's make sure we keep them, make sure we don't get put out to pasture for a stupid mistake. You following me?"

"I do. And I can promise you that I'll be with my team every step of the way."

"We don't usually do this. If anyone knows the law, it's the FBI. But they still need guidance at times. So you're their boss."

"I can do that. I don't like the idea of losing all of my cases, though."

"Sorry, Michael, it's just a matter of priorities. Yours is now the Linda Burrows murder case. Any ideas about where you'll begin?"

"What's the most obvious path?" I asked.

"The husband?"

"You said it," I said. "You read my mind."

"He's a cop, you know."

"I know. I was there at the memorial and heard him read the Bible."

"Which could be pure cover-up."

"Agree. We'll look in the most obvious places first. Then we'll go from there."

"One other thing you need to know, Michael."

"Yes?"

"My sources at the Metro PD tell me that Harry Burrows was the first cop on the scene of Linda's murder."

The air went out of me. I inhaled then whistled softly. "Wow. I had no idea. What a horrible thing for him."

The USA looked at me—squinted. "Or was it?"

"You're thinking—"

"I think you could do worse than to begin with the husband. Nine times out of ten the murderers and rapists are family members. But you already know that."

"We'll have to talk to him right away."

"Yes. You know what else has my attention when I lie awake nights?"

"Sir?"

"Linda cheated with maybe one, maybe two men in our office. What if the killer, who, let's say just for giggles, is her husband—let's say he knows who those men were."

"And he comes after them next. I doubt he would."

"I don't doubt a damn thing. Nothing surprises me now, Michael. I would've thought, after all your years in the trenches, that you'd be of the same mind."

"I am, I am. I just meant that he would be damn stupid to go after a lover. That would point us at him."

"Agree. As for me, I'm already pointed there. I hope you are too."

"He'll be my first stop, Mr. Boudreaux."

Amazing. Hadn't he seen the file I'd received? Evidently not, or he'd have known his name was at the top of any list. He's the one who'd had the confirmed affair with Linda; there were no other known "men" from the office—leaving me off that list. Our moment need never come up. That left me with Niles and Harry Burrows. Beyond that, I was chasing maybe someone Linda had prosecuted, sent away to prison, and who was now out and about and carrying a grudge against her. After Boudreaux himself, this was probably my second choice for a suspect, although the ex- might have been slotted there too. Time and lots of shoe leather would tell.

"All right, then, Mr. Boudreaux. I thank you for this assignment. I'll handle it with the greatest care."

"And solve it by the end of the month. That's what would make me ecstatic. Then I could call up President Sinclair and make him think of me the next time he's looking for an Attorney General. Or FBI Director. I'm a political animal, Michael. I make no bones about it. Women hate me; I fill in the blank spaces in my life with my career. That's all I have going for me now. So make me proud, Michael. Make me proud."

"I'll do my best, Mr. Boudreaux."

"Niles."

"Niles, okay."

"Mr. Boudreaux is dead. My father died ten years ago. I go by Niles with my friends."

"Got it. Thank you again."

"Go call up some cops and some FBI. Make some plans, follow-up, make me proud. We'll talk again soon."

"Fair enough. I'll get started in the next thirty minutes."

"Fifteen minutes, Michael. Daylight's burning."

"Very well. I'm off."

"S'long."

8

That afternoon I called in the first two members of my team. They would bear the chief responsibility for leading the FBI teams (Jack Ames) and Metro PD (Ronald Holt). Ames was an ex-staff member with the U.S. Attorney's office and would serve as the liaison between me and the Metro PD. Holt was now a detective with MPD. Holt and I had worked together before. I wanted him directing all MPD efforts as he was familiar with the PD's rules and procedures and had the trust of the D.C. detectives and coppers.

We met in my office.

Jack Ames went first. "I'd like my partner, Marty Longstreet, on my team."

"Done," I said. "Just task him. He'll be running special assignments for me as well."

"I've worked with you before," Holt said to me. "I'd like to do witness statements with you."

"We can do that. You'll also be working with Rusty Xiang when I'm tied up."

I looked at my two principal investigators. They were opposites. Jack Ames was a much younger man; Ron Holt was a large black man whose physique resembled that of a grizzly bear. His face had a rough-hewn look, widespread eyes, a perfect smile—which was often —and a mind always ahead of everyone in the room. He was one of the brightest cops I'd ever met and had been invaluable to me during earlier investigations we'd worked together. Jack Ames had been around long enough that there was a bit of a bulge around the mid-section, a fact which I guessed he overcame with stretchable waist-bands. Jack was plodding and thoughtful and very fast at taking the correct position in any situation. Ron was an old hand at law enforce-ment, having served seven years in the USAO before leaving to join the Metro Police.

I also wanted Rusty Xiang on our team. Rusty's story was a long one and included me. He had at one time worked for the CIA and had run into trouble in Russia. I had ventured to Russia on that case and defended him. With lots of luck and a large helping of ass-in-chair kind of research, I managed to walk him out a free man. He was beholden to me, and there was one more thing: I was also his biolog-ical father. It's a long story, but he was conceived one night when the man who raised him—my roommate—was hospitalized and his girl-friend and I wound up in bed together. Not a story I'm proud of by any means; my only excuse is that we were young and I was bursting with testosterone, and she was beautiful and easily seduced. Or maybe I was the one seduced. But from that night on I carried the shame of betraying my roommate, and we had grown apart over the years until Rusty's arrest in Moscow when his father called me for help. So, those were the pieces I had called together that day after my meeting with the U.S. Attorney, Niles Boudreaux.

"One other thing," I said. "Staffing among you guys will shift and move around. Don't complain to me about it, please. We're all adults here, and staffing will depend on my needs, not yours."

"The FBI runs investigations," Jack Ames interjected. "You better check again with Boudreaux about that."

I stared at him, and he stared right back. "All right, I'll do that," I said. And I left it there for now. Our first disagreement.

There were no personality conflicts among my guys: they were all too professional to allow petty grievances to interfere with their work. Which was a relief to me because deep down I hate having to manage people, particularly when pettiness degrades our ability to produce timely results. Don't slow me down. That was my mantra that I recited to my troops. Just don't. Anyone who violated this rule would have been summarily drummed out of our corps. It went without saying, and everyone got it.

"So here's what I have in mind," I began. "Mr. Boudreaux wants me to participate in the investigation. This means assisting with witnesses, getting searches and seizures done according to the latest case law, and locating and prosecuting the perp as fast as possible. It seems he is getting beaucoup pressure from above and they're clamoring for a quick arrest. So that's my problem, not yours. But I'm telling you this, so you're not wondering why an AUSA is out taking witness statements with you or breaking down doors—which I don't expect will happen. Who knows?"

They nodded their understanding, though I could tell the FBI wasn't ready to go along with me heading up their investigation. Talk about turf-jealousy.

"So here's Round One. Ronald, you and Rusty will proceed to the grocery store and obtain witness information. Jack will be my Special Agent for special detailing. Jack, you and Marty will track down the customer witnesses and employee witnesses. Jack and I will interview the police and CSI investigators. Marty will be locating and cataloging all physical evidence. He will also handle the medical examiner and the lab techs. I think we're going to find this is a pretty clear division of labor as there were maybe thirty shoppers inside the store when Linda was murdered."

Ronald whistled softly. "Wow. We've got our work cut out for us, Rusty."

Rusty nodded. "I'm ready. This is a terrible case for our office. People are scared here. They're afraid there might be a connection between Linda and the fact she's an assistant U.S. Attorney. As for me, I think it's something else."

"What's that?" I asked.

Rusty didn't hesitate. "Many of the staff believe it was someone close to Linda who was fed up with her promiscuity. Maybe a jilted lover who wasn't finished screwing her. I'm inclined to this point of view, though I'm trying hard to remain open-minded."

"Let's talk about this," I said. "Do you have a feel for which of our colleagues were sleeping with Linda?"

"No."

"Then let's leave that alone. I think that's your basic office gossip with no basis in fact whatsoever. People are catty and love to target single women. Forget it for now."

"Who gets the husband?" asked Jack.

"You and I get the husband," I said. "He's our number one suspect, going in. At least that's my thinking."

"What about Annie? Is she in?" asked Detective Holt.

I smiled. "You bet she is. Today's Tuesday. I would like all documentary evidence pulled together and on my computer by Friday. I'll turn it over to her, and hopefully, we'll have a profile by the end of next week."

"Shouldn't we wait until then before we begin?" asked Agent Ames.

"Ordinarily I'd say yes. But I'm getting enough pressure from the U.S. Attorney that I want to strike out now. I know it's more random than what we get with Annie, but so be it. Everyone with me so far?"

I looked from face to face. Nods and agreement all around.

"We'll meet here again at one o'clock Friday afternoon. This is mandatory. I want Annie to sit in while we do a brief review of what we have so far. Any problems making it?"

No one had a problem with making Friday's meeting.

"All right," I said, "let's get to it.

9

Rusty Xiang's report reached our office network. His first interview. I was excited to read it: we were finally underway.

Delores Cheney was the name of the checkout worker closest to the front doors when the killer walked in and hurried past the registers. Detective Holt and USAO investigator Rusty Xiang met with her in the store manager's office on Wednesday morning following the Tuesday meeting at Michael Gresham's office.

Delores was a matronly mid-forties woman whose face was still beautiful but quickly identified as one who had gracefully settled into family life and being okay with aging. She had nothing to hide, was Holt's first thought, he told Rusty.

"Can I smoke in here?" she asked the investigators.

"It's not our office," said Rusty. "Does your manager let you smoke in here?"

"I've never asked."

"Then let's not smoke while we're here," said Rusty. "I don't want us to get run out of town on a rail."

"Okay, that's cool," said the clerk. "I'm just nervous. I've dreaded talking to you men. I haven't slept very well since you called me and scheduled."

"Why's that?" asked Holt.

"I mean, think about it, sir. It's murder! I've never been around anything like that. I don't know how I can help. I didn't even look up when the man came in."

"Did you look up when he left?"

"Yes. We all did. There had been shots fired inside our store, and everyone watched him leave. We were all crouched behind our checkout stands. But I took a peek. He was wearing a police officer's uniform. Was he the killer?"

"We don't know. That's what we're here to find out," Holt assured her. "But you have nothing to fear. Your statement is confidential. He'll never see it. Now, can you describe the man you saw leaving the store?"

She sat back and briefly drummed her fingers on the glass desktop.

"Well, he had very dark sideburns, very bushy. He was wearing eyeglasses. And his eyebrows were bushy and dark, too. He didn't look our way when he hurried by. In fact, he was looking off to his right as he went outside. So it was hard for me to get a good look. My description could be wrong. It's what I think I saw."

"Was he carrying anything?"

"Like a bag of grapes?"

"No, like a gun, maybe?"

"No, there was no gun."

"But he was wearing a police uniform?"

"Definitely. At first, I thought he had come inside to investigate and was going back out to his car to get something. It never occurred to me that he had done the shooting."

"What else do you remember about his looks?"

"He was very tan—bronze, almost. Like he just came back from Bermuda. In fact, he was too bronze, if you know what I mean. Nobody gets to looking like that from the sun."

"What else?"

"His hair was black and stuck out from under his police hat. It was curly. Like those guys that got perms back in the Seventies."

"But you don't remember him entering the store?"

"No. Sorry."

"What about after he went outside? Did you see where he went?"

"He went out and got in his car, I guess. Which made me a little crazy. I mean, why would a cop be leaving the store when there had been gunshots fired? It didn't make sense. I thought he was going out to use his radio, but then I realized he had one of those microphones on his shoulder. So that wasn't it; he wasn't going out to use the radio."

"Let me ask you this. Did he ever return to the store?"

"I didn't notice if he did. We all heard a big commotion coming from aisle eleven. We hurried back there to see. That's when I saw blood all over the cans of vegetables. And the woman lying on her side. She was plainly dead."

"How did you know, dead?"

"Mr. McIntosh was there, feeling her throat. He shook his head and looked up. He had tears in his eyes, and his hands were shaking."

"Who is Mr. McIntosh?"

"He's second-in-command. Assistant Manager."

"Anyone else with him at that time?"

"Another manager came. He called out for someone else."

"What was that all about?"

"Mr. McIntosh had hollered for a cleanup on aisle eleven. He was in shock. I mean nobody was gonna come clean up a dead woman. It was a crime scene, for crying out loud. We all knew better. Everybody watches CSI. You don't enter a crime scene. Oh, yes. A cop came up behind us just then and began stringing yellow crime scene tape all around. He told us to move back, and we did."

"Who's 'we'?"

"I don't remember. Other employees, maybe a customer or two. But I don't remember for sure."

"Now, think about this hard. Was the cop with the crime scene tape the same cop you had seen leaving the store just after the shooting?"

"You know what? I've been wondering about that. I mean, he didn't look the same: no sideburns, straight hair, no eyeglasses. And he wasn't at all bronze like the other cop. I'd have to say they were two different people."

"All right," said Rusty Xiang. "Anything else that might help us?"

"No. I went into the break room with other staff, and several of us were crying. We can smoke in there, so we lit up."

"Then what happened?"

"The detectives took all our names and numbers, and Mr. McIntosh sent us home. The store closed the rest of the day. When we came back in the morning, everything looked normal again. But there wasn't the usual nitpicking and joking. It was very grim."

"I'm sure," said Detective Holt. "Okay, I think that's all we have for now. You've been a huge help, Delores. One more thing. Would you take my card and call me if you decide to move or change phone numbers or quit your job here? That's very important to us. You're a key witness."

"All right. I'll keep your card in my wallet under my driver's license. If anything changes, I'll call you."

"Thank you."

"Okay, g'bye."

"'Bye.'"

Holt and Xiang were left alone in the manager's office.

"I don't know," Holt said. "I quit five years ago, but I could use a cigarette right about now."

"Forget it," said Rusty. "Cigarettes kill."

"You know what else kills? I think we've got a rogue cop that kills. That's just too coincidental."

"He shot her then went back out to his car and removed the makeup and mustache and sideburns?"

"Maybe so."

"I was thinking that, too. And I didn't even need a cigarette to arrive at that."

"Don't be a smart ass, Rusty. No one likes a smart ass."

"Let's write this up. I think Michael's going to be very interested in what Delores has to say."

"Agree. But first, let's talk to McIntosh. Seems like he was first to the dead girl."

"Let's do it, then."

10

Harry Burrows appeared at my office as requested. With FBI Special Agents Jack Ames and Marty Longstreet ready to square off with him, as well as me waiting to handle him gently and extract what information I could, Burrows was outnumbered by about ten to one although there were but three on our side. We moved our meeting into a small conference room two doors away from my office at the USAO with the intention of removing the intimidation of meeting on my turf.

We were careful to equally divide the table with bodies, Jack Ames taking the seat next to Burrows so he wouldn't feel outnumbered. Marty and I sat across. Jack produced a tape recorder, hit the red button, and announced that we were ready to proceed.

"Officer Burrows," I began, "you understand that you have the right to have an attorney present while we ask you some questions?"

"I do."

"You understand your statement is being recorded?"

"Yes."

"And you waive any objection to recording?"

"Yes."

"You also understand that your answers may be used against you in a court of law?"

"I do."

"And knowing you have the right to remain silent, you are choosing to waive that right and are willing to voluntarily answer our questions?"

"Sure. Why not?"

"All right," I said with a smile. "Now, you're a police officer with the D.C. Metro Police Department?"

"I am. Eighteen years now."

"So you've almost got your twenty in?"

"Yes."

"After you have your twenty, what are your plans?"

"Well, before we got divorced, Linda and I wanted to move out to Montana and get a small place in the country. She wanted to raise llamas. I wanted to raise cows and sell them for slaughter. The divorce ended that dream. Now I have no plans."

The word hung in the air: slaughter. It seemed to have a special significance.

"You and Linda. Can you describe your relationship with your ex-wife at the time of her death?"

"Pretty average, I guess. We were both committed to our jobs. I'm a sergeant now. She was close to getting her own team." A huge gasp for air overtook him at that point, and he turned his face away. His shoulders were clenching and unclenching. Apparently, the man was overwhelmed and—wonder of wonders—he wasn't faking. I let him gather himself and then plunged ahead.

"What did you have going on when you were together?"

"Happiness. Financial success. A growing feeling we were going to escape the rat race. That was the most important thing. Like escape was going to happen for us. We were working hard for that. We were a team."

"You yearned for that change, correct?" I asked, trying hard not to lapse into a series of leading questions, which would have reduced his answers to monosyllables. We wanted him to explain their life together, to expand, to give us words, not monosyllabic grunts of yes and no.

"We yearned for it? That's an understatement. We had dedicated ourselves to escape. And we were talking about getting back together. Almost there when this happened."

"For the record, what happened?"

"My wife was murdered."

"Mr. Burrows, do you have any knowledge about who may have murdered your ex-wife?"

"No, I do not."

"Do you have any guesses about that?"

"Maybe. Yes."

"Give us your best guess about your ex-wife's killer."

"Someone from this office, I'm thinking. Look, Linda wasn't robbed— her purse and wallet were under her where she was found. Her engagement ring was on her finger. That was my mother's two-carat diamond. So rule that out. What's that leave? I'm thinking jealousy."

"Why do you think jealousy?"

"Linda had a hard time staying away from Niles Boudreaux. He killed her love for me."

"What does that mean?"

"My wife was crazy about Boudreaux. You guys know that. Everybody knew it. I'm thinking maybe she was throwing him over and he got jealous and murdered her. She was pretty close to coming back to me."

"Do you have any evidence about any of this?"

"I have my suspicions, and I have a truckload of evidence."

"Tell us about that, please," I asked.

Burrows sat back from the table. The muscles in his jaw jumped. His eyes peered up at the ceiling, and he began slowly shaking his head.

Then with a long sigh, he said, "Niles Boudreaux. I caught them together."

"The U.S. Attorney? You saw him having sex with Linda?"

He smiled. It was a crooked smile and reflected the irony of the situation. "I caught them together at the Hyatt Hotel because I followed them there. I played like I was room service and Boudreaux opened the door, and I walked in. My wife was in the shower. Boudreaux was wearing a silk robe and drinking scotch straight out of a bottle on the table."

"Scotch? How do you know that?"

"I sat down at that table. I was wearing my uniform."

"Boudreaux tried to make a joke. I wasn't laughing. I even considered shooting both of them right then and there myself. Then she came breezing into the room, nude. I turned to look, and you could've knocked her over with a feather. Her knees buckled, and she almost fainted on the spot."

"What happened next?"

"I ordered Boudreaux to get dressed and leave."

"What did he say?"

"Nothing. He was already throwing stuff in his athletic bag and heading out. The door closed behind him, and I made Linda lie down nude on the bed. It was unmade—that much I remember. I then walked over to her and fucked her. Meaning it was against her will, and she even cried. She said she still loved me, but Boudreaux had promised they were only going there to the hotel to talk. She begged me not to hurt him."

"You believed her when she said she was only there to talk? How does that explain catching her in the nude? Was she drugged? Was he pointing a gun at her?"

"I know, I know. I never bought it either. But I was in a rage, and I knew I was close to hurting someone."

"You admitted you raped your ex-wife. Were you going to hurt Boudreaux too?"

"Neither of them was worth me doing time in the penitentiary. I finally just got up and left. I guess she went back to work."

"Harry, how did it make you feel when you saw your ex-wife and Niles Boudreaux together?"

Agent Ames added, "And she was naked."

"How did I feel? Seriously? I felt stunned. And I felt like hurting someone. I felt like shooting him."

"What about her? Did you feel like shooting her?"

"Never. I loved my wife. She had this horrible thing about Niles Boudreaux. Like she was under his spell. I hated him, but I still loved her. I would give both my legs to have her back right now."

"What about Niles Boudreaux? Have you spoken to him since that day?" I asked.

"I tried to. But he refused to see me. Which made me even angrier. I hope for bad things for him."

"Do you have any plans to hurt him? To strike back?"

Burrows leaned forward and placed his elbows on the table. "Yes, I'm going to beat the shit out of him if I ever get the chance. He has it coming, don't you agree?"

I looked at Agent Ames, and he looked at Marty Longstreet. They shook their heads and dropped their eyes. Ames finally said, "I would be furious, for sure. But I wouldn't say he has it coming, not a beating. Maybe a lawsuit to embarrass him but no physical violence."

"Not a bad idea," Burrows said. "I like that. Sue the bastard for alienation of affections. I can do that. I will do that. Thanks for the idea."

"Don't thank me," Ames said, "unless I helped keep him from getting shot. You'd go to prison for life over that. You can thank me for steering you clear of prison."

"Thank you. But I still want to split his head open with a sap."

"Well, that's your business. I know we're only talking here. I know you won't attack him."

"I'm glad you know that. I sure as hell don't know he's safe."

Ames then began with his line of questioning.

"Mr. Burrows, were you at the scene of your ex-wife's murder the day it happened?"

"I was patrolling in the area. I think I was the first Metro PD car on the scene."

"What did you do?"

"Saw Linda, went into shock, double-timed out to my squad car and grabbed a roll of crime scene tape and taped the crime scene. Then I began keeping people away. Within ten minutes the medical examiner's crew was there along with a few cops. It was all pretty standard stuff after that."

"What else did you do?

"Just secured the scene until CSI and backup and detectives came pouring in. Then I left the scene and went to a Denny's and shook and tried to calm down. I would break down crying and then stop myself. My waitress was afraid to come over. Then I drove home in my squad car. I've never done that before, taking a duty car home. But I didn't give a damn what anyone thought about it. They figured out right away that I was better left alone just then. I'm sure Boudreaux gave everyone the order to stay away from me because he knew I was a loose cannon. So I spent that first night on my own. The second night, my sister arrived from New York. She stayed with me for a week, mainly helping with the kids and cooking for me. I owe her big time."

"Have you discussed the case with any police officers? MPD detectives, for example?"

"No one will talk to me about it. They're all staying far away. When they see me coming in the station, they turn and head the other way. I'm an outcast because my wife cheated on me. Go figure, eh?"

"I guess," Ames said. "It doesn't seem fair, for sure."

Burrows winked at Ames. "You're getting it now. Good for you."

I took it over again. "Why would you think Boudreaux would shoot your ex-wife?"

"I know, it doesn't make any sense. But I don't trust that bastard. Would you?"

Ames and I shared a look. Then we both shook our heads. Boudreaux was a political animal above all else. Who could say what he might do to protect his career in Washington? We wouldn't trust Boudreaux if we were in Burrows's shoes. It went without saying, and we all knew it.

"Why would he do it? Motive?"

"Maybe she told him she was coming back to me. That doesn't sound much like what would set him off, though. I guess I don't know. But I know what effect she has on men. She's a tiger!"

"Or quite loving," I said. "She sounds like someone you loved a lot."

"I did. No doubt about that."

I sat upright and looked deep into his eyes then. "Mr. Burrows, one more question and I'm done here. You obviously were in the area where she was murdered. You obviously had the opportunity and the motive. How do we rule you out?"

"I've never been arrested. No history of violence on my work record."

"Domestic violence: that's on there."

He spread his hands. "Look, killing someone is not who I am. I just wouldn't ever do that. I might feel like kicking her ass or shooting him, but hurting Linda only happened once even though she was sleeping with another man. Give me credit, okay?"

"Fair enough," I said. "Jack?"

Ames shook his head. "I think I'm done. At least for now."

"Marty?"

Agent Longstreet looked down the table at me. "I don't have anything. Except for one thing. Mr. Burrows, have you given a statement to any law enforcement officers? I'm talking specifically about detectives from the MPD where you work?"

"Not officially."

"What's that mean?"

"It means we met during lunch one day. It was a taco stand with outdoor tables. It was just me and two dicks. They poked around for a minute or two and then started talking about football. They weren't interested in me."

"Anyone else?"

"No."

"Can you provide us with a copy of the report filed by the detectives?"

"Go to our records clerk. You need to get it from them."

"I will," I said. "I lied before; I do have one more item. Is Niles Boudreaux safe from you? Do we need to put a detail on him to keep him alive?"

"Are you asking me do I have any plans to hurt him?"

"Yes."

"Not at all. It's all on Linda. Boudreaux just happened to be in the right place at the right time."

"Thank you, Officer Burrows."

"You're welcome."

"One last thing," I hurried to say as he was getting up. "This conversation is very preliminary. We'll need much more in-depth soon. Maybe even grand jury testimony, depending."

"Depending on what?" Burrows asked.

I drew a deep breath. "Depending on how guilty you end up looking. Depending on who else looks like a candidate. Depending on lots of things."

"I see. Got it."

The cop left us alone then, walking up front by himself. The FBI agents and I just sat there staring at dots on the walls. He had to be our first suspect. We all had to agree on that. We didn't even need to say it out loud to make it so.

"Do you want a detail on him?" Ames, at last, asked me.

"Guess not. Boudreaux might want to get protection, but that's his problem."

Ames looked into my eyes. "What?" I asked.

"Nothing. I'm just concerned about other staff who might have boffed Linda Burrows."

"Forget it," I said. "We can't protect everybody."

"May they all get syphilis and go blind," Longstreet said from out of the blue.

"No chance," I said. "I've seen the medical examiner's report. She had no STD's. And I don't believe there were other men. Just bullshit gossip."

"If you say so."

"But she was pregnant."

"No shit?" the two FBI agents said in tandem.

"No, no shit."

11

Edmund Rasmussen was the Metro PD detective leading the investigation of the grocery store murder of Linda Burrows. At least he was until Niles Boudreaux assigned the case to me. Special Agent Jack Ames and I met with Rasmussen in my office to exchange information. But there was one public relations piece of business to address before we began.

"Ed," I said as soon as we were settled at my desk, "I want to apologize to you for taking over your case. That was the call of the U.S. Attorney for political reasons, and I had nothing to do with it."

"Forget it," said Rasmussen. "It's just one more file I don't have to process."

A man after my own heart.

"I appreciate that, Ed. Well, for whatever reason, I apologize again. It came down from above. And that's all I have to say about it."

"Okay," Rasmussen said with a smile, "how can I help?"

"We need to know what you know," Jack Ames said. "We need a brain dump."

"I was one of the early responders," Rasmussen began. "I believe I was the third cop on the scene."

"Who was the first cop there?"

"I think that would have been Harry Burrows. Found his ex-wife dead in the canned goods aisle. He's doing horribly, I'm hearing. Finding Linda shot to death has thrown him into shock, and he's barely making it day to day. He's taking all his accumulated sick leave. He refuses to speak with family and friends beyond a casual 'okay' when asked how he's doing. He is definitely in another space. But who can blame him?"

"Definitely," I agreed. "So what happened when you arrived at the scene?"

"Harry had secured the scene with yellow tape and was holding the gawkers back. He had made the call that brought us all running. Amazing man: he had laid his coat over Linda's face. And he had strung the crime scene tape—all without breaking down then and there. He deserves a medal."

"Let's hold it right there. How did it come to be that Harry was first on the scene?" I asked, ignoring the comment about the medal he might deserve.

"As I understand it, Harry was on patrol in that part of town. He's frequently assigned to patrol duties there."

"It just seems too circumstantial to me," Agent Ames commented. "In fact, we're all asshole buddies here, so let me postulate: what if Harry himself shot her dead? What if he walked in, shot her, walked out and then returned wearing his uniform. Maybe he was wearing street clothes at the time he shot her, went back out to his patrol car and returned looking like an on-duty police officer. Maybe that's what happened."

"I've thought of that," said Rasmussen. "Burrows should be interviewed about this."

"He has been," I said. "He came across as clean."

"He did? Then fair enough, Michael. I won't ask what he told you."

"And I can't tell you," I said, "since you're no longer working the case."

"Sure," said Rasmussen less convincingly that he had all day. "I do not need to know at this point."

Ames and I only looked at each other. It was a less-than-savory moment for us, considering we had all but ripped the investigative file out of Rasmussen's hands. We were beginning to feel very bad about that.

"Let me skip around just a bit," I said. "What about physical evidence at the scene?"

"Well, the gun that killed Linda wasn't found."

"So someone is walking around with evidence of a murder that could come back to bite him or her. Not smart to keep a murder weapon, as many of my old clients learned the hard way."

"Looks that way."

"What about store video? There were cameras out front?"

"There's a whole row of cars parked between the video camera and the vehicle the cop was driving. As the cop walked toward the store, he never raised his head enough that we could see his face. Apparently, he saw the video camera."

"Store interior video? What's up with that?"

"No coverage on aisle eleven. The manager promised the security company would be fired over that."

"Too bad. What else?"

"I talked with two cashiers, two stockers, and a shopping cart retriever out front of the store. He probably came the closest to being any real help because he saw Linda Burrows come into the store wearing a very short skirt that caught his eye."

"What about her?"

"He was important because he confirmed that between Linda going into the store and the gunshots going off probably no more than five or six minutes went by."

Ames looked at me. "Which probably means someone followed her to the store and then followed her inside."

"Exactly," Rasmussen agreed. "So I asked if he saw who might have entered the store after her. He said no one except a cop. But he couldn't remember if the cop entered before or after the gunshots."

"That's a shame. I think we'll talk to him again," I said. "Maybe he's had a chance to think about it. It would be too much to ask for if he can confirm the cop entered the store before the gunshots, came out, then entered again."

"Exactly," Rasmussen said. "There's your case if he can do that."

"If he can do that, the case is over," Ames agreed.

"So tell me a little more about the shopping cart retriever."

"It's all set out in my report. Maybe twenty years old, Hispanic, unmarried, honest enough. He didn't try to stretch it or say something just to make me happy. Or just to make me go away."

"We'll follow up with him next. So who else did you talk to?"

"Delores Cheney. First cashier closest to the sliding front doors. She saw a cop come in; strange description she gave of him. He then left the store—you couldn't miss him. But she did see another cop come in after the shooting. Different description. He was the one who hung the yellow tape. Didn't recognize him."

"Did she describe the second cop?"

"See my report for that; I honestly don't recall. But what I do recall is that she wondered if the two cops might have been the same guy. The theory might not be a hard sell to a jury if you're looking to finger someone."

"Let me ask you this. You said Delores saw a cop enter and gave you a bizarre description."

"It's in my report."

"Did any of the witnesses see anything that suggests cop number one was disguised?"

"No."

"Did you come away thinking that might have been the case?"

"Definitely. We all know Harry Burrows had a motive for killing his promiscuous ex-wife. Maybe you or I would too, given the right circumstances. So if he had a motive, and he was at the scene, how big a leap is it to believe the first cop, the shooter, and the second cop, the investigator, were the same person?"

"I'm inclined that way," Special Agent Ames said. "But I do have one reservation."

I looked at him. "Such as what?"

"Why shoot her in a public place like a grocery store where there's bound to be plenty of eyewitnesses? Why not shoot her out on some lonely road somewhere?"

"I give up," I said. "What are you thinking?"

"I was wondering the same thing," said Detective Rasmussen. "Not exactly an easy kill to work."

Rasmussen shrugged. He looked around the office, then said, "Maybe he wanted an alibi—such that he was setting it up to look like a cop or someone else shot her and that it couldn't have been him because he was one of the good guys, a first responder."

"So he was creating eyewitnesses who could exonerate him. Whereas if she died out on some lonely road without eyewitnesses to exonerate him, then it wouldn't be a great leap to connect his motive with his opportunity to kill her. I can run with that."

"I think I can too," said Ames. "I think you can sell that to a jury, Michael."

I spread my hands. "Remains to be seen. All right, Detective Rasmussen, anything else we haven't asked?"

"See my report. Call me for follow-up. That's about all I have."

"Thanks for coming," I said. "Why don't you take off and let me and Agent Ames talk a little now?"

He stood up and buttoned his suit coat, then walked out without another word.

"Well?" I said to Ames.

"The simple explanation solves most of these shootings. I think the two cops are the same guy."

"Me, too. Disguise. Motive. It adds up."

"So who do we talk to next?"

"Next we meet with Annie. I'm having all files copied, and all witness statements typed up. I want us to meet with her tomorrow and turn over all that we have. Then let's stand back and let her do what she does. We'll go from there."

"Sounds good."

We broke off, then.

All we had were theories. But they were limited by our imaginations.

We needed someone who wasn't limited by the ordinary human imagination.

We needed Annie.

12

My bio-kids are Mikey and Dania. Dania gets her name from her mother, Dania—Danny. Mikey gets his from me. These kids are under ten. Then comes Annie, who's thirteen. When I arrived home after the interview of Edmund Rasmussen, I found my family in chaos, thanks to friction that exists between the two younger kids and Annie.

Nobody was speaking—meaning the kids, not Verona, who was the United Nations trying to heal bad feelings between them.

My feelers were twitching when I walked in and took the emotional temperature of my family. Dania was pissed at Annie. So I took her aside in the kitchen and asked her what happened.

"She refuses to talk to us," Dania said. "I know you think she's special but I don't. I think she's a jerk."

"It must be tough trying to interact with Annie," I said. "But I have to remind myself that Annie was born this way. She's different, like a child who was born deaf and can't hear people talking to her. Can you give her space to be what she is? Like you would a deaf child?"

"Why should I?" she sniffed. Her voice was reasonable, but her demeanor said otherwise: she was acting her age, and that meant to her that her new sister was a jerk. "I don't like her, Daddy. I say send her back where she came from."

"We can't do that," I said. "Her family was murdered. There's no place to send her back to. We're all she has."

"You're playing on my feelings, Michael," Dania said, startling me with her insight. I *was* playing on her feelings, and she had called me on it. My girl was growing up.

"I am playing on your feelings," I admitted. "And I'll tell you what I'm counting on, and this goes no further than this kitchen. I'm also counting on you to be the mature one. You're the—how should I say this—you're the healthy one. No, that's not what I mean to say. What I'm trying to say is, you're the one who isn't the deaf girl. You hear everything, and you expect others to as well. But it's never going to happen, not with Annie. She was born emotionally deaf, and we just have to accept that."

"Just make her give Ralph back, and I'll try to get along."

Ralph was Dania's turtle. Woe to anyone who threatened Ralph. He was off-limits to us all, and we knew it.

"Annie has Ralph? How did that happen?"

"Well, I didn't exactly see her take him. But he's missing from his terrarium. Who else would take him except my new, weird sister?"

"So you're accusing her without having any proof?"

"Yes, I can suspect her. I'll bet you have suspects you're after every day you're at your office."

She had me there. The logic of children can be stunning. Consider me stunned.

"All right, I do have suspects, you're right. But this is different because we're talking about family. The people I'm after as a prosecutor have done terrible, terrible things. These are not turtle suspects. It's much worse than that."

"Oh?" she said, shooting a querulous look at me. "What sort of things have your suspects done?"

"Well, they've killed other people. They've taken kids like you across state lines to abuse them. Stuff like that. Way beyond turtle theft, if you see what I mean."

"It's all relative, Dad. Turtle theft might not be a big deal to you. But it's a huge deal to me. Give me credit for having the same feelings about Annie that you have against the bad guys who take kids across state lines."

She had me. "It's all relative?" I asked myself. Where did that sophistication come from? My kid was growing up right in front of me, and I was missing it. I resolved to get more involved with her—with them. I resolved again to be a real person for my family.

"Okay. I understand. So let's ask Annie about Ralph. Okay?"

Her face brightened. "Okay. Right now?"

"Yes. Let's go talk to Annie."

We found her in her bedroom, her computer open on her lap as she sat on her bed, her back against the headboard. She didn't look up when we entered—after knocking on her closed door and getting no answer.

"Annie," I began. "Will you talk to me?"

She looked up. "About what, Michael?"

"About Ralph."

"A stupid turtle? I don't want to talk about that."

"Well, have you seen Ralph lately?" I plunged on.

She looked at me, fixing me with a look that was noncommittal. She was feeling nothing. I hated the look, but no one would ever know. I was human, too.

"A stupid turtle? Do I look like someone who might be tracking a turtle around, Michael?"

"No, you don't. But you look like someone who might've seen Ralph just because you live here."

"I don't know what you're getting at, Michael. Now if you're finished, I'll get back solving the mystery of the errant ex-wife. The dead errant ex-wife."

"All right," I said. Honestly, I didn't know what else to say to Annie. She had me.

I gave Dania a futile look. But she wasn't finished.

"How about you coming clean and give Ralph back to me?"

No response from Annie.

"And quit ignoring me. I hate you when you ignore me!"

No response. Annie wasn't home just then.

"Fuck off!" Dania said and ran out of the bedroom. I could hear her crying as she made her way down the hallway.

Annie was gone. She didn't respond to my attempts to smooth things over. So I stood up from her desk chair and walked out. I had known the feeling before, the feeling I had just then. Forlorn, foresworn to failure. There was no way to deal with Annie except to accept who and what she was. With that adult resolution in my heart, I left her there with her laptop.

Then I found Dania in her room, her music turned up to ten.

"Can you turn that down?" I asked.

She dialed it back. Grudgingly. Maybe to eight.

"Where did you learn that word?" I asked. I was referring to her "fuck you" to Annie.

"Face it, Dad. I don't go to school in a bubble. I hear stuff. Like any kid hears stuff."

"Well, I don't like you talking like that to your sister. Please apologize to her."

"Why? Stupid won't hear me apologize. She can go to hell."

"Come on, Dania. This isn't like you."

"How do you know what I'm like when Ralph's missing? It never happened before she came here."

"True." She had me there. I was frustrated by the rift between Dania and the girl who wasn't there. Nobody—especially not me—possessed the kind of tools it would ever take to fix that. So I gave up. I nodded at Dania and backed out of her room. It was just going to have to resolve itself. My attempts were futile. It turns out I didn't understand either girl.

So much for getting home in time to solve my family's problems. Shot down by a teen and a pre-teen, I went looking for Verona. She was my anchor, the steady one in the boat.

I longed to hold her and shut my eyes for a minute with my head on her shoulder. Let the world pass me by.

"Fuck you?" I heard myself repeat. We've come to that point in our family's story?

I couldn't find Verona fast enough.

13

Friday afternoon, one o'clock, and we were all together again, the team I'd assembled. Our purpose was to step through the documentary evidence and let Annie listen in. Would she get anything out of it? I honestly didn't know. I hadn't tried a review of documents with Annie present. We'd just have to see.

First up, Harry Burrows' personnel file from the Metro PD. Ronald Holt had obtained the file, and we knew to handle it with the highest confidentiality. We worked through it first. Burrows' file was pretty much unremarkable. There was one shooting of his gun on duty—but he hadn't hit anyone. It was during a chase-down on foot, and he had fired off a single round to protect his partner. It was just commentary in his file, nothing serious.

Police personnel files are unlike other personnel files I've seen over the years. Unlike others because police files go much deeper than ordinary employment files. So I was amazed to view the short history of Harry's problems with his wife due to his jealousy. He had been "handled" so that Harry seemed professionally unfazed by his jealous assaults. Of course, there was nothing in there about him punching his wife and cracking her teeth. The PD couldn't afford that kind of negativity in a police officer's file should he get himself and the department sued by a civilian. A well-oiled file when it was all said and done.

Annie, who had proved she could judge human doings without embarrassment, commented that while Harry's accommodations of his crazies were laudable, she wondered why the assault and battery weren't recorded. Broken teeth are recordable events, in her--and my--view. "I want to see more on his violence and jealousy. Let's get her medical records," she said to me. "I'm far from convinced by his personnel file that his jealousy didn't overwhelm him. I've found dozens of cases like Harry's in my studies. Assaults recorded in personnel files are devastating to careers. So I'm not giving him a full pass. Not yet, Michael."

I noticed that Annie was addressing her comments to me alone. She wasn't speaking to the others: she was speaking, in fact, as if they weren't even there. I could see in the others' faces that they knew they were watching something spectacular in how this thirteen-year-old worked. But no one was going to interrupt. They were smart enough to keep still.

"I need to spend quite a bit of time with Harry's file. Has he been interviewed?"

"He has," I said.

"Recorded?"

"Yes."

"Good. I need the transcript, and I need the recording, too. His voice and vocabulary and tone will go a long way in helping me understand him."

"I'll make sure you have both," I said.

"What else do you have for me?"

"Witness statements, mostly. The cashiers, the stockers, the shopping cart handler, other police officers, CSI's and so forth. Then we have the full autopsy and forensic analysis from the M.E."

"Your voice is dropping out when you tell me this, Michael," she said. "Is there something else I should know about the autopsy? Or the forensics?"

She stared me down. So much for Annie's unwillingness or inability to maintain eye contact when she spoke to me. Just then she was managing full eye contact. I was her prey.

My team was looking at me with great interest. I could feel eyes on me, judging, taking in my emotions, realizing there might be more to me than anyone had first imagined.

I had become more than casually interesting to them.

Which describes the whole arc of my life. I've never been good at coverup. I've been a terrible actor. Because of this, I've always kept to my side of the street, played it honestly. There was no other path for someone like me, someone who telegraphed his sins to the world.

But now this.

I only stared blankly at her. Words would've failed me. There was no hiding in words. So I clammed up and decided how to proceed to get everyone's eyes off me and focused somewhere else.

But I couldn't pull it off. I couldn't think up a way to escape with a new topic sentence in my conversation with Annie. I was stuck, suspended, everyone's focal point.

Just as I was about to announce the session with Annie was finished, she raised her eyes to me and kept them on my eyes. Then she looked down as if disowning me.

"You're going to hate me," Annie said softly.

"Why would I hate you?" I asked.

"Because."

"Because why?"

"Because a profile doesn't immediately rule you out, Michael."

I sat there stunned. I blinked hard, once, twice, three times. The cops and FBI agents couldn't take their eyes off me. It was as if Annie had trained a spotlight on me during a stage play. It was my moment to make my speech to the audience except for one huge problem: I had no speech. I never had in my wildest dreams imagined Annie would say such a thing.

But her words made me believe more than ever in her talents as a profiler.

Why?

Because I too had been with Linda. In fact, it happened during a weak moment after work late one night when we went out for a drink. I violated everything I stood for that evening and went to bed with her. She was just too sexual and too, too inviting for me to resist that one night. I've done things before I wasn't proud of. I've done things that have followed me around in my guilt all my life, things I would never get over. And Linda and I were one of those things.

But there was much more at play here than even that. Linda's autopsy had revealed she was pregnant. I had only just learned that from the medical examiner's report of the autopsy.

Which was bad enough. But consider this: I was one of the last men with her.

The fetus—the baby—was very possibly mine. DNA testing was inevitable. Comparison of the fetus' DNA to the DNA of the men in our office was also inevitable.

Was there any evidence about her killer that could be more damning than having gotten her pregnant?

If there was, I didn't know what.

I had become my own best candidate for her murder.

I suddenly ended our meeting with Annie, trying to make it look as if her words hadn't shaken me up one bit.

But I could see it in the eyes of my team.

None of them believed it. They knew how shaken I was.

I only hoped Annie didn't. I couldn't stand for her to carry the guilt of turning-in her father.

That had to be avoided no matter the cost to me.

So I acted. I acted as if nothing had happened.

And the other men on my team—they acted too. They saw what was at stake for Annie. They wouldn't confront me just then, not in her presence. But I knew it was coming once we were away from her.

Brother, it was really coming.

14

After debriefing with Annie, my team and I met up at Denny's two miles away. I was dreading what was about to come.

Ames and Longstreet settled into the booth opposite me. Ronald Holt sat beside me; I had claimed the spot nearest the aisle, which was predictable: I had this wild notion I might have to make a run for it. Crazy autopsy thoughts.

The waitress brought menus and, after we told her our selections, we tried to look busy with staring out the window beside us. The waitress thanked us and left. Then she returned with coffee.

Once she was gone, Jack Ames spoke up first.

"Michael, is there something you want to say to us?"

I hung my head. But then I decided shame wasn't the best thing, that I would have enough time for that later. So I pulled myself together.

"I slept with Linda," I admitted. I sipped my coffee. Then I watched the remaining curls of cream dissolve in my drink. There was no going back from there: the mix was done.

"Figured," said Marty Longstreet. "But I wouldn't commit suicide just yet. Just screwing her doesn't mean you're going to turn around and kill her."

Ames looked at me very carefully. Then he said, "Unless she was carrying your baby and you didn't want that to get out. Especially not to your wife."

"I'm not married."

"Don't start," said Ames. "You know damn well what I mean, you and Verona."

"You knew she was pregnant?" I stupidly asked.

They didn't respond. Then Holt said, "Michael, you think you're the only one getting records? We've all seen the autopsy. We knew she was pregnant. But we didn't know you might have been the customer who did the deed. We didn't know it might be your kid. At least I didn't. Not until today."

"Same here," said Ames and Longstreet in unison.

"I don't know what to say," I said. I didn't.

"I don't think anyone suspects you," Ames said slowly. "Except maybe for Annie. Your daughter hasn't ruled you out. Ironic."

"We do need to alibi you," Holt said, meaning they'd need to check out my alibi.

"I was in court," I said. "Easily verifiable."

"Did you kill her?" Longstreet asked flat out.

"No. No, I didn't kill Linda. But after I cheated with her and betrayed Verona I felt like killing myself."

"I'm not impressed," Longstreet replied. "You're guilty of gross stupidity. So what? That doesn't exonerate you. In fact, you know what? I'm keeping you on my list of possible perps. I want to know more about your alibi, and I'm going to check it out. Just saying, so there's no misunderstanding here."

I nodded. "I expected no less. I'd do the same thing if I were in your shoes."

"Of course," said Longstreet.

Our orders arrived. We had ordered hamburgers, except Ronald Holt, who chose bacon and eggs. I knocked ketchup out of the bottle and bit into a french fry. No taste. Just a leftover feeling of grease on my tongue.

But Longstreet wasn't finished with me. "I want you on the lie box, Michael."

"Lie detector? I'm happy to do that. Set it up."

"It's standard operating procedure for agents who get too close to the flame," Ames explained to me.

"No problem. I'm eager to clear myself."

"We'll set it up for next week. Monday okay?"

"Aren't dawdling, are we?" I said. I couldn't forego the sarcasm.

"What?" said Longstreet, who wasn't playing games with me. "You want Tuesday instead? Wednesday? What?"

"Monday's fine," I said in a voice that sounded small and far away.

"I'll let you know what time," Longstreet replied. "Just following procedures."

"I get that," I said. "Don't feel bad. I don't."

"How long were you screwing her?" Longstreet pressed.

"Just that one time. It was a huge mistake, and I didn't go back for seconds."

Longstreet smiled. "You're the only one of her suitors who didn't. Once a guy dipped his wick in that he was a goner, from what I can figure out."

"Well, let's just say my resistance was higher. Also, you should know I don't believe Linda was promiscuous like the office gossip has it. I don't believe that at all."

Ames slipped in, "Your behavior contravenes your claim."

"Touché," I said. "Nice, Jack."

"We're all big boys here, Michael," Ames added. "You dished it out. Now you have to take it."

I chewed another fry. The burger looked very unappealing. Nothing like the picture on the menu.

"Let's say I take the lie detector and pass. Are we all ready to move on then?"

"If the DNA test clears you," Longstreet said. "No problem after that."

"Same here," said Ames.

"You know I believe you've done nothing wrong already," Ronald Holt said. We'd worked cases together before. Maybe he knew me better. Whatever; I was happy for his support.

It was time to move on.

"The top guy on my radar is Harry Burrows," I said. "Any ideas on how to proceed with him?"

"First off, you should let me put a tail on him," Holt said. "I'm thinking around-the-clock."

"Why a tail?" I asked. "Linda's dead. He won't kill again."

"No, but I want to know everything about him," Holt replied.

"Do it," I said. "Jack? Marty?"

"I like the tail," Jack said.

"Me too," said Longstreet. "Plus I say we get him on the lie box too. Might as well see where he's at with that."

"He might lawyer-up if you ask him," Holt said.

"Then I'll take him to the grand jury," I said; it was refreshing that the focus was off me, now.

"You know what?" Longstreet said. "I think I want you off the case, Michael. I think I might be more comfortable with someone who hasn't fucked the victim."

"If there is any guy in the office who hasn't," Ames said, entirely out of character for him. He was disappointed in me. And disapproving. We had been friends up to that moment. Now I wasn't sure.

"Well, I'm not resigning," I said. "I didn't kill her, and I want this case. It's too important to the office to let anyone else do it."

"Special snowflake are we?" Longstreet said. I winced at his sarcasm. "No, I want you off."

"Well stick it up your ass, Marty," I said. "Because I'm not leaving."

"Fine, I'll just go to Boudreaux."

"Careful there. You might find Boudreaux's implicated too."

Longstreet gave me a long look. "Seriously? The U.S. Attorney was banging her too?"

"Just be careful," I said. "Ask Boudreaux for yourself. My guess is he'll surprise you."

"Jesus," muttered Longstreet.

"Oh well," I said. With all sarcasm, I added, "How's everyone's burger? Tasty?"

"Fuck off," Longstreet said with a smile. "Every guy in the office is a suspect?"

"Until I say otherwise," I smiled. "Linda was a beautiful woman. Most guys are like me: they never get a chance at a beauty like that. When it's offered we take it—that's the problem. Don't marry anyone prettier than you. Rule One of the Michael Gresham Sandbox Rules."

"Funny man," said Ames.

"Go to hell," Longstreet said. "I'm getting you off the case, and that's that."

"Good luck, Marty. I'm not leaving, and Boudreaux won't make me. Maybe I'll get you off instead."

"It might surprise you to know that's my second choice, my backup plan," Longstreet said. "This case is doomed before it even starts. I'm sure Jack's with me on that."

I looked at Ames. He shrugged. "I think I'm with my partner on this, Michael. Sorry."

"Your SAIC won't let you off my team," I said with a smile at both men.

"Meaning?"

"Meaning it was my request that brought you onboard. Your boss understands the politics of the case. You're not going anywhere, so lean back and enjoy the burgers. We're all in this together for the duration. Now, having said that, who wants to interview Niles Boudreaux?"

No one looked up.

"Good, then Holt and I will take it," I said. "I'm done here. I'll catch the bill on my way out."

I stood up and abruptly set off for the checkout stand. Twenty-five dollars later and I was free to go.

I inhaled a lungful of clean air outside.

Twenty-five bucks was cheap.

I would've paid twice that to walk out of there a free man.

15

We were located in the polygraph room at the FBI offices, and I was forcing myself to look calm.

The polygraph examiner fastened the lie detector's leads and contacts to my body. Then he went behind me so I couldn't see him. I was aware when Marty Longstreet came into the room; I could hear them whispering. It was time for me to prove my innocence.

Without introduction, the examination began. The detached voice of the examiner started with a question that suggested to me this was going to be a piece of cake.

He asked, "Is your name Michael?"

"Yes," I said, knowing I got at least one right.

"Are you fifty-eight years old?"

"Yes."

"Were you born in 1959?"

"Yes."

"Is today Monday?"

"Yes."

"Do you live in Washington, D.C.?"

"No."

"Do you have a mortgage with Bank of America?"

"No."

"Have you stolen more than four-hundred-dollars from an employer?"

"No."

"Do you have an illegal drug history?"

"Yes."

"What was that?"

"Marijuana in college."

"Have you committed an undisclosed serious crime?"

"No."

"Are you a lawyer?"

"Yes."

"Are you married?"

"No."

"Do you have two children?"

"Three."

"Based on your personal bias, have you ever committed a negative act against anyone?"

"Yes."

"During a domestic dispute, have you physically harmed a significant other?"

"No."

For the most part, these were very obvious relevant questions. But note that "undisclosed serious crime" is vague enough that it might easily be confused for a probable-lie "control" question." They were tricky, the FBI.

Another control question followed:

"Did you ever lie to someone in a position of authority?"

"Yes." Like all lawyers, I had lied to so many judges I long ago lost count. Or cared.

Another control question:

"Before this year, did you ever put false information on an official document?"

"Yes." Again, like all lawyers, I had prepared legal pleadings that I knew contained falsehoods. It was standard procedure in lawsuits.

Another control question:

"Before this year, did you ever betray someone who trusted your word?"

"No."

Another control question:

"Did you ever do anything that would place your integrity into question?"

"Yes."

"Describe what you did."

"I had sex with a woman while I was living with another."

Another control question:

"Before this year, did you ever take credit for something you didn't do?"

"No."

Another control question:

"Before this year, did you ever deceive a family member?"

"No."

Then we were evidently finished with the control questions. Now the real meat was served.

"Did you kill Linda Burrows?"

"No."

"Did you have sex with Linda Burrows?"

"Yes."

"Do you know who killed Linda Burrows?"

"No."

"Did you want Linda Burrows dead?"

"No."

"Do you know Harry Burrows?"

"Yes."

"Did Harry kill Linda?"

"I don't know. Maybe."

"Have you lied to the FBI about the murder of Linda Burrows?"

"No."

"Are you withholding information about Linda Burrows' death from the FBI?"

"Not that I'm aware of."

"Yes or no, please."

"No."

"Have you ever lied to Marty Longstreet?"

"No."

"Have you ever lied to Jack Ames?"

"No."

"Have you ever deceived Marty Longstreet?"

"No."

"Have you ever deceived Jack Ames?"

"No."

"Are you the father of Annie Gresham?"

"Yes."

"Did you adopt Annie Gresham?"

"Yes."

"Did you know her father?"

"Yes."

"Do you know who killed her father?"

"I think so."

"Yes or no, please, Mr. Gresham."

"Yes."

"Have you deceived anyone about who murdered Gerry Tybaum?"

Gerry was Annie's birth father. I did know who killed him and I prosecuted him for it. But I also knew another person who might have been involved, and I didn't prosecute him. I didn't prosecute him because I was protecting money Annie had received. So, yes, I had deceived others about who murdered Gerry Tybaum. The problem was, I didn't want to admit that. But I couldn't lie.

"Yes."

"You have deceived someone about who murdered Gerry Tybaum?"

"Yes."

"Have you ever lied to a judge?"

"Yes."

"Have you ever lied to a jury?"

"Yes."

"Do you believe in God?"

"Yes."

"Do you believe God will punish you for lying?"

"No."

"Are you lying to me today?"

"No."

"Have all your answers been truthful?"

"Yes."

"Have all of your answers been complete?"

"Yes."

"This ends the polygraph exam. Thanks for participating."

I didn't respond. The less the Fibbies knew, the better.

After the exam, I turned to the examiner while he was freeing me from his wires and patches.

"Did I pass?"

"That's confidential."

"When will I find out?"

"You won't."

"You mean I'll never find out if you think I'm lying or not?"

At just that moment, Marty Longstreet came around and faced me head-on. "Let's put it this way, Michael. You're still on the case."

"You don't want me removed?"

"No."

"You don't have any reservations about me?"

"No."

"Are you willing to take the polygraph, Agent Longstreet?"

"No."

I smiled. Longstreet returned my smile. Then he shook his head and walked out of the room.

I followed shortly after in the company of a person I'd never seen before. I passed through the outer office and then outside onto the steps.

I had passed, and I was free.

16

Agents Ames and Longstreet followed me outside minutes later and told me they wanted to give me a ride back to my office. It beat a taxi, so I accepted, reminding myself to keep my guard up.

On the way, Jack Ames broke the silence.

"We want Niles Boudreaux next. I suggest we work our way from top to bottom."

"I disagree," I said. "We should work bottom-up. That way we're loaded and ready to pounce by the time we get to the U.S. Attorney himself."

Ames, riding shotgun, shook his head. "We have orders to begin at the top, Michael."

"So someone is protecting the U.S. Attorney? Making it easier on him? Is that it?"

No answer. Then Longstreet said from behind the steering wheel, "No one is giving anyone a break. You've chosen us to head up the investigation. Your role is to attend interrogations and other investigations if you want. Your role isn't to run the investigation. The FBI always runs its investigations, Michael. How long have you been a prosecutor?"

"Not that long. I'm a lateral hire."

"I would've guessed that. The rest of your colleagues know the FBI decides in what order we interview witnesses. Now you know, too."

"And if I want to complain?"

Longstreet found me in the rearview mirror and made eye contact. "Are you always this difficult?"

"Which presupposes I'm difficult," I said and looked out the window. "But the answer is 'No,' I don't consider myself difficult. Just committed, Agent Longstreet. That should make you happy, as anxious as you are to nail the killer of Linda Burrows."

"All opinions are gladly received," Longstreet said. "But remember that they're only opinions. The bottom line is that the investigation belongs to the FBI."

"I would've thought we could work together on this, make joint decisions."

He smiled in the mirror. "Not the way it works. Please schedule Mr. Boudreaux for a meeting with us. Let me or Jack know when and where. We've decided Jack will ask the questions. It keeps you out of the hot seat and might save your job."

"All right," I said with a long sigh. I was tired after the exam and was getting nowhere arguing with Longstreet. The FBI has its methods. My job was to fall in and soldier along with them. My job wasn't to plan the witness order. Now I knew.

TWO DAYS LATER, our foursome was prepared to take the statement of Niles Boudreaux. We had gathered around a conference table in CR

6. Time to begin. We agreed that Jack Ames would ask the questions. Then I would follow-up with any questions I might have.

So it began. Right out of the gate, I could see Ames was going to use an open-ended approach with the U.S. Attorney:

"Mr. Boudreaux, independent of the investigation you have Mr. Gresham here running, have you or anyone working for you done a parallel investigation into Linda Burrows' death?"

Boudreaux shot me a look that said I wasn't going to like his answer. "Yes, I have sources at the Department of Justice looking into this. Sorry, Michael."

"Why 'Sorry, Michael'?"

"Because I feel like I'm betraying Michael by not telling him. But the real truth is, we always do this in personnel death cases."

"Always? You mean there have been others?"

"Not on my watch. I'm talking generally."

"I understand," said Ames. "That's why I asked the question."

He had me there. I wouldn't have known to ask that question.

"What has that parallel investigation turned up?"

"I'd rather not say. That's why it's a secret investigation."

"I'm okay with that," Ames said. "I understand. Let's do this, though. When you're finished with that investigation will you give me a report at that time?"

"Yes. I have no problem doing that."

"Good, good. Now, we're here to shotgun these questions. I mean, this isn't supposed to be like a cross-examination. Just a series of broad, open-ended questions. So let me ask you straight out: do you have any idea who might've killed Linda Burrows?"

"No idea."

"Someone from the office here?"

"Maybe. I honestly don't know."

"Someone on the outside?"

"Same answer."

"Her husband? Might Harry Burrows have killed his ex-wife?"

"Very possible. Harry was a hater and a hitter. Jealous little snot. You know that."

Ames didn't respond, didn't corroborate what he knew or didn't know. The sign of an adept questioner.

"So you don't have any leads?"

"Not yet. I have suspicions but no leads."

"Why don't you tell me your suspicions?"

"Well, the husband seems a very likely candidate. He had motive— she made the mistake of falling out of love then falling back in love-- but with someone besides Harry. He had opportunity—first on the scene of her murder, a cop was seen leaving the store before the first responder. I'm guessing it was Harry Burrows who left. I'm quite interested based on those two hits. If I were you, people, that's where I would start. Check out his alibi. Check out his clothes for blood spatter; you know what to do."

Ames didn't respond verbally, but he did allow a small smile. Oh, yes, his smile said: we do indeed know what to do.

"What about the other men in the office? Have any lovers been identi-fied among them? If so, would you give us a list of them?

"No. We've turned up no others. But we all need to keep in mind that there are men outside the office who might've enjoyed a night or two with our Linda."

"What evidence of that do you have?" I asked.

"Zero. Zilch. Your point is well-taken, Michael."

"Any leads on any of those men?" Ames asked.

"Haven't looked into them yet."

"Here's a question that has been nagging at me," Ames began, headed in a new direction. "What about women? Did Linda have relations with women? Anyone know?"

"That's random," I said sarcastically.

"We've considered that," said Boudreaux. "Right now we have no names, but we're keeping our ear to the ground. I hope to hell there are no women—something like that might keep us tied up for a year or more. President Sinclair sure as hell wouldn't like that."

Then Ames asked, right out of the blue: "What about you, Mr. Boudreaux? Did you have relations with Linda?"

Niles Boudreaux tried to maintain his calm, but he knew we had talked to Harry. He knew Harry had talked to us about the meeting between Boudreaux and Linda at the hotel when Harry caught them. So Boudreaux tried to downplay his involvement with Linda.

"I think I spent one night with her. I'm not proud of that but remember I'm also not married. I should've known better, but hell, Agent Ames, did you ever see the woman we're talking about? She was a pure sex kitten."

"Why did you keep her in the office? It sounds like she was nothing but trouble."

"You can't fire someone based on their sexual predilections. Or for their choice of sex partners. So we had no basis to fire her. But there was one other consideration too. Linda was a terrific prosecutor. I think she was like forty-to-two when she died. She was winning every case she took to trial."

Ames must have known the federal law on firing someone and discriminating against them. It was for damn sure the lawyers in our office knew the law—we had a civil rights division. Firing for sexual behavior would've left the office wide open for a lawsuit. No one wanted that, especially not Boudreaux and especially not the president, either.

"So I have to ask this, Mr. Boudreaux," Ames began, his voice much less edgy. "You have an explanation for your whereabouts the day she died? Is there an alibi?"

Boudreaux nodded as he considered his answer. Then, "Actually, I usually work on Sundays. But that day I was away from the office shopping for my mother's eighty-second birthday. There was a gift to buy; there was a cake to order; there were her old friends to ask over."

"Was anyone with you?"

"No. But I'm sure my credit card will have receipts that prove my whereabouts."

"Can you get those to me?" Ames pressed. "It's just an item on a list we need to check off. I'm as confident about your innocence as I am about the sun in the sky today as we sit here. But if you don't mind, we need that account print-out."

"Sure, sure. Not a problem at all. In fact, I've had my secretary dig it up already. She'll get you those records on your way out."

"Do you mind if we get them from her right now so I can go over any questions I might have while we have you here?"

Without responding, Boudreaux picked up his phone and told the other end what he needed. A woman in a gray flannel coat and skirt came in moments later. She distributed a thin, two-sheet compendium to each one of us. Then she left without a word.

"Fire away," said Boudreaux.

"Well, just a quick glance tells me the credit card charges we're looking at on the day Linda died were all around the noon hour. Linda was killed before noon."

"She was?" said Boudreaux. "I guess I didn't pay much attention to that."

"So these credit card statements almost rule you out, but not totally. Let's just say they don't alibi you, Mr. Boudreaux. What about witnesses? Was anyone with you on the shopping trip?"

"No, I was alone."

"What about that afternoon? What were you doing?"

"I took my purchases to my mother's nursing home. They put the cake and ice cream in the refrigerator. I delivered her present to her. But told her not to open it until her birthday. She loves having presents she's forbidden to open. She loves the drama of waiting."

"Sure, sure. Would she be able to give us a statement of that afternoon's goings-on?"

"No. She has dementia. She couldn't do that."

"So sorry to hear that. What about sign-in records at her nursing home? Did you have to sign-in?"

"No, they don't require that. You just show your ID, and they wave you on back. They know me now so when I come to visit they don't even ask for ID. They just ignore me and nod as I pass the desk. Depending on how busy they are. But mostly it's come-and-go without checking in or out."

"Okay. Well, if you can think of how else we might establish your whereabouts that afternoon, please get back to me on that."

Boudreaux sat up when the line of questioning was exhausted. "Will do," he said in a distant voice.

Jack Ames then looked at me. "Michael, any follow-up?"

"Not really," I began but then a subject came into focus for me, and I stopped. "Wait, there is one thing. Mr. Boudreaux, was Linda threatening you in any way when she was murdered? Was she threatening to reveal your relationship with her, for example?"

He shook his head. "Not at all, Michael. As an unmarried man, I'm almost embarrassment-proof. Plus she wouldn't have wanted to reveal our time together because it might've gotten back to Harry, who was crazy in love still. So it just doesn't make sense for a couple of reasons. Is that all?"

"Well, it bothers me that you're saying you had nothing to lose because you're unmarried. How about the fact that you're having sex with an employee? Wouldn't that have been an embarrassment to the office?"

"Tell the truth, I never really thought of it that way. I've always operated from the point of view that my private life is nobody's business. Especially when my partner isn't under duress or fear about job loss."

"Speaking of the work environment, what about sexual harassment? Did she ever threaten you with a sexual harassment lawsuit?"

"Good grief, no! Linda was a survivor. That would have taken her down, too."

He was about a beat too quick in giving that answer. I know I noticed and if I did, so did the FBI. So I acted as if nothing had happened.

"Like Jack here I'll be very interested in hearing about anyone who might corroborate your alibi. Please let us know in the next little while."

"I already said to Jack I would, Michael. Did you miss that exchange?"

"No, I didn't miss it. I'm just trying to emphasize how helpful it would be to my team and me to have such corroboration so we can cross you off our list."

"What list?"

"Of people with motive and opportunity."

He smirked. "What motive?"

I stared straight into his eyes. "I haven't established that yet. But neither have I quit looking."

I had waited until the very end to spring my surprise on him. "Mr. Boudreaux, I've spoken to Harry Burrows. He told me he caught you and Linda together in a hotel room. Linda was nude, you were or probably had been. She had been showering. Do you recall Harry walking in on you?"

"Not walking in, no. I opened the door, and Harry pushed his way in."

"So you don't deny being with her and being discovered together by Harry?"

"I don't deny it. I was unmarried. Yes, I was discovered by the ex-husband, and he probably has a hatred of me today that makes him dangerous to me. But that doesn't mean I killed Linda. Why would I?"

"We're looking into that," I said. I shouldn't have responded to his bait, but I did. And immediately regretted it. Not professional of me, not at all.

"All right," said Jack Ames in his best overview voice. "I think we're finished."

"Fair enough," said Boudreaux. He gave a smile, but his eyes told the truth: he was eager to chew me up and spit me out.

"Shit," I muttered to myself as we single-filed out of his office.

In for a penny, in for a pound. I had crossed the line with my boss.

We closed his door behind and paused in the hallway.

"Damn, Michael," said Ames with a sharp shake of his head. "Crossed him off our list? What list?"

I stood there, and my mouth moved, but no words came out. Then I managed, "Our list of possible suspects."

"We don't have a list like that. We're still interviewing. No one's a suspect. Not yet."

"I know that. I was just intimidating him."

Jack Ames turned away with a toss of his head. "There's a man who doesn't intimidate. He has more power in his little finger than the four of us have combined. Suggest you re-think that approach for future reference."

"She threatened him with sexual harassment. I could see it on his face," I said quickly.

"Sure, genius," said Longstreet in a mocking tone. "And how you gonna prove that with her dead?"

I had no reply.

Then we split up and went our separate ways—me back to my office where I closed my door and sat at my desk and shut my eyes.

Maybe I had missed the whole point. Maybe if there was a list, maybe it was Boudreaux's list, one he kept.

And maybe I was on his list now instead of the other way around.

17

The FBI crime lab came to my office the next day and took a swab of my nose and a blood sample. They were looking at the dead baby's DNA and comparing that to the DNA of all male staff members. It was very hush-hush, and we were threatened that the test and comparison should never be discussed outside the office. No leaks, absolutely no leaks, said Boudreaux's memo to all staff members. We got the point.

A week later, I got a call from Jack Ames. He and Marty Longstreet were on their way to my office to speak with me. "Don't leave your office, please," Ames told me before hanging up. Now what? I wondered. I had all but forgotten about the DNA testing.

We assembled in my office and Longstreet was the first to speak up. He was beaming and excited. I had the sick feeling he could hardly wait to deliver a bombshell.

"You're the dead baby's father," he said, proudly bearing my bad news as one who has cracked a challenging case. "Now you've become a person of interest."

"What?" I said, stunned at the news. My heart started racing as

Longstreet delivered the hammer. Now my palms were sweaty, and I felt a chill wrapping around me. This news was devastating; it just couldn't be. Hadn't we practiced safe sex that one night? Hadn't we?

I thought back over what had happened. There had been way too much pinot wine. We had taken in a wine-tasting in Georgetown, and we had settled on a pinot that went down way too smooth and had enough oak taste to make me come back for seconds. Then thirds. One thing had led to another and—that was it. We made love in my hotel room after tearing off our clothes and collapsing on my bed. Oh, my God, I remembered—with Jack Ames and Marty Longstreet sitting across from me, gauging my reaction to the news. I thought I was going to pass out. This just couldn't be happening: Linda and I had traded passion for passion and were soon having unprotected sex. That kind, yes. It never crossed my mind, not even once, that we might be making a baby.

But here they were, telling me Linda had died with my son inside her.

I sat back hard in my chair and stared numbly at my desktop. I could hardly move my arms. But I did, sipping my coffee mechanically and with zero enjoyment.

"Who else knows?" I asked lamely.

Ames looked at Longstreet. They laughed. "Get a fucking life, Michael. Are you kidding?"

"Pretend I didn't just say that," I said, still in shock.

"So where does this leave us?" I asked.

"This leaves you with a pretty strong motive to see Linda dead when she refused to have an abortion," Longstreet crowed.

"You've got the wrong guy, Marty," I said. "I'm not like that. I would rather raise the kid alone, on my own, than have a lover get an abortion. Don't forget who eats fish on Fridays, Mr. Omniscient."

"You want me to believe no Catholic has ever had an abortion, Michael? Seriously?"

"Guys, guys, guys," Jack Ames broke in. He was determined to get between us: "Marty, where does this leave Michael? Michael, where does this leave you? Marty goes first."

"As I said, it buries him in motive. Now, all we need was opportunity. Oh, that's right, he can come and go in his job as he pleases. So, he had the opportunity to kill her, too."

"One problem with that, numbnuts," I hissed at Marty. "I don't kill people. Not even people I hate."

He feigned shock at my words, "I feel so safe with you, Michael. Always have."

"Gentlemen, I'm going to break this up now if we can't quit doing petty. I've had about enough from both of you. Michael, for the record, you're not a person of interest to the FBI. Marty was speaking out of turn when he said you were. But let's do think about your alibi too on the day Linda died. Can you get back to me on that? We might as well dot the i's and cross the t's."

"I'll get my calendar out and shoot you my activities that day. I'm sure it's mostly court stuff, so there's a record of my appearances."

"That would do it," Jack said. "That would be all we'd need. Thanks for doing that."

"And don't leave town without telling me," Longstreet added, just the hint of a smile in his eyes.

"Fuck you very much," I said not playfully but without real anger. Just holding up my end of an acrimonious few minutes there.

"Okay, no one else knows this so far, Michael. The FBI plans to keep it that way."

"Then I won't enter it into my file memos. If I did, it would spread around this office like wildfire."

"Forget it, you two," Longstreet said dismissively. "Everyone in the office will know before they go home tonight."

"I don't think so, Marty," Ames said. "I nixed the DNA report coming over here by mail. Michael has the only copy of the report in the office right now."

"Okay," said Longstreet. "Well, Michael, I'm almost certain you won't be announcing it."

Ames smiled. He sat back and placed his palms on his knees. "Exquisite." Then he clapped his hands as if finished, started to stand, then abruptly sat back down. "Seriously, Michael, what were you thinking with this girl?"

I shook my head. "I remember I was lonely. And I hate to admit this, but here it goes: I'd never been so turned on before. Linda was fantastic."

"So we've heard," said Ames. "Glad I missed that."

"You should be," I agreed. "Or maybe not. I've never had those feelings before or since. Now you know all my secrets. I'm embarrassed."

"I'll bet," said Longstreet.

"Well, here's the thing," Ames said. "We've got this little secret, just us girls, Michael's little dalliance and baby. We don't want the rest of the team to know. That would only muddy the water."

"Agree," said Longstreet.

"Same here," I said. "Plus it would be embarrassing. I don't know how I'm going to face you two again, much less the whole team—the whole office, rather. Everyone inside this building would know in less than an hour if we let the cat out of the bag."

"I hear that," said Ames. "So we leave it here."

And so we did.

~

THAT AFTERNOON, I went to confession. I let it all out. The loss of my baby was something I couldn't excuse myself; it took a much higher power than me. Anger at myself, shame, embarrassment, the sadness I had for Linda. Then I launched into my cheating on Verona. Was it a sin since we weren't married? I didn't know about the Church's view of what I'd done. But this much I did know: it had happened before Verona moved with the kids to Washington. It had happened because I'd had wine—I rarely drink—and because Linda was alluring and I was lonely. These were things I couldn't say to the priest: these things were excuses and damn weak ones at that. In the end, the priest did his magic, and I walked out of the booth a technically cleansed and forgiven man.

But in my heart of hearts, I knew better.

My lust might very well have, in some small way, contributed to Linda's death.

Maybe her ex-husband had found out she was pregnant. Maybe he killed her in a rage when he heard.

Maybe, maybe, maybe.

I left the church, grateful for forgiveness in spirit.

But full of loathing for myself in the flesh.

Always the goddamn flesh.

~

AFTER DINNER that night I went into my home office and shut the door. I told Verona I needed an hour alone.

I accessed our office network and decided to take a look at Harry

Burrows' statement. I pulled up the police report filed by Harry, who stated in the very first sentence that he was the first responder on the scene of Linda's murder.

He wrote that he arrived on the scene under an all-cars call from his dispatcher. The time of the call matched the dispatch tapes: 11:44 a.m. She had been shopping for deli items. In her shopping cart was a barbecued chicken, a half-pound of olive loaf, a bottle of ten-dollar wine, Peet's coffee (two k-cup boxes), raisin bran, milk, half-and-half, and four sugar donuts. Nothing on display in Aisle Eleven was found in her cart, leading Harry to speculate she had just begun walking the aisle. Maybe, I thought as I kept reading the report, and maybe not.

The report continued, describing the horror Burrows experienced beginning with finding his ex-wife shot to pieces and trying first to revive her with CPR then stopping to issue a panic call from his shoulder mic requesting medical services and police backup. He had resumed CPR but no luck. Harry had been around. He knew she was dead even before he administered CPR, but the inability to accept her death required that he at least try. When she didn't revive, he sank down and sat beside his ex-wife and took her hand in his. Shock had taken over.

I read on through the report, looking for some mention of time or place or event that might trigger some memory of what I had been doing that day. Finding none, I moved to the detectives' reports, the CSI reports and evidence collected and processed, and then I read and re-read the autopsy.

Finding nothing that triggered a memory from all of the police and technician filings, I browsed to the *Washington Post* archives and immediately found what I was looking for. I loved Bluegrass music, and Verona wanted to hear it for herself. So we had attended a revue hosted by Chris Thile, a musician I considered to be at the very top of the Bluegrass food chain. Through Saturday there was a lot of plucking, fiddling and harmonizing involved with Chris Thile's "American Acoustic Festival" at the Kennedy Center. The composer, singer and mandolin virtuoso curated the four-day festival of Americana music, which included a handful of workshops, family shows, and a free late-night jam session.

Times and prices varied for the performances. So I looked up my orders on the ticket sales website. Sure enough, we had tickets for the Punch Brothers matinee show beginning at noon on June 24, 2017. Local Bluegrass players were appearing starting at noon as warm-ups. We knew we couldn't be out late after being gone all afternoon and the show time worked perfectly for us.

Which led me to my cell phone. I had snapped some pictures. Pictures of the auditorium, the stage, the groups, and even a short video of Thile himself launching into one of his incredible mandolin solos. Last but not least, a selfie with the stage at my back. I was obviously enjoying the music, judging from the huge grin. Bingo, I had my proof.

A warm glow passed through my body. I wouldn't be a person of interest after all.

That had been close.

Oh, so close.

18

Friday night I was restless. Verona could sense it and saw me ignoring the kids. Instead, I was in my home office, poring over police reports and CSI reports and test results and studying Linda's employment file from the USAO.

Around ten o'clock I made a decision. I would go to the watering hole where I knew the people from my team hung out drinking and laughing after a week of tough work. Maybe I could learn something.

When I walked in, they were surprised to see me there, but chairs around their table were immediately shoved apart to make room. The usual questions and commiseration followed; my team liked me and had a million questions, which I tried to answer.

Around eleven o'clock a young woman known to me as Janice—a paralegal from Antonia's team—came up to my chair and bent down to whisper.

"I'm very drunk, and you just got here. Would you take me home, so I don't kill someone with my car?"

She was young enough to be my daughter. Still, I didn't particularly like the notion of being alone with her.

"Why me?" I asked. "Aren't you here with someone?"

"I came here with Piers Litton, but he left." Piers was one of the attorneys on Antonia's team. I vaguely knew him. I could only wonder why he had left Janice there alone, knowing she had been drinking heavily. But I didn't know Piers that well, so I couldn't imagine his motive. Whatever, I finally agreed to call Janice an Uber and send her off.

"Please," she said, "I've been assaulted before. I don't want to be alone late at night with any driver."

"Even Uber?"

"Even anyone."

She hooked me with her reticence: she was a hell of a good-looking young woman, and she was intoxicated. Maybe that did make her a target. So I relented and agreed to take her home. My car was right around in the parking lot. We pulled on our coats and went outside.

I noticed a motorcycle cop parked with his engine idling in the parking lot at the end of my row. But I didn't give him any thought. For one, I had been drinking Coca-Cola, no alcohol. For another, I was an assistant U.S. Attorney: police weren't as scary to us as they might have been to civilians.

He was watching us, I realized. So what? He saw us come out of the bar with my arm around a much younger woman as I tried to keep her from falling. That didn't mean anything in the grand scheme. But the cop pulled the faceplate down on his helmet and hit the starter on his bike. It roared to life, and the twin pistons began loping along, winding up as he twisted the throttle. Neither Janice nor I turned to look. Instead, we climbed into my Mercedes. I had to help her buckle up.

We cautiously pulled out of the lot. Maybe ten seconds later I saw the motorcycle cop in the rearview mirror.

Now the cop was running forty feet behind us. I goosed it up to five over the speed limit, and he readily caught up. I did it because we were in a commercial area that was well-lighted and if we were going to be pulled over, I wanted the stop where it was as light as possible. Just as I predicted, the cop hit his red lights and waved me over. Seconds later we were pulled over to the curb, and the biker was dismounting.

THE COP APPROACHED my driver's side window. I looked over. Janice was relaxed in her seat, her head back against her headrest, her mouth wide open, snoring and unmoving. The cop rapped a gloved hand on the glass. I lowered the window and found myself staring at the black faceplate of a police officer who hid his identity. Suddenly I recognized the situation, and a rush of ice traveled my spine. It was a setup—though I had no idea why I was being singled out. I felt for my gun and remembered I hadn't worn it because guns aren't allowed where alcohol is served. I turned to shout at Janice so she could witness whatever was about to happen and, as the first word came out, the cop raised his sidearm to the window and fired a single shot into my chest. I remember sliding into unconsciousness. I came to in a split-second just as I felt my hand clutching a cold object. Janice failed to see the motorcyclist reach through the open window and plant the .38 pistol in my hand—so she would later testify. In fact, she was trying to unbuckle and jump from the car, without any luck because she was unable to fumble open the seat belt. The cop shook his head. "Not today, honey," he whispered. Then he turned and walked back to his motorcycle and climbed aboard. He had left it running and now leaned hard to the left and twisted on the gas. He made a long, looping U-turn and jetted away from the vehicle and the chaos and horror inside.

Then he was gone.

Here is what Janice told me later. She managed to fumble her phone out of her gold purse and dial 911. It was only a short time before the first police car swooped in on our sedan. The cop bailed out and drew his weapon. Carefully approaching the vehicle as he had learned at the academy, he got close enough to determine what was happening inside. When he drew abreast of the driver's window, he heard Janice's screams. I was lapsing in and out of consciousness although I couldn't move and my mouth didn't work.

"What happened here?" the cop shouted. "Who did this?"

Janice cried out, "A motorcycle cop stopped us! He walked up and shot Michael!"

The cop, lighting up the front seat of my car with his flashlight, pried the gun out of my right hand.

"Whose gun is this?" he asked.

"I don't know," Janice sobbed. "I was trying to get out! It's Michael's, I guess."

A patrol car swerved in front of us, and its brake lights flared. An ambulance arrived. I was lifted out and placed onto a gurney. Then I was wheeled to the ambulance and rolled inside. Doors slammed, a siren erupted, and we were off. It was all a dream to me, coming and going, an enormous pressure forcing my chest to fight for air.

Then I was out.

I AWOKE hours after the surgery. Water was my first whispered request as I couldn't swallow. The endotracheal tube had done its work, leaving my mouth and throat parched.

"Michael, can you hear me? It's Verona."

I blinked several times. Ever so slowly her face came into focus. "Hey," I whispered.

"Hey, yourself."

A nurse leaned into my field of view. "Are you in pain, Mr. Gresham? Do you need more morphine?"

My brain scanned my nerve endings. No pain and I told her so.

"Okay," said the nurse. "You're in ICU. I'll be checking back every few minutes. Just say you have pain and we'll help with that."

"Water," I whispered to her.

"Ice chips. I'll get some."

"Okay. What happened?" I whispered to Verona.

"The bullet pierced your body just over your lung. He was shooting at an angle, so the bullet angled across your chest and exited forward of your armpit. You were fortunate, Michael."

"What about—what's her name??

"Janice? Janice is fine. She told me what happened, that you were taking her home because she'd been drinking. She said to tell you how sorry she was. She said she'd come see you tomorrow."

"Not necessary," I said.

"Michael, the police officer I talked to. Was he the first one on the scene? He told me you had a gun in your hand. Why did you take your gun tonight?"

"I didn't. Someone put it there."

"Who?"

"It must have been the cop who shot me. Who's that cop who shot me?"

"They're working on that. Janice didn't see a badge or a nameplate. She's very little help."

Then it hit me. "Backup, Verona. They say I was holding a gun?"

"Yes, a silver gun."

"I felt something put in my hand. I swear it wasn't mine."

"Let's forget about that. Let's keep you comfortable and let you rest."

Two days later, when I was released to go home, the cops didn't know any more than they did when I was rushed to the hospital.

But the crime lab did. Agent Jack Ames stopped in and gave me the news.

"Where did the gun come from, Michael?" he asked in that steady FBI voice.

"I don't have a clue. It wasn't mine."

"Well, here's the bad news. It's the same gun used to murder Linda Burrows."

"You must be joking."

"No, the crime lab did its workup. Same firearm."

"Oh, my God."

"Boudreaux is in shock, and I don't like some of the things he said."

"Such as."

"Well, he told Marty and me the gun makes you a suspect in Linda's death."

"What did you say?"

He spread his hands. "What could I say? I said I didn't know. I said we needed more time to assess what we knew. We needed to talk to more people. I stalled."

Which was where we left it because Verona arrived to take me home. Then the wheelchair arrived, and I was whisked to the elevator. As we rode down together, Ames told me he'd keep me updated.

I only stared ahead without speaking.

The lawyer inside of me had my attention and had told me to keep my mouth shut.

Nothing I could say could make this go away.

The gun that killed Linda found in my hand? The detectives investigating my shooting were of the opinion that I had pulled it out to confront the cop who shot me. But how could that have happened? I wondered. I wouldn't pull out a gun on a traffic stop. It was ridiculous, and everyone should know it.

Shouldn't they?

19

After release from the hospital, there was a period of rehab. Verona drove me home. As we threaded through heavy traffic, I found myself checking my outside mirror, looking for any sign of a tail. I was frightened and weak--which left me knowing I couldn't defend myself if something did come up. Then there were several days around the house until, at last, I began circling the block with the aid of a cane, getting my strength back. Not long after, I left the cane in the umbrella stand and hoofed it without support.

I was back.

It was time to see Annie. I needed direction because I had never felt so lost in a case. I did have a list, whether my team had one or not. My list included Harry Burrows, who had motive after Linda had gone on with her life and taken a lover, which Harry Burrows had been unable to accept. Would he kill his ex-wife? I knew that he had struck her—seriously injured her before. And Harry had the opportunity. Would he go to the next level and take her life? It was possible.

My list also included Niles Boudreaux, who had a political motive to kill her. After all, she could've been a huge embarrassment to him and his office if she had filed a sexual harassment claim. He'd have been dead in the water before he even started if that had happened. Even President Sinclair has raked him over the coals for that. So he had a strong motive to see her dead. Who else?

There was always the possibility—and a strong one—that we didn't have a clue about who killed Linda. This was the wild card, the possibility that someone she had once prosecuted wanted her dead—payback. The list of people Linda had sent to prison was very long. The list of people she had helped send to their death was much, much shorter; but it existed, as some federal crimes are punishable by death, and Linda had prosecuted her share of those. Angry family and friends, left behind, were capable of anything.

I didn't know whether I had enough data for Annie to do her workup, but it was time to present her with what we did have. Obviously, I needed all the help I could get, so I paid her a visit at her cubicle in the USAO's office. She was busy with another case. I waited until she looked up and asked me what I needed. I explained what we had from the 20,000-foot view and left everything with her.

Two hours later, she entered my office without knocking. I immediately was confronted by a grim look on her face—wrinkled forehead and pursed lips. Plus the eyes—she was sparking.

She plopped down and fixed me with her eyes.

"Does Verona know, Michael."

I realized she had seen what she was bound to see. It didn't look good for me.

"No, she doesn't know."

"What were you thinking? That you could get Linda pregnant and no one would notice?"

"First, I had no idea she was pregnant. Second, I had no idea someone was going to murder her."

Annie was young but mature far beyond her years. And confident. She sat back and casually draped her arm over the chair beside her. "Well, this makes my job lots easier. I have you in my sights, Michael. You're someone I would like to know lots more about if I were the FBI."

"Okay. Go on."

"But I know you. You're Catholic born and raised. You wouldn't hurt an unborn child if your life depended on it. That alone rules you out. You didn't pull the trigger."

"But nobody is going to give that the weight you do because you know me. Others don't."

She was nodding her agreement. "You should consider recusing yourself from the case. I don't see how you can carry on. Especially now with the gun thing."

I let out a long sigh. My daughter. I was a suspect according to her logic. This was going to go downhill fast.

It was early in the day. I knew it was only a matter of time before Niles Boudreaux called me into his office and told me the same thing. I was about to lose my case. That didn't bother me all that much besides the fact no one likes to have a case jerked away. But what did bother me was that I would become a target for whoever took over the case. I would become a person of interest. I would have a bullseye on my back. Even my daughter had her doubts about me.

I responded to her suggestion I recuse myself.

"I probably should bow out. It's only a matter of time before Antonia, and Niles Boudreaux take the case away."

She scoffed. "You think that's all? Ten-to-one says they put you on admin leave, too. You're about to become persona non grata around here, Michael. Which begs the question: where does that leave me when you become a suspect? You're my father. My first loyalty is to you. I can't keep working here. Plus they wouldn't use me on the case again. You know that. So I'm toast too. Too bad; I was starting to like it here."

She hadn't said this much to me in months. She was invested here—to my surprise since she had never evinced any love for the place—and I had ruined it for her.

"Let's leave it alone until I find out what the powers-that-be are going to do with me. Stop working up the case, Annie."

She tossed her head, miffed. "Whatever."

THEN THE HAMMER CAME DOWN. At one o'clock that afternoon I was called by Boudreaux's secretary to a meeting. The boss wanted to talk. Antonia Xiang would be in attendance. I rode the elevator upstairs and plopped down in a waiting room chair.

"Not here, Michael," Joanie, his secretary, said. "Room eight-oh-two. They're waiting."

"They?"

"Just go on, Michael. You know I can't say."

I walked next door to 802 and steeled myself before turning the knob. Then I stepped inside.

Antonia was there at the small rectangular conference table. She sat at the far end. Mr. Boudreaux was across from where I would apparently sit. So I sat and seemed to satisfy them with my selection of chairs.

"Thanks for coming, Michael," Boudreaux said as if we were gathering to share lunch.

"Sure," I said.

"Antonia," said Boudreaux, "Why don't you lead things off?"

She grimly began. "Michael, reference the Linda Burrows case. We've seen the DNA workup. We know you impregnated her. We also believe you tried to bury the DNA report. Now the gun that shot her is found in your possession. We don't know what all this means. Personally, I think it's a setup. But, long story short: it disqualifies you from working up her case any further."

"I thought that might be it," I said.

"But there's more, Michael," Boudreaux said in a voice that was ninety degrees less friendly than when I first stepped into the room just two minutes ago. "I'm putting you on administrative leave until this gets sorted out."

"That doesn't surprise me either," I replied. "I'm in a very awkward position."

"'Awkward' isn't the word I would choose," Boudreaux said. "I would say you're compromised, and that places you at risk. It's all about motive, Michael. It could be argued—by a competent prosecutor— that you had a motive for killing her. She could've ruined your life and ruined your job with a sexual harassment claim. And the gun that killed her found in your hand? How does that happen, Michael? Don't answer—you need to talk to a lawyer."

Sexual harassment? Plus the gun? We were both vulnerable to sexual harassment claims. Which was when I realized that I wasn't any more vulnerable than the man who had just put me on administrative leave. Boudreaux had ten times the exposure I had, given his long-term affair with his employee. Plus, Linda's harassment complaint— if she had filed it—would have seen him fired. I had no idea of where they were romantically, but what if they'd had a falling out and she was head-hunting? He would've been at total risk. But now I had put the spotlight on me with the pregnancy. He probably would've kissed me if Antonia wasn't there, for taking the heat off him. As it was, he played true professional.

I couldn't resist, though I should have. "So I'm your whipping boy. Focus the case on me, and that moves the focus off of you, Mr. Boudreaux," I said. "Nicely done."

He didn't flinch, and he didn't give away anything. "You'll have your chance to make that case if you're unlucky and find yourself indicted, Michael. Right now is neither the time nor the place to try to switch the blame to me. It wasn't my child she was carrying."

He had me. It wasn't the time or place. The pressure was getting to me. I loved my new job, loved the brain trust I got to work with every day. I loved having the FBI at my disposal to help make my cases, and I loved the power the whole thing gave me. I had become a power freak to some extent, I realized just then. Not good.

"So clean out your desk and turn in your ID. I expect you to leave my office immediately."

"That's it? Am I still on the payroll?"

"Of course. You haven't been convicted of anything. However, I do have just cause for firing you. But I'm not going to do that—yet. It wouldn't look right."

"What's that mean, 'look right'?"

"It means your employer, the prosecutor's office, shouldn't just throw you to the wolves. That would be very bad for morale. Plus it would make me look like a chickenshit. We can't have that."

"Great," I heard myself say.

"Sorry, Michael," said Antonia.

"It's okay," I said. "Not your doing. I was stupid. Not guilty of anything but stupidity, Antonia."

It was a defense—but not a legal one, only an emotional one—that I would hear myself interposing many, many times in the months to come: guilty of stupidity, yes; of murder, no.

We broke off, and I left the conference room. Boudreaux and Antonia stayed behind. I wasn't ten steps down the hall until I felt my ears burning.

They were talking about me.

And I didn't like it.

Worse, I was scared.

20

Events in my life never happen in the order I'm expecting. And some events happen that I never see coming. One of these was the re-entry of my brother Arnie into my life. Expected or not, here he came one night while I was on admin leave. It was a telephone call to me. He wanted to follow that up with a visit. Or a short stay with me. A stay akin to a rest cure. Oh hell: Arnie had gone off his meds again, and his shrink had put him into rehab, but now he needed a halfway house kind of setting. I was the chosen one for that.

When Arnie refuses to take his meds, I get panicky calls like that one, the night after I was semi-retired from the USAO. The other type of call I get will be from his partners at his law firm begging me to step up and make Arnie behave. As if I or anyone could ever do that. What can a brother do for a brother who won't medicate?

Arnie's actual diagnosis depends on which psychiatrist he is seeing. Sometimes he is bipolar, and that explains his mania. Other times he is agoraphobic, and that explains his refusal to leave his apartment for days, hanging out in his pajamas and refusing to shower. Other times he is suffering from a dissociative disorder that explains the new personality my brother suddenly has speaking for him. I don't know; maybe he's all three. My parents are gone, for all intents and purposes; there are no other siblings, so Arnie falls to me. Which is fine; truth be told, I all but worship my brother. One day, science will solve the mysteries of Arnie's psychology, but it hasn't done so yet.

He called that night, and his voice sounded small and far off. I hardly recognized him until he said, "Michael, it's Arnie, your brother."

"Arnie!" I emoted into the telephone. I sounded much happier than my reality when I greeted him. If the call came over the Christmas holidays, I usually knew the glad tidings season had worn him down. If it came over New Years, I knew he was into the liquor cabinet—an absolute no-no for someone with Arnie's potpourri of psychological problems. If it came around his birthday he would be suffering from an annual trauma that always began, "I'm one year closer to dying, Michael...." But this call was around none of those special times. This call was unexpected. So what had pushed him over the cliff this time? Why had he once again stopped taking his meds?

"Hi Michael," he replied. "I hate these calls I have to make to you. But Dr. Mickelson insisted I needed a support group when I got out of treatment. You're the only support group I have, little brother. So I'm throwing myself on your mercy."

"Slow down, Arnie. I'm reading between the lines, and I'm thinking you had a med relapse. How close am I?"

"I got overloaded, Michael. The futility of my life hit me in the face, and my world came crashing down. I stopped the meds so I could hear the music. So I could hear the inner voices that tell me which direction to proceed."

"That doesn't sound medically sanctioned to me," I replied. Of course, it wasn't. The last thing any of Arnie's doctors wanted for him was a divorce from his Risperdal, his Zoloft, his Lamictal, and so on. "So what straw broke the camel's back for you this time?"

"I was doing fine—my partners at the law firm voted me a two-hundred-and-fifty-thousand dollar bonus. Sweet, as they say. I took a two-week holiday to Santa Barbara. While I was there, I decided to try out medical marijuana. You know all the stuff you hear about it—even the veterans are using it now for PTSD. So I figured it wouldn't hurt to try."

I knew a little bit about it. I do my share of reading about new treatments for people like my brother.

"Medical marijuana isn't indicated for bipolar disorder, Arnie. It can have unwanted side effects. Trying it in your case wasn't very smart."

"Who said anything about bipolar, Michael? Has anyone made that diagnosis? You know they haven't. My diagnosis remains undetermined to this day. Of course, there is a small group of physicians that believe I suffer from aspects of schizophrenia. And some who think bipolar is a real possibility. But the truth-tellers won't go that far. Anyway, I decided to give pot a try. I thought it couldn't hurt. So I bought a vape of CBD and started puffing."

"What happened, Arnie?"

"Within fifteen minutes my headache was gone. Another fifteen and my limbs were relaxed and not jerking all the time from the Risperdal. Thirty minutes later, my back pain had relented like seventy-percent. It's a miracle drug, Michael. Unfortunately, Illinois doesn't recognize it for any of my ailments. I can't get a medical marijuana card where I live. I figured the hell with Illinois and began laying out plans to move to California. It was a smart move from where I was sitting."

"Except there was the law practice waiting back in Chicago. What were you going to do about that?"

"Move my practice. Live and work out of California and commute to Illinois for key depositions and court dates. I had it all planned out."

"Sounds doable so far. So why are you calling me?"

"I decided to step up the salutary effects of marijuana. I added in some THC, which you know is the psychoactive element of marijuana. I might have added too much because I suddenly found myself elated. I smoked it continuously over a weekend, and by Sunday night, when I was waiting for *Game of Thrones* to start, I realized I hadn't had any of my pills since Friday. The floor was rising up to me, and suddenly I came crashing down through space and wound up in the emergency room. They said I was seen downstairs in the hotel lobby completely nude and trying to change to a long-term room. That part escapes me—I have no recall and can't argue with them. So I called Dr. Johansson, and he sent an assistant who accompanied me back to Chicago. I was admitted to rehab and spent the last month there, getting my meds back in place. I'm doing better now. But I need to stay with my support group for at least two weeks now."

"And I'm your support group. Got it."

"Do you resent that? Do I hear resentment in your voice, Michael?"

"Not at all," I honestly could say. "You're my brother, and I love you. You're always welcome here."

I was already counting bedrooms, wondering where we'd put my brother up for two weeks. In a flash I realized: he'd be taking over my office. A rent-a-bed was in the works.

At one time I wrote to Arnie's new doctor:

Ever since we were playing Tonka trucks, my brother has been a study in spotty mental hygiene. I am younger than him by five years and have followed his career in and out of the offices of mental health professionals for almost fifty years. His inner life seesaws between mania and psychosis; he takes meds for these things only because his outer life goes to hell the minute he stops and it frightens him. Until it doesn't. Like me, he is a lawyer. He runs the litigation group at Eden Shaw Robles, a 400 lawyer firm in downtown Chicago.

That just about summarized our time together on Mother Earth. Him using, me stabilizing where possible. Or him not using and me chasing him down, getting him the help he needs, then me stabilizing him again.

One thing was true: I would never fail him. My home was always open to Arnie.

"Of course come here and chill with me as long as you want," I said a second time. "Do you need me to purchase your ticket?"

"Of course not, Michael. My SEP-IRA is at five million right now. Nobody needs to pay for anything for me."

"All right, just asking. When are you coming?"

I could hear him speaking to someone else. Then he returned, "My doctor wants me to come tomorrow. He doesn't want me alone in my house for even one night."

"That's perfect. You'll be sleeping in my home office. Hope that's okay."

"Whatever you have to offer will be fine. I don't take up much air."

"I know that. But you always know, *Mi casa es su casa.*"

"Then I'll be there tomorrow. Email me the address. I'll grab a cab over."

"I'll do that as soon as I hang up. So come on ahead, brother, and we'll have a few laughs and let you get your feet under you. You're welcome for as long as you want."

"Tomorrow, Michael. Goodbye for now."

We ended the call.

At that time I wasn't accustomed to the calculus of having two mentally-challenged people under one roof with an amateur like me directing traffic, real and imagined. Annie added to Arnie equals what? I remember thinking as I drifted off to sleep beside Verona that night.

I was asleep before the answer revealed itself.

21

Our usual meeting place—when we didn't want attention—was the Washington Monument benches. Talk about inauspicious, as if thousands of people a day don't visit there. But that was just it: we could lose ourselves in the crowd.

I'm talking about Antonia, my supervisor at USAO, and my friend from our time in Russia freeing her husband.

Long story short: she called me. "We need to talk," she said from a calling number I didn't recognize. Probably a burner phone. Or maybe a payphone—I didn't know. One thing for sure: it wasn't her office phone, and it wasn't her cellphone, and it wasn't her home phone—numbers I already had stored.

It was Tuesday afternoon, biting cold outside but clear skies, so I dressed in my jeans and Patagonia shell with a flannel shirt. She arrived maybe ten minutes after me. She wore a black dress, a necklace of small pearls, expensive heels, and a Coach purse. A long black winter coat, open down the front, heightened her tall, slender Vogue look. And there was the requisite neck scarf, strategically selected to tie together her ensemble. Her sunglasses and visored cap were out of place—at least to my eye—but they hid her features well. I wouldn't have recognized her ten feet away. She sat apart from me maybe four feet. We both stared straight ahead.

Then she opened her purse and made a big production out of blotting her lips with a tissue. She spoke to me from behind it.

"Boudreaux has you in his sights, Michael."

I said nothing, just stared straight ahead.

"He's convinced you killed Linda. He found a file on your computer with Linda's home address and her cell number. Why would you have those?"

Honestly, I couldn't say. "Were they part of a program? Database?"

"Your contacts list. Boudreaux suddenly caught fire when Linda's autopsy and DNA reports showed up."

"I'm clueless why it was on there. Maybe—I don't know. I can't even speculate, but I don't remember putting it there."

"Interesting. Maybe it wasn't you who did put it there."

"Meaning?"

"Maybe the office's forensic computer geek put it there."

"Now why would he do that?"

"I don't know. Because Boudreaux told him to?"

Seriously, I hadn't even considered that possibility. But I had crossed Boudreaux—at least in his eyes. It was the day Jack Ames established Boudreaux had slept with Linda, the day we took Boudreaux's statement during our investigation. It was also the day I learned Boudreaux had mounted his own, secret investigation. He had told us that was standard procedure whenever a member of the staff was assaulted—or worse. The purpose of doing it was to negate at trial any suggestion by defense counsel that someone in the USAO might have been the perp. If the USAO did its own internal investigation, Boudreaux could come into court and testify an independent study turned up no complicity by a staff member. It was smart business and very important to a case.

I said when she suggested Boudreaux might've slipped Linda's private info onto my contacts list, "Then we've all got a bigger problem than any of us knew."

"Michael, not all of us trust Boudreaux. He's a politician first and a human being second. He'll tell you he's got your back, but that doesn't mean anything. More than one staff member lost their job when Boudreaux blindsided them."

"I even liked him at first."

"As I said, Michael, he's political. He can be very likable."

"I didn't know."

"Now you do. Watch your back, my friend."

She stood up to leave. We hadn't spoken face-to-face yet.

"If I were you," she said across the wind, "I'd make every effort to get to the bottom of Linda's murder...and fast."

"Sounds smart. Am I about to be indicted?"

"No way of knowing. But if you are, you're miles ahead to have the phantom perp in place to point the finger at when you go to trial. Capiche?"

"Totally."

"So long, Michael. Watch your back."

"Thank you, Antonia."

"You'd do the same for me. I have no doubt."

I milled around once Antonia was gone, but after a couple of minutes

I fell in behind her, following from a great distance.

She evidently was on foot for we crossed through the Washington Monument parking lot and kept going. We headed up Fourteenth Street and took a right at Constitution Avenue. We then made our way north on Sixth Street where, halfway up, she ducked into the Wolfgang Puck restaurant called The Source. I knew it to be a cool Asian place; I waited outside, a block away, for her to finish our little walk. As I waited, I counted faces and checked them out again and again. I wasn't an expert, but if she was being followed, I thought I would've picked up on it. It was important to me because I needed to know whether the FBI had eyeballs on us.

I then walked north, beyond the restaurant, and crossed the street. A bus bench was unoccupied, so I took a seat. Now I could watch the entire opposite block.

Ten minutes later she came out onto the sidewalk, her purse over her shoulder and her hands holding a plastic bag in which I would've bet there was a Styrofoam takeaway container. Then she did a funny thing. She went back inside the restaurant. Five minutes later she hadn't reappeared. I stood and crossed back the way I'd come but went straight at the corner rather than turning back right toward the restaurant. Halfway up the block, an alley cut off to my right. I turned and followed it halfway down its length. Sure enough, there was the back entrance to The Source. The restaurant's back door was wide open—presumably to let fresh air into the kitchen.

I knew I was too late. Antonia had exited through the back door and was long gone. Which was fine. The USAO was only a few blocks away, and I had come to see what I had seen: no one following after her. And what about after me?

I went out the far end of the alley, made a right, and suddenly pressed my back up against a wall and waited. A good ten minutes.

Then I decided that if someone were pursuing me, they were damn patient.

22

The next day dawned to find me up and drinking coffee like it was going to be taken away. I was on my third cup when Verona traipsed downstairs to find me in the kitchen at our circular table. She brushed aside my feet, which had been comfortably resting in the chair next to mine.

"What's up?" she asked.

"Same old, same old."

My thoughts about my administrative leave, the possible roads Boudreaux's investigation might take, and the possibility I would become a hard suspect in the investigation into the murder of Linda Burrows had become a daily meditation.

"You're up early," said Verona.

"I am. I'm thinking, which I've realized since I've been staying home, I wasn't doing enough of before."

"Penny for those beautiful thoughts."

"You don't wanna know."

"But I do," she said and poured coffee into a porcelain mug from the Moscow airport.

"I'm thinking there's something I have to tell you. But I'm afraid you're going to leave me if I do."

There, the cat was half out of the bag. I felt an immediate release of pressure in my chest but at the same time dreaded the hammer that might come down on my head when I told her the truth.

"Uh-oh. Should I be packing my bags, Michael? Or can you give me some credit for knowing how lucky I am to be with a beautiful man like you?"

"Oh, that makes what I have to say hurt even more."

"Just say it."

"I got someone pregnant."

"Anyone I know?"

Understatement; that was my Verona.

"A woman at work."

"Let me guess the rest: she meant nothing, it was a one-time thing, you had been drinking, you had been working late together, I was still in Chicago with the kids. How am I doing?"

"You stole my speech."

"That isn't a speech. That's a string of excuses. This is what I want to hear: are we still good? Or is your guilt going to drive us apart?"

Really? I wanted to cry out with joy. Was that going to be the end of it? Who was this incredible woman who shared my bed?

"My guilt isn't driving me away from you. That's between my priest and me, and I've already made that stop on my way back to you."

"Well, good then. Can I fix you a nice cheese omelet today?"

Seriously? You'll cook for me. I've known women who would be throwing carving knives my way.

"You're amazing," I said.

"No, not amazing. I'm fifty-three with no brighter prospect in my life than you, Michael. I love you. I can't afford to lose you over my pride or hurt feelings. So I won't let that happen. With cheese or without?"

"With. I love you, Verona."

"I know that. How that reconciles with your news of the day, I'm not sure. I'm not sure I even want to go there. I think I might just leave it beside the road in a pile called Life's Little Mysteries."

I clammed up. Then I couldn't stand it, "But you'll never know—"

"I'll never know how much you love me? Yes, I will. I'll know. We'll have a minor setback or two, but so far you've been pretty good to me. I'm good with you. Hash browns?"

"Maybe toast with marmalade."

"Done. Now pour yourself another coffee and some OJ. Your breakfast is two minutes away."

And like that, it was done. We went on to discuss Arnie—she'd never met my brother, but she was anxious to welcome him and offer any help she could.

I cleaned the garage the rest of the morning. Arnie would be arriving in the late afternoon. A rental bed delivered just after lunch fit alongside my desk perfectly. Verona cleaned out two of the drawers in my office desk so Arnie would have someplace to keep a few things while he was with us. Then she checked the bathroom off the office and gave it a good going-over. She then got me to remember some of Arnie's favorite foods and set off to the grocery store.

By two o'clock I was close to having a breakdown after allowing the Linda Burrows case to churn up my mind for two hours. It was more than unnerving; it was impossibly complicated in so many ways that I found myself helpless and trapped in a snare of my own making. I wanted to call Antonia and check in, but I knew she couldn't and wouldn't discuss the investigation with me. Plus, that would obviously amount to taking advantage of our friendship if I called. She and Boudreaux were going to do what they were going to do, and there wasn't a damn thing I could do about it. At least not from their side of the street. But what about my side? What could I do to protect myself?

The answer was obvious, and I finally was able to see it: only by finding the real killer could I exonerate myself. So I committed to doing just that. I needed to apply every skill and asset to finding Linda Burrows' killer.

For openers, I needed an investigator. Rusty was still working at the USAO, and I didn't blame him. It was a real job with security and professional challenges, and if he ever did go on to law school, he would have the perfect entrée into a great job there. No, Rusty couldn't help me.

So that left my old standby, Marcel Rainford. Marcel had been with me for years. But after Russia he had taken a different path, winding up working for Interpol in Europe. Now I needed him, the most capable snoop and facilitator I'd ever had working with me. He was gold. Would he drop whatever he was doing and come to Washington and save my stupid butt? I didn't know. Only one way to find out.

I still had his cell number. My hands shook as I dialed it. This had to work, or I was sunk.

I waited for him to answer, thoughts racing through my head.

Marcel was with me almost fifteen years before going to Interpol. We date back to when we got called up to go to Iraq during Bush Two's misadventure. I was Reserve. I served ten months in-country in the JAG Corps; Marcel served two tours as General Dumont's logistics officer—meaning he was a bodyguard who didn't get to shoot anyone because he was guarding a four-star Army general. We both came out frustrated, but we had gotten to know each other at beer call, and we had hit it off. When we returned to the states—this was Chicago—, I had a law practice I gave CPR. It wasn't quite dead because I'd had two friends of mine, lawyers from Chicago, keep my phone lines open handling calls on my work-in-progress—for a split in the fees, of course. When we left the Army, Marcel had no place to go, so he tagged along, got his investigator's license, and began working up criminal cases for me. It worked out well; we were tight until years later when we handled a case in Russia. At its conclusion, we left Russia, and he went to Europe while I returned to Chicago.

A familiar voice finally answered. "Hello, Michael. Long time, little brother."

"Long time yes. You okay?"

"Haven't been shot at in weeks now. You?"

"I was doing okay. Now I'm not so sure."

"You went to D.C. I follow you, Mikey. You went to the U.S. Attorney's office? How's that working out? Putting lots of bad guys in jail?"

"I was. But then I hit a wall. I got a co-worker pregnant, and someone murdered her. DNA tests pointed back to me as the father of the baby. Now everyone at the office and the FBI is investigating the case with me as a person of interest. Or even a suspect, I don't know. It was stupid of me to fool around on Verona, I've already been to see the priest."

"What about Verona? She hanging with you?"

"Surprisingly enough, she is. She's pretty amazing, and I'm damn lucky to have her. My little dalliance won't ever happen again."

"You should tell her that, Michael."

"I have, brother. I have."

"So what else is new?"

"I adopted a twelve-year-old girl after her family was murdered. She's thirteen now. She doesn't talk much, but she's a savant. She's shown a particular gift for profiling people. So she was working alongside me at the USAO. When I got put on admin leave, she came with me."

"How the hell is she working? Why isn't she in school?"

"She has some emotional things going on. A judge said she could be home-schooled and work too. Verona's been doing the home-schooling. She taught at Moscow State University, in case you've forgotten."

"What about Dania and Mikey? They're good."

"Can hardly keep them in clothes, they're growing so fast. But they're great."

"Getting over the loss of Danny?"

"Who, me or the kids?"

He paused. "All of you."

"I guess so. Tell the truth, my feelings about Danny and the pain I'm still feeling are what led me to cheat on Verona. Sounds like an excuse, I guess. But the pain was real. I was trying to douse those old embers I still carry for Danny. But it didn't work. I know that now. She's gone, and I just have to live with that. It hurts every day, Marcel. It hurts lots."

"I'm sure it does. Now, how can I help?"

"I need your help finding the person who killed the girl I got pregnant."

Long pause. "You're sure it wasn't you? Sorry, I have to ask."

"Positive. You know me; I don't operate that way."

"I do know you. But people can do crazy things when they're in psychic pain. So I needed to cross that off my list. Now, you want me to come to Washington?"

"Do you have any vacation time you could use to come here? Anything like that?"

"Nope. But it doesn't matter. I've been thinking about coming back to the States anyway. Europe has changed since the jihadists came to town. The whole place reeks of fear. Not for me."

"Sorry to hear that."

"No, it's just the way of the world right now. So I was thinking of calling you up anyway and see whether you had anything stirring. Anything I could hire on to do."

"Well, the writing's pretty much on the wall for my U.S. Attorney job. I doubt they're ever going to want me back."

"So where does that leave you? Back to Chicago? Stay in D.C.? Some-place else?"

"Haven't got that far. But Chicago is done. I sold the practice."

"Okay, cross that off. What about the West Coast?"

"Too old for that. *Surfin' USA.* Beachy blond hairdos no longer get me going. No, I'm thinking right here in D.C. There're more lawyers per capita than horse flies on a sweaty cow. Besides, there's so much to see and do. I wouldn't mind the kids growing up here and taking in all it has to offer. They could do much worse."

"True that. So what kind of timing are we talking about?"

"ASAP. I need you yesterday."

"I'm on my way. Let me tie up a few loose ends and explain to my lady friend why I'm leaving."

"Hell, bring her with you."

"She's got kids in school here. It would be a mess."

"I'll look around for office space. Let's hit the ground running."

"Same salary as before? I hate to ask, but the lottery still hasn't ironed out my financial wrinkles."

"Same salary. Which means I have to start drumming up some defense work. I'll give my notice at work."

"I'm on my way."

"I'll email my address. Come here, and we'll work out a place for you to crash until we're all financed again."

"I just might take you up on that. But I do have a bit of money squirreled away. So I'll come to see you as soon as we touch down, but I'll probably start looking for my own place the next day. That work for you?"

"Absolutely. I wouldn't want to stay long with me either, three kids and all. Oh, and guess who else is coming to town?"

"Arnie?"

"How'd you know?"

"It was about time for Arnie to go off his meds again. It's been at least a year since last time, right?"

"About that. So he's with me for the next couple of weeks."

"Good, then you'll have something to do after work."

"Get serious. Who can even work with Arnie on-board?"

"We'll have to talk about that. He might be able to fit right into our little scheme if he's still got a license to practice law."

"He does. You're not suggesting using him on the case they're probably going to file against me?"

"He's a top litigator in Chicago's snake den. He's got the brains and the experience."

"All right, we'll discuss that when you get here. But don't expect too much on that. I don't trust Arnie even when he's right in front of me. But that's just me."

"Maybe he needs a leave of absence from his firm. That's all I'm saying. Nothing permanent."

We talked a few more minutes then we said our goodbyes.

When I hung up, I had to pinch myself. For the first time in days, I felt pretty good. I felt like I had some hope again.

Marcel does that for me.

Rock solid, thorough, and has my best interests at heart.

What more could I want?

23

Arnie was in an expansive mood, and he was determined to make a friend of Annie. Arnie had been in town all of two hours and back at my house forty-five minutes when Annie came into the kitchen for a glass of ice. Arnie and I were across from each other at the kitchen table. He had been providing me with the full history of his current problems. I was a good listener to my brother. He was older: we still did that thing where the eldest gets to talk first.

But when Annie strolled into the kitchen, Arnie's antennae shot up.

"This is Annie," I said. "Annie come meet your Uncle Arnie."

She neither acknowledged me nor turned to see her uncle out of pure curiosity. She held her glass under the refrigerator's ice dispenser, and a fistful of cubes chugged into her glass. She held her head high as she turned around and began to walk out.

"Hey," I called to her. "Annie, please come here and talk to your dad."

That worked. It almost always worked.

"Look, Michael, I'm swamped right now. I don't have time to talk."

"Give me just two minutes. This man is my brother. Remember when you had a brother?"

"Of course I remember my brother. And my sister. But what does any of that have to do with your brother?"

She had me there. But I plunged ahead.

"If you can remember how deeply you felt about your brother and sister then I'm hoping you can understand how much I love my brother. And how much I love you and want you two to be friends."

"Friends?" she said. She swirled the ice around in her glass. "I don't have time for friends, Michael. What's the point?"

"Sit down, Annie," I said with a sigh. "Let's take a few minutes and talk friends."

She advanced to the table then halted a step short. She was on my right shoulder, so I gently took her hand and pulled her down into the seat beside mine. She didn't pull away, but she also wasn't joining the companionship emanating from a table around which family and friends gathered. Of course, she wouldn't; she didn't know Arnie, and she didn't have time to dilly-dally anyway, to hear her tell it. Just then my heart went out to her, and I felt sorry for Annie. She was sentenced to a life without close relationships with people all because of a—a what? A congenital disability? Some disease in child-hood? Genetics? I didn't know, and it was very frustrating at such times. I secretly still harbored the very last remnants of a belief that I could cure her, that I could deliver her back into the world to take up where others of her age were. But of course, it never worked that way and never would. Maybe I was the only one to feel her loss, too. Talk about co-dependent. But that's what being a parent is all about: being co-dependent in your kids' lives but getting a pass on it. I don't have to attend Co-Dependents Anonymous meetings because co-depen-dency with your kids is expected--my attempt at humor. An exception to otherwise unhealthy relationships. Anyway, I was thinking all of these things in the instant between Annie sitting down and Arnie fixing her with his eyes. Together at last. I held my breath.

"So, my niece," Arnie slowly began in his South Chicago drawl, "what are you up to these days?"

I could almost see her eyes glaze over. This was going to be a dry well for Arnie. She looked neither right nor left. There was no eye contact possible—Arnie should've seen that right off. But Arnie doesn't always succumb to obvious social signs either. Arnie can be—how do I say it—very, very pushy. He's used to getting his way, but endearingly because he cares about other people and wants to be emotionally close to loved ones. Annie was buying none of that. She just wasn't built that way; there was no "caring" about other people. Perfunctory and goal-driven. That's how I described my newest child.

"Annie doesn't like to talk a lot," I told my brother. "She's a very quiet child."

"Does she know I'm talking to her?"

"Yes and no. She probably knows, but it doesn't register inside her mind as a trigger to reply. She isn't like that. Just enjoy having her around."

"Annie," Arnie said, coming from a new angle, "I was in rehab. I went off my meds, and whammo, I was loony as a psychiatrist's waiting room."

No response—of course. But that didn't stop Arnie.

"They say I'm bipolar. And maybe a little schizoid too, I don't know. What's your working diagnosis, if you don't mind your very interested uncle asking?"

"I'm going to my room now," Annie muttered at me. Then she stopped. "You're my dad's brother?" she said to Arnie. I felt a thrill run down my back. I'd never actually seen Annie respond to another except for her brother and sister when they were alive. Here was a first and I sucked in my breath so as not to interrupt.

"I am your dad's brother. His older brother, I should add. I'm the head of what's left of our family. Where is your family?"

She shot me a look. She waited. I responded, "Annie's family was attacked. She's the only one who survived."

"Oh, oh, that's very sad. But Michael, you've had a tragic loss with Danny, so I expect you have something in common with Annie that's created a bond."

Sometimes we need to listen carefully to our nearby angels. They can be very insightful.

"I've thought that," I said to Arnie. "We hit it off just immediately when we met."

"Like I hope we will, too," said Arnie, "You see, Annie, like you I'm also drifting through life. Rudderless, no clear direction forward. A headful of medications but a heart craving freedom from all chemicals. There's been a good deal of loss for me, too."

"Not the same thing, Arnie," I said with a frown. The frown meant he should take what she'd given—a few words—and let her go before he ran her off with a bunch of psycho-babble. Arnie's psycho-babble was a learned tongue, accumulated by sitting a few times too many in the offices of mental health professionals. My brother had earned every bit of that jabberwocky.

"Okay, Annie," he finally said with a shrug. "We'll talk more after I've had a rest. We have plenty of time. This has been good."

"Like I tried to tell you," I started in with Arnie after Annie had left us alone, "she's low-verbal. Very low-verbal. But she can do things with the database occupying her mind that mere mortals like you and I can only aspire to."

"What kind of things?"

"She knows things about people. Lots of things, just by looking at them. And she also has a capacity for predicting perpetrators' profiles by studying police reports and feeding that kind of data into her computer. I don't know how it works. But I can tell you that she knows more about you at this very minute than anyone else, except yours truly. She's amazing."

"That could come in very useful in your case, Michael."

I had given him just a skeletal view of my legal difficulties when he arrived. It's the wise attorney who has access to Arnie and takes a few minutes to run his most challenging case by him, and I knew that. After he had mulled it over for a day or two or three, he would offer up some advantageous points about my dilemma. I hadn't, however, followed up with him on what Marcel and I discussed: enlisting him to help as counsel in my case. I hadn't anywhere near gotten that far, and I wasn't sure I wanted to. First, before making any decision like that, I needed to know where his head was. When he's really off his rocker, he can hardly string two thoughts together to make a sentence. I needed to be sure he wasn't still operating out of what I would almost call his pre-cognitive state if you will. That would be the state of his mind before new drug prescriptions took hold and produced logical thought processes inside Arnie's tortured brain. I loved my brother, but there were times when it was good to share info with him and times when you definitely should clam up.

Just then, Verona came into the kitchen and sat just across from Arnie. "Your bed's all set up with clean everything," she told him with a broad smile. "I think you're going to be very comfortable here."

Without even a thank-you, Arnie said, "So what's the deal with you two, Verona? Are you pressing my brother to get married? Pressure doesn't work with Michael. I'm sure you've found that out by now. Or maybe you're smarter than that. Maybe you won't apply the thumbscrews until after you've got his last name?"

"My God, Arnie," I said, raising my voice, "let's leave the mating of my family outside in the driveway, shall we?"

Arnie looked hurt. "Overstepping, am I?"

I had my answer. He wasn't ready to join me in the investigation of Linda's death and the defense of any case that might be filed against me. No way was he ready. Nor was I anywhere near ready for him.

Verona took it in stride. "I don't know, Arnie, let's ask Michael, shall we? Michael, do you feel I'm pressuring you into marriage?"

"If anyone's pressuring, it's me," I said. "And I have been for nearly two years now."

Arnie shook his head. "That doesn't sound like you, Michael. I'm not sure I understand the two of you at all."

Verona fielded that one. "That's okay, Arnie, you don't have to understand us to stay with us awhile and get your life sorted out. We're just going to love you regardless."

"Well, that's sweet of you to say." He turned to me. "I like her, Michael. No wonder you're begging for her hand."

There was no winning with Arnie. So I just smiled dreamily at the refrigerator and played like that topic was exhausted.

"So, Michael, how's it going at the office?" Arnie asked.

Verona got up and ran water into the sink. She turned to me. "Michael, are you going to share with your brother that case about Linda Somebody and you investigating her death? Did you tell him they might consider you a suspect too? I'm sure Arnie will have lots of ideas about all that."

Damn it! What the hell just went cockeyed in her brain? But the cat was out of the bag. Arnie wasted no time.

"You might be a suspect in a murder case? Is this true, Michael?"

I closed my eyes and let out a long stream of air before answering.

"It's nothing. I think Verona meant to say that I'm pursuing the suspect, not that I am the suspect."

Should she turn around to correct me, I was ready.

Instead, she said, "You seemed very worried about it the other night, Michael. I don't think I've seen you fighting back the tears since you told me how Danny died. Poor baby, Arnie. Your brother has had some rough times these past years. And now he's a suspect. I hear you're a legal giant. Maybe you can help him."

"Michael, we need to talk about this—tomorrow. My nighttime meds are kicking in, and I need to get some sleep. Night, all."

We said our goodnights and Verona and I were alone at the kitchen table, her with her last few sips of wine, me with a mug of coffee gone cold. I shook my head as I glared at her.

"Did you have to?" I asked.

"I'm worried. You told me Arnie is one of the greats. I'd like to have him on your side. I did it because I love you."

"You did it because you're just a little bit controlling, yes?"

She sat upright and toyed with her glass. Then, "Did I control you into bed with Linda Burrows? What, I didn't? Maybe your wrong choice makes me feel you need a little more controlling. I'm sure you don't blame me."

We were in bed after Stephen Colbert's show. Two hours later, I finally dozed off.

We were even, Verona and I.

Well, not really.

That would never be.

24

We took my boat out on the Potomac the next day at noon, Marcel, Arnie, and me. It was time to discuss the case. My latest toy was a Sea Ray 45 Sundancer, a new boat that still smelled new and that had never been in salt water—although you could hear the locals argue saltwater versus freshwater all night. I had my Sundancer dressed to the nines: Joystick Propulsion, full teak cockpit, twin Raymarine GPS's with radar and sonar, and Sat TV—huge overkill but fun stuff. Cummins twin Zeus diesel engines put out 918 HP—enough to lose the Coast Guard if that particular chase scene ever tickled your fancy. (So far it hadn't mine.) I took meticulous care of that boat, cleaning and checking and testing. Plus there were all the fun electronics upgrades. That boat could've navigated to Alpha Centauri and back.

We ran south for twenty minutes and found deeper water. Five miles south, I dropped anchor while Marcel prepared a spread of the smoked oysters and crackers with a small pot of french mustard. We would graduate to char-broiled ribeye—but that was later. No alcohol was ever onboard my boat—aptly named *CONDITIONS OF RELEASE*. Drinking and boating don't ever mix—not in my book. Too much can go wrong too fast. So we stuck to coffee made fresh in the cabin and served by Arnie.

Arnie and Marcel went way back. Marcel had helped me at one time with getting control over Arnie several years ago. That would have been the last time Arnie went off his meds and stayed off. Until this time.

We were lounging on the fantail after hors d'oeuvres thinking our thoughts when Marcel casually asked for me to present the Linda Burrows case. He sealed the deal by passing out three Cuban cigars that went for about $60 apiece: the Arturo Fuente Opus. I wasn't a smoker, but expensive cigars were Marcel's weakness, so who could turn him down?

After we were happily blowing rank smoke across the breezy river, I started by telling them the facts of Linda Burrows' death. I described aisle 11 of the grocery store--not a common place for murder. I explained how she was gunned down with no defensive wounds—meaning her murderer caught her unaware, billfold and purse still with her, no cries for help or screams of terror—nothing. The first cashier saw a police officer come into the store and leave. She heard the shots ring out after he came in and before he left. Then I explained Linda's predilection for romance with Niles Boudreaux and a "couple of others."

Arnie's eyes narrowed and his feelers went up. "Does that by any chance include you, Michael?" he asked.

"One time. I was weak."

"You always were," said Marcel with a snort. "You haven't changed."

"I thought you were off the market, with Verona around and all," Arnie remarked. I cringed. That was too damn recent. I became determined not to respond in any way. I hated big brother just then.

"So, you slept with her. Did her ex-husband know?"

"Not at first."

"What does this mean?"

"At the time I took his statement, he didn't know she was pregnant and didn't know her unborn child's DNA matched my own. When it came back and nailed me as the father, the husband knew at that point. This was after his interview, but just barely. He called me at the office and told me to watch my back. He was crying. But he had been drinking."

"You haven't been worried he would come after you?" Marcel asked with alarm. "What if he killed her and was guilty of murder already. How much more could it possibly cost him to kill you too? Not that much, I'm thinking, not in his frame of mind. These are always the cases where the aggrieved husband comes to the deposition armed with a MAC-10 and blows the walls down. Arm yourself, Michael."

"I have. I just about always carry my nine millimeter when I go out."

"Your concealed carry card still valid?"

"Yes," I said to Marcel. "All good there."

"From now on, I will drive you. Wherever you go—at least until we solve this case. Do you understand?"

"I do," I said.

Marcel puffed mightily on his cigar. He flicked his ash overboard.

"You've interviewed the usuals—CSI, detectives, uniforms, medical examiners, eyeballs?"

"Yep."

"Any tendencies there?"

"Well, there's the ex-husband again. In all fairness, he's a nice enough guy when he hasn't been drinking. But I can't imagine how it tore him up inside having the woman he loved, out kidnapping

Boudreaux's dick for a night. That was horrible for him. I'm sure I would've wanted to kill someone."

"We all would," Arnie suggested. Marcel and I nodded.

Then I added, "Oh well, I've also interviewed him and—this will get you—the U.S. Attorney himself, Niles Boudreaux."

"What the hell for?" Marcel said. "Something leap out at you?"

"He doesn't get a pass just because his politics are right. Besides, he's the one who put me on admin leave when he found out I was father to Linda's fetus."

"Jerked his little chain, did it?" Marcel laughed.

"It did."

"What about Annie?" Arnie asked. "Isn't she your go-to criminal profiler?"

"She is, and I'm glad you mentioned her, Arnie. She deserves my recognition and my long-term gratitude so far. She even weaned me off cream in my coffee and guessed my height and weight and where I was from and where I bought my suits and the fact I was unmarried. She did all this the first time we ever met. She hadn't seen me for fifteen minutes before she was able to do this with my profile."

"Amazing. Is Annie a looker?" Marcel innocently asked.

"She's thirteen-years-old, you sly dog," Arnie chided.

"Ouch! Didn't get that going in," Marcel said, directing the comment to me.

I eased him along: "Well, no one would ordinarily expect to find a profiler younger than maybe twenty-five or thirty. Annie's a remark-able study in what savants can do with their gifts."

Arnie stood up, stretched, and gazed off at the shoreline. He shook his head, turned back to face us, and told us what he was thinking.

"Michael, I've listened to your presentation on this Linda Burrows. And what I can say is this: you're in trouble, number one. Number two, I can't join with you in this because my doctor put me on medical leave with the Illinois Supreme Court for one year. So I can't practice law and save your young ass. Not at this time. Also, I have business in Chicago, and I'm headed back there in the next day or two. But here comes number three: I know just the woman who can. Her husband was elected to Congress, and she moved from Chicago to Washington D.C. to be with him. She lives here now. Her reputation as a trial lawyer is second to none. Her name is Joy Heavens."

"I know Chicago. I practiced there half my life. Never heard of her."

"She was civil law. That explains why you've never heard of her. You were simple criminal law."

Arnie stared wistfully beyond me. "Joy Heavens. Everyone feared her —even me."

"What kind of cases did she handle?"

"What kind? Joy is all litigator, and strictly civil. Contract disputes, business torts, tax appeals, even some high-profile divorces. Makes me shiver to think of her. She's exactly who you need to keep you out of the hoosegow."

"I'll call her," I said. It sounded like exactly the kind of firepower I needed just then. Joy Heavens.

What are you doing now?

And will you help me?

It's going to take all of us and more.

25

I called Joy and introduced myself over the phone. It was tit-for-tat: she'd never heard of me, and I'd never heard of her. We had a good laugh over that.

I felt right about meeting Joy. I liked her almost instantly. She had proven her mettle in Chicago; she was charming and honest—telling me she could try to help, that her friendship with Arnie almost required her to help. I was happy and relieved for her to join with me.

I told her I had a place where she could join me in my new office and put her expertise and brain-power to work. I told her she would be helping me solve my most difficult problem ever. Why was it the most difficult problem ever? Because Niles Boudreaux was motivated by political goals rather than the logic of the law. If he had been following the logic of the law, he would've had to admit that I made a lousy candidate as the man who killed Linda Burrows. It just didn't fit who I was. And that case would have been much easier for me to defend because it would have been a legal case where the important things were witness statements and crime scene evidence. Unfortunately, that was not the case. His case against me was based on political maneuvering. He was a man who would stop at nothing to placate his president and save his job. So I would never see it coming, his knockout punch. For that there's damn little a person can do except be prepared to turn on a dime, as it were when the case suddenly takes off in a direction no one could have predicted. The law was predictable and followed the rules. Politics, however, was unpredictable, opportunistic, and followed no rules.

That was where I found myself the morning Joy reported for her first day on the job.

Our new receptionist, Tammy Eubanks, showed Joy back to our conference room where Marcel and I were laying plans for our first day. She walked in with a big, happy smile and took the seat next to Marcel without waiting for an invite. I liked her already.

"So," I said, "welcome to our humble law firm."

"Thank you," she said, her eyes sparkling. "I haven't been out of my house for three days. I feel like I'm on parole."

"See, boss," said Marcel, "she does know the criminal law lingo. Not everyone knows parole."

"Joy, Marcel. Marcel, this is Joy. But you already knew that."

They both said hello and brusquely shook hands.

I wasted no time. "Let's talk first about how we're going to approach the—let's call it the Linda Burrows case. I sent Joy all of the discovery and reports, so she's up to speed. So, what's our first move?"

"We need investigations. I've got that," Marcel said with a sly smile. "It's what I do," he said to Joy. "I've been with Michael for eleven years now. Or is it more, boss?"

"Something like that. And I'm ready for another eleven. At least."

"Good," Joy said with a smile. "Then I'll know who to come to when I need something investigated."

"Okay," I said, "let's break this case down into its parts. First, there are eyewitnesses. Second, there are suspects. Third, there are legal challenges. Let's look at each one of these."

Tammy stuck her head in. "Coffee's ready. Should I bring some or do you do that yourselves?" she asked.

"We do it ourselves unless we're under the gun," Marcel said. He knew all about how we work in my law offices. "Then we might ask for help from you if we're hung up on something and can't leave our desk or deposition or whatever. For now, we'll help ourselves. You're also not expected to make the coffee every day. We rotate. You did it today, I've got it tomorrow. Then Michael then Joy."

"This place is different," Tammy commented as she left us.

Back to me. "First come the eyewitnesses. My staff at the U.S. Attorney's office and I had interviewed everyone involved. But there's a big problem with this. Back at that time, we were acting as prosecutors and police. Looking at ways to convict someone. Well, now we need to go back to those same eyeballs and interview them a second time. Only this time we're looking for ways out. We're looking for defenses, meaning ways we can keep me from involvement in Linda's death. By the way," I said with a slight smile, "I wasn't involved. I hardly knew Linda and had zero wish to harm her. Marcel knows me: I don't go around hurting people like that. Even if I was embarrassed for my time with her—which I was—I don't relieve any pressure on myself by taking it out on her. I'm the guy who starts with himself and looks to see where I went wrong. Am I a saint? Hardly, but when I know that I've created a problem, then fixing it must begin with me. Make sense?"

They returned my look. "Yes," they replied.

"Good. So, Marcel, you're the investigator and the best at witness statements I've ever worked with. You take the eyewitnesses."

"Got it."

"Number two is the suspects. Joy, I would like you and Annie to work up the suspects and commit your logic and rationale to memos. That way we can all have quick access to your thinking and are mindful of connections we might be trying to make in the real world with witnesses."

"Suspects, Annie and me. Got it."

"Number three is the legal challenges. I've purposely assigned this to myself because it keeps me isolated from the witnesses and suspects. If I get indicted, I don't want to hear testimony that I've personally been out talking to witnesses. Except when I was with the U.S. Attorney, of course."

"So who are our suspects going in?" Joy asked.

"Good question. Ready to take down some names? Let's begin with Niles Boudreaux. He's the U.S. Attorney for Washington, D.C. He also admitted to me he'd had a fling with Linda. He hates me. He'd like to pin her murder on me."

"Why?" asked Joy.

"I'm not sure, except I embarrassed him when I was interviewing him. And remember, he's appointed by the president to serve as U.S. Attorney. He serves at the president's pleasure. If he displeases President Sinclair, he can easily be replaced. My guess? I'm thinking Linda's death and the death of Piers Litton, another AUSA, has embarrassed the president. Put him in a bad light. So he's raised hell with Boudreaux. I'll let you add to that as you peel away the layers."

"Will do."

"Your second suspect is, of course, Linda's ex-husband. His name is Harry Burrows. Harry is a police officer with the Metro PD. He has more motive than anyone to see her dead since she was cheating on him--it's a long story--and it was probably killing him inside. However, my intuition tells me it wasn't him."

"Okay."

"Here's an interesting one. Interesting because the name I'm going to give you is a guy who's been murdered since Linda. He was also working with our team at the USAO. Piers Litton, Jr. was a second-generation career prosecutor, a young man who worked for the U.S. Attorney's Counterterrorism team. I liked him, what little I knew about him, and heard he was death on terrorists. Piers was only twenty-six and had only been with the office for two years at the time of his death. But he had maintained a long-term love affair with Linda. I think he was actually in love with her, from what I've pieced together. That doesn't excuse his guilt in sleeping with a married woman. But he's the least of the suspects as I can't imagine a motive for him. Still, he's dead under the strangest of circumstances, so there's more to this than I've been able to figure out."

"That's three suspects," Marcel mused. "Who else are we looking at?"

"Well, there's me. You must treat me like a suspect and then turn on a dime and establish what my defense would be. Track me down—on paper—then get me off. You following me here?"

"Yes," Joy said. "Look for all the reasons you might have killed her then come up with the facts that prove you didn't do it."

"Exactly. You'll be doing most of this, Joy. I'm counting on you."

"I'm with you a hundred-and-ten-percent," she said. "Can we pause for coffee? I need to pee and have some caffeine."

"We'll take five," I said. "But let's get our coffee and then return here, so we don't lose time. I want you guys tasked and jumping all over your assignments before ten o'clock this morning."

"Done, boss," said Marcel. Joy nodded as she hurried out of the room.

When we had supplied our coffee needs and re-situated ourselves around the table, we continued.

"Joy, here's another thing for your suspects file. Which is this: we might not even have the suspect on any list so far. What I'm saying is—"

"You're saying it might have been someone who so far has remained undetected?"

"Exactly. Let's think about how that might work. First, there are the phantom lovers. The phantoms stem from office gossip that she slept around. Not a shred of evidence of it but we're keeping an open mind. So you, Joy, will need to follow up with these rumors.

"Okay. Now hit me with your questions."

Joy started us off. "Have you heard anything from your peeps at the USAO? Any news on how their investigation is coming along? Any indication you're still in their sights?"

"I do have a resource there," I said. "This person will alert me if the noose is tightening around my neck. So far, I haven't heard that. But that doesn't mean it won't."

"Can you give me your contact's name?"

I didn't hesitate. Either I trusted Joy or I didn't. "Her name is Antonia Xiang. She works there, and so does her husband, Rusty Xiang. They're both friendlies."

"I won't contact either of them—that's your call. Unless you decide on down the road that you want me to. But not without your direct order."

"Good."

We broke up then and went to our separate offices and began the task of settling in: office supplies, phones, Internet, and all the rest of it. Technicians and suppliers were coming and going for the next three days as everything got connected and systems began talking to each other. So did we, the people. By Wednesday we were feeling like this might work; by Friday we were a team.

I spent that weekend with Verona and the kids. We toured the Smith-sonian—or what you can see of it over a long morning/early after-noon, and then returned home. I took a nap. Verona joined me a little later, and she watched me sleep the sleep of the exhausted.

I was getting too damn old for this.

26

Marcel reviewed my notes and files. Next, he began his work for me with a trip to the Foggy Bottom Grocery. Through the front door he walked, up to the first register, where he pulled aside the clerk he recognized from one of the file photos. Delores Cheney was her name. Delores was the cashier closest to the front doors when the man in the police uniform walked in and hurried past the registers. Marcel politely asked if he might speak to her. Believing that it was yet another detective, Delores, with a long sigh, assented.

They caught up in the break-room where Delores went to grab a snack and step outside on the dock for a smoke. Marcel followed her out there.

Introductions followed; she kept her distance. This man wasn't from the police; she didn't know where he was from and she didn't trust him right off the bat. So he handed her a hundred-dollar bill for her time. She pocketed the cash and looked over her shoulders. She and Marcel were alone.

"All right," she said, "shoot."

"I work for the attorney who had this case at the U.S. Attorney's office.

He doesn't work there now. His name is Michael Gresham. My name is Marcel. Michael wants me to ask you a few questions. Do I have your permission to turn this recorder on?"

"I guess."

He clicked it on. Delores stated her name and confirmed that the tape recording had her knowledge and consent. Then it began.

"Did you see the man come into the store just before the gunshots?"

"I didn't even look up. I was busy with the register. Just doing my job."

"Let me show you a photograph," Marcel said and whipped out my picture. "Have you ever seen this man?"

"No. That's not someone I know."

"Look at him carefully, please. Did you see this man the day Linda Burrows was murdered in your store?"

"No, like I said."

"Have you seen him since that day?"

"Again, as I said."

"No?"

"No, I haven't seen him since. And not before."

"His name is Michael Gresham. Can you initial this picture on the back, so we all know which photograph we're talking about?"

"Yes."

She applied her initials. At the top of the photograph, backside, it was labeled, "Michael Gresham."

"Then let's talk about who you did see that day."

"Sure."

They then proceeded to more or less go over Delores's prior statement—which I had copies of on my laptop even before I was put on admin leave, so Marcel had it, too. Funny thing was, no one ever asked me about my laptop when I was being bum-rushed out of the USAO. I was ordered only to turn in my files, keys, and ID. Nothing was said about my laptop. But it was mine, I had paid for it, and they never caught it. So there I was, the USAO's entire investigative file on my computer. This wasn't as big a deal as it might sound like to the uninitiated. I would have these same materials if a case were filed against me. The prosecutor would have had to turn all these items over to me during discovery. If they weren't turned over the prosecutor couldn't have called anyone listed in them as witnesses—court rule. Nor could exhibits and documents be used that were mentioned in the withheld investigative items. It was tricky but it worked, and it was fair. No longer do we have trial by ambush in America. Both sides know what's going to happen before the jury is ever selected. But having those documents even before any case was filed—now that was unusual, and it was a great help in our investigation.

"I want to specifically ask you about men or women you saw entering or leaving the store around the time of the shooting. Okay?"

"Okay."

"I believe you said to the investigators from the U.S. Attorney's office you saw a man leaving the store right after the gunshots. That man had very dark sideburns, very bushy. He was wearing sunglasses. And his eyebrows were bushy and dark, too. He didn't look at you when he hurried past. In fact, he was looking off to his right as he went outside. So it was hard for you to get a good look. Still stand by that?"

"Yes."

"Need to make any changes?"

"Have the police gone over the video of this man? Have they shown it to you and asked questions?"

"Yes. But the video stinks. The guy's disguise blocked out all features."

"So the video isn't useful to you?"

"No."

"I believe you also told the investigators something about the man's hair?"

"Well, and his skin color. He was very tan—like golden, deep-fried chicken."

"His hair?"

"Black and curly like a perm. It stuck out from under his police officer's hat. Like a Brillo pad."

"So he was wearing a police uniform when you saw him leaving the store?"

"Yes."

"And you also saw a police officer enter the store just minutes later, correct?"

"That's right. They asked me whether it could have been the same cop I just saw leave. I guess it could if the guy was wearing a wig and bronzer. How hard would that be to do? Why, are you guys thinking it might be the same person? Because it wasn't."

"How were they different."

"Well, the two were the same size, about six feet tall."

"But one was bronze, and the other was white. One had bushy facial hair and the other did not. One looked you in the eye; the other did not."

"So you saw what the second cop's face looked like?"

"Sort of."

"Let me show you this picture of Michael Gresham again. Is that the man you saw leave and then re-enter wearing the police uniform?"

"As I told you, I've never seen this man before. He wasn't one of the cops. Mr. Gresham's face is scarred. The cops weren't scarred. I always notice things like scars right away."

"Good for you. Now for the final question. If we asked you to come to court and say these things, would you come?"

"Would you get an excuse from my manager?"

"Yes."

"Would you pay me my salary for that day?"

"Yes."

"Then I'll do it. I just can't afford to lose this job, and I can't afford to lose any salary. I have two kids."

"Please give me your cell phone number."

She gave the number and then Marcel thanked her, turned off his recorder, and went to question other employees. There had been a significant turnover in staff since then, which, he found, wasn't unusual in the grocery business. Produce managers and butchers and people like that, not so much. But cashiers, stockers, cleanup crews— they came and went almost daily.

Just as he was leaving Delores there on the loading dock, she tugged at his sleeve, and he turned back around.

"I just remembered one more thing."

"What's that?" Marcel smiled, pleased she had decided to volunteer information.

"One of the stockers said she saw the woman get shot. She was one aisle over, and she saw it happen between the shelves she was stocking."

Marcel froze. He withdrew his tape recorder and had Delores repeat what she'd just said.

"Do you know her name?"

"Agnes something."

"Does she still work here?"

"I don't think so. I haven't seen her for a month or so. We used to smoke out here on the dock. She was from somewhere in California. Maybe San Diego."

"Did you ever tell the police about her?"

"About Agnes? No."

"Why not?"

"They didn't ask me."

Marcel blinked and fought down the impulse to shake his head. He pushed on, instead.

"Do you know anything else about her? Where she lived, what kind of car she drove? That sort of thing?"

"Not really. She smoked Marlboros, just like me. She preferred Lights. She was trying to quit because she had a little boy at home she wanted to see grow up and graduate from college. The store would have her records."

"Sure, sure. All right, Let me talk to your manager and see what he can tell me."

"She. She can tell you."

"What's her name?"

"We call her Sag."

"Sag? Any other name?"

"Yes, Sag-butt. I don't know her real name."

"Is she here today?"

"Oh, yes, up there watching everything from the eye in the sky."

"All right. I'll track her down."

"Okay. Is this information worth another hundred bucks?"

"It is," Marcel said. He slipped her a second hundred-dollar bill.

"Cool," she exclaimed as Marcel was walking out the door in search of Sag.

Five minutes later, Marcel had located the manager on the second floor. She was sitting in a cramped office. But Marcel was struck by her great view of the store down below. She could look down on an aisle in the store or any cash register by changing location on the narrow plank walkways. That way she could pause and view the action below. It was a typical feature of larger grocery stores.

Marcel introduced himself and asked if she were Sag.

"No," she replied in a distant voice, "I'm from Sag Harbor, Washington. But I know how my people use the word and make it about my butt. I'm onto the little bastards."

"Sag Harbor? How'd you get all the way back here to D.C.?"

"My husband's in the Navy. We move every three years."

"You were on duty the day Linda Burrows was shot to death in aisle eleven?"

"I was."

"Did you witness anything that day?"

"Haven't we been over this before?"

"No."

She pulled away and eyed Marcel suspiciously. "Hey, let me see your badge."

"I don't have a badge. I'm working for a private investigation company.

We were hired by one of the people who might be accused of the crime."

"Oh, you were? Well, what if I threw you out?"

"We'd just subpoena you and take your deposition," Marcel lied. We don't have the right to take depositions in criminal cases.

"Okay. Did I see anything that day? I saw a helluva mess in aisle eleven. A dead body, blood all over, customers screaming and running and knocking displays over. It was pandemonium there for a while. I got on the PA and tried to calm things down. Then I ran for aisle eleven to see what I could do."

"All right. Did you have an employee on duty that day whose first name was Agnes?"

"Sure. Agnes Streith. She's gone now."

"Did you ever talk to her about the shooting?"

"No, why?"

"Did the cops ever talk to her?"

"Now that I couldn't tell you."

"Do you know where she is now?"

"I know where we sent her last check."

"Can you give me her address?"

"Sorry, that's confidential."

"What if I offered you five-hundred-dollars? Is it still confidential then?"

Her eyes bulged. Her hand twitched. "Show me the money."

Marcel fanned out five one-hundred-dollar bills. Crisp and snappy. That's what they always went for.

"First the money."

He passed her the bribe.

Then she rolled her chair over to her desk and picked up her mouse. She stared diligently into the monitor and clicked and talked to herself. "Okay," she said. "Here it is. Forty-five-ten Muir Street, San Diego, California, nine-two-one-oh-seven."

Marcel repeated the address. "That's right," said Sag.

"Spell her last name, please."

"S-T-R-E-I-T-H. First name Agnes like it sounds."

"Okay."

He didn't push what she knew any further. To do so would have required telling her that Agnes was a witness to the shooting. He didn't want to do that, fearing the cops would find out and beat him to Agnes. So he broke off.

"Thank you for your help."

"Thank you. Goodbye, sir."

"Goodbye."

And that's how we located the woman who claimed to be an eyewitness to the murder of Linda Burrows.

Marcel had Tammy making reservations for a flight to San Diego before he got back to the office. He would be leaving that night.

27

I sat in on Joy's phone call to Helmut Richard, an investigator in the U.S. Attorney's office.

She had retrieved his name from the files I made off with. Richard and Linda had a fling at one time, however fleeting. Long story short: he had bedded her. More than once? That's partly what we were trying to find out.

"Helmut Richard," Joy began, "My name is Joy Heavens. I'm an attorney with Michael Gresham."

She clicked on the speakerphone just then.

"Michael? I didn't know we'd hired any new attorneys. But I guess his team is expanding. Every team in here needs more hands. I know I do."

"What is your position?"

"Michael didn't tell you? I'm a SEC investigator on loan to the USAO."

"I think he might have mentioned that. I'm wondering if we could meet up and I could ask you a few questions."

"Sure. About what?"

"About Linda Burrows."

"Well."

Long silence. Then he cleared his throat. "Why me?"

"We've heard that maybe you went for drinks with Linda once or twice. Stuff like that."

A long pause.

"I could meet you someplace. Just not here."

"We can do that."

They went ahead and set up a meeting. After she hung up, Joy turned to me.

"He thinks you're still with the USAO," she said.

"I heard that. He thinks you're working on my team at the USAO, too."

"Well," she said, "We don't want to disappoint him with the truth. I've never let the truth come between me and the truth. How about you, Michael?"

I had to smile. "The truth comes between the you and the truth. Nicely done." She smiled. I continued, "You're meeting him this afternoon? Do you want me to ride along, maybe stay in the background? We've never formally met so I don't believe he'd recognize me."

"No need. Besides, he's an investigator. He'd make you in a hot second."

Three hours later, Joy returned from the meeting. She had dictated her file memo on the meeting on her way back. I began reading.

They met at Jim's Corner Tavern in the near north neighborhood of Silver Spring. Jim's Corner Tavern was your basic neighborhood bar: a dozen tables scattered around a postage-stamp dance floor; jukebox; one bartender; thirty-foot mirror behind the bar; enough neon beer signs to start a stampede at an AA meeting (Joy's words). The permanent fragrance of vomit and cigarette smoke.

She went inside and settled into the first booth on the right—as agreed. Helmut Richard was late. She waited fifteen minutes, finally ordering a Diet Coke before the bartender's patience ran out. Five minutes more and she watched a young man in a blue suit with vest and gold chain slide into the bench opposite her.

She held out her hand. "Joy Heavens. You're Helmut?"

"I am." He shot a look around. "We alone?"

"I haven't seen anyone. Relax, no one from my team knows we're here."

"You say you're with Michael Gresham?"

"I am. Two weeks now."

"Why haven't I seen him around the office lately? I always see him in the lunch room before everyone else comes in at noon. Is he okay?"

"He's been rushed working up a homicide case. I've never seen him so busy."

"That must be it."

The bartender looked over and spread his hands.

"I'll have coffee, Maxim," Helmut shouted to the man. "And bring her another—"

"Diet Coke."

The bartender didn't acknowledge he'd heard but turned directly to fixing our drinks. Then he brought them over sans tray. Handing the coffee to Helmut in a red-rimmed mug, he then passed me the frosty mug containing the diet drink and gave me the once-over. "How's a thug like you get such lovely women up in here?" Maxim asked Helmut.

"Never mind. My secret."

"I'm having trouble keeping them straight," he joked and punched Helmut lightly on the shoulder.

Helmut shook his head and didn't respond. The bartender made his way back to the bar.

"Why I asked you to meet me, Helmut, is I have it from one of my sources that you might've spent some outside-time with Linda Burrows a few months ago."

His jaw clenched. He abruptly stopped stirring cream into his coffee. "Whoa! We're here to talk about Linda and me?"

"It goes down easier away from the office than if I confronted you there. This is private. No one ever has to know we met. I'm just looking for some information. You are not a suspect. You are not a person of interest."

"Well." He sipped his drink then poked at his lips with a napkin wet from the freshly-wiped table on his side. "What kind of questions do you want to ask me?"

"Tell me about your time with Linda. Where and when?"

"That's easy. We met twice in the parking garage underneath our building. We met both times in my Dodge RAM. We had sex, straightened our clothes, and went back inside the office."

"Just a wham, bam, excuse me, ma'am?"

"Pretty much. She was something else."

"In what way?'

"Oh, just so needing to be loved. She wanted to be held and kissed."

"What was her reputation at the office?"

"She was banging the boss. Niles Boudreaux was her favorite."

"Why was that?"

"I don't know. Power trip? Because he was the big guy? I don't know. And I don't care. Is that all you want to ask?"

"No, please give me a few more minutes."

"Five minutes."

"Did you have any feelings for Linda?"

"Other than when I was banging her brains out? No. Zero. Zip. Nada. She was just someone from work."

"Did you know whether she was married? Divorced?"

"I didn't pay attention. Maybe I did."

"What would you think if she had slept with other men in the office?"

"What would I think? I would hope they're using protection. I never bang anyone without a top-hat. Who wants to die from AIDS?"

"What I'm driving at is whether you felt any jealousy when she went with other men?"

He launched into a low, guttural laugh. Then, "Not hardly. That wasn't how it was with Linda. Remember that poor, desperate girl from high school who would jump into bed if she believed you loved her and wanted to be with her? That was our Linda. She was just a warm body."

"No jealousy?"

"Shit, lady. Please."

"What about her husband or ex-husband? Ever meet him?"

"Not that I know about."

"Did you ever work on any cases with Linda?"

"Nope. I'm SEC. She was local crime."

"Tell me about Niles Boudreaux and Linda. How do you know about that?"

"We all watched them leave the office in different cars around the same time every afternoon. They'd both creep back in—separately—around four, four-thirty. Both flushed. We weren't stupid, Ms. Heavens."

"No, I'm sure you weren't. How long did this go on?"

"Hell, up until the day her old man shot her, I suppose. They never did quit."

"Her husband shot her?"

"Yes. Why?"

"I just wonder how you know that?"

"It makes sense. He had motive, that's for damn sure."

"Can't argue with that, Helmut. He did have motive."

"I woulda shot my wife, too. I should have when she divorced me. Would've saved everyone lots of trouble."

"I'm not going to put that in my report. But don't mention it again, okay?"

He pulled far away from the table. "Whoa! Are you wearing a wire?"

"No, no wire. I would tell you if I was recording our talk. I'm not. I'm just jotting down some notes."

"Well, I'm done here anyway. So when are you going to arrest Linda's old man?"

"You'll have to ask Michael about that. I'm just a gopher."

He shook his head sadly, partners-in-crime, he and Joy Heavens. Lowly investigators who did all the work and got none of the glory.

He felt a kinship with her. So much so, that he said, "I was drinking with some FBI last Friday night. They said her husband didn't do it."

"Really? Who did they say did do it?"

He screwed up his face and shot a look around the tavern.

"You ready for this? They say she was gunned down by Michael Gresham. Your boss."

"Did they say why Michael would shoot her?"

"Don't quote me on this, but they said Michael got her pregnant. It was going to wreck his career, get him fired, run his wife off. So he shot her. Hey, you didn't hear it from me."

"No, of course not."

"And if you say I said it, I'll say you're lying."

"Sure. It's not even going into my notes."

"Michael Gresham," he repeated. "You might be smart to ask for a transfer before he gets canned and you're looking for a job."

"Yes. I can see how that might work."

He shook his head as if he'd just passed White House blueprints to the Russians.

"Wow," he remarked under his breath. "Just wow."

"Yes, wow."

I finished reading Joy's notes and hit her buzzer.

"Yes?"

"We gotta talk."

"Two minutes."

She came into my office like she said, two minutes later.

"They're going to indict me," I said, and I felt the scowl that had taken over my face permanently now.

"Sure sounds like it," she replied. "Or maybe it's just FBI letting off steam."

"No, they were talking out of school. I can promise you Special Agent Marty Longstreet was there. He hates me and would love to spread the word about me all over town. But not as much as he'd like to send me to jail. They were talking truth when Helmut heard them Friday night."

"Sounds like you know the FBI."

"No, I know Marty Longstreet. He's on a par with Niles Boudreaux. They both want to nail me. I'm even wondering if there's something there between Boudreaux and Linda's ex-husband. I need to think about that."

She gave me a puzzled look. "Between the U.S. Attorney and Harry Burrows? How would that work?"

"Don't know. A deal to take the heat off the husband in return for—for the husband not telling the newspaper the U.S. Attorney was banging his wife."

"That's iffy, isn't it?"

"Yes," I said.

"You're frightened right now, Michael."

"I am."

"What's your alibi?"

"Verona and I went to a concert. We have lots of pictures and videos showing me."

"Good on you. That makes me so happy. Are they in our file?"

"Yes, inside my folder."

"I looked there and didn't see any photos."

"I'll double-check. They should be there."

She smiled just then, an unexpected, broad smile, flashing white teeth, and soft red lips—I caught myself. Soft red lips? Where did that come from?

You couldn't ignore her just by ignoring her.

Joy Heavens was beautiful, to me, in her own fifty-two-year-old way. There, I said it, and that would be the end of it. Except it caused me to forget to post my concert photos and video in my file online.

I was still human even though I was about to be indicted.

28

MARCEL RAINFORD: FILE MEMO

RE: AGNES STREITH INTERVIEW

I flew into San Diego and drove my rental car to Muir Street in Ocean Beach. OB is an oceanside suburb at the end of the Eight freeway in San Diego. It is a smallish town, something out of the 1960's with plenty of sidewalk restaurants, black light head shops, antique consignment stores, surf shops, and nail and hair establishments filled with Vietnamese and Filipino hair and nail technicians. Muir Street is just north of downtown Ocean Beach and, as I scouted out the area, I found myself driving from the beach to Agnes' address about three blocks away in less than four minutes. Then I parked a block away from her address and snooped the front and back of her house. Seeing nothing unusual, nothing threatening, I opened her front gate and went up onto the deck on the front side of her house. I rang the bell and waited. Standing there on her deck I could look right inside through the sliding glass doors. A young woman was reclined on a small sofa watching the TV across the room, all of maybe eight feet away. I rang again, and she raised her head and turned to see who was calling. She slowly stood up from the sofa, stretched, and made her way over to the door.

She unlocked and slid the door open twelve inches.

"Yes?"

"Sorry to bother you," Marcel said in his sincerest voice, "but I'm looking for Agnes Streith. Are you Agnes?"

"Yes, I am. Are you from the city? That tree that split in the thunderstorm Saturday night?"

"No, I'm an investigator from Washington, D.C."

"Oh." Pause. "Then you're here about the grocery store shooting. Do I have to talk to you?"

"It would be easier for everyone if you did. Then we wouldn't have to subpoena you to return to Washington and give a statement on the record."

I hated to do it—play like we had subpoena powers, but I did it anyway. It just seemed like the easiest thing for everybody.

She slid the door fully open. "Come on inside. Let's get it over with. Wait, do you have ID? A badge or a card or something?"

"I have my driver's license with a picture ID." I showed her my license, and she seemed okay with that. She stood aside and waved me on in.

"Let's sit at the kitchen table," she told me. We did as she said. Her back was to the galley kitchen; my back was against the west wall. "Okay, me buck-o, ask away."

"I'd just like to start with your job at the grocery store. That would be the Foggy Bottom Grocery. The date was June twenty-fourth, 2017."

She gave me a puzzled look. "I thought someone said it was June twenty-fifth. Does that make any difference?"

"Huge difference. The shooting occurred on June twenty-fourth. On that date were you employed by the Foggy Bottom Grocery? We're talking about the day of the shooting."

"I was. I was a stocker."

"What did that entail?"

"Keeping every shelf and end cap in the store fully stocked during my shift. You'd start on one side and get to the other side and go back and start over again."

"What's the highest turnover item in your store?"

"I heard it was milk, but I didn't do dairy, so I don't know. The refrigeration cases were outside my job."

"What time did you come on that day?"

"Ten. The first crew came on at four in the morning. Ugh! Who can do that?"

"Do you recall what time the shooting occurred?"

"Sometime after I started. Maybe an hour? Maybe two?"

"Tell me what happened. When did you first notice anything unusual?"

"Well, I was working aisle ten. Midway down the aisle is the coffee plantation."

"Plantation"

"It's what the stockers called it. All kinds of coffee and a grinder. It smelled delicious along there, and I don't even drink coffee."

"Okay. What did you first notice?"

"I heard a woman say, 'No! No!' I turned my head sideways and looked right between the shelves. There was a man with a gun who raised it up and shot her. Three times. I wet my pants, I'm sorry to say, but it scared the piss right out of me. Then he turned and walked off.

When he turned, he was facing me for about two seconds. I saw his face."

"Did you ever talk to the police about this?"

"No."

"No? Really?"

"I don't think they knew I was there. I didn't tell anyone I was there. No, that's wrong. I told my best friend, Delores. But she promised not to tell. Except she told you, is that it?"

"Yes, she told me. I told her how serious the case was and she thought we deserved the truth since there was so much at stake."

"Sure, sure. Bitch. No, I don't mean that. She was like me, probably, just trying to get it over with and get rid of you."

"Are you trying to get rid of me?"

She grimaced. "Not get rid of you, exactly. I just don't like complications in my life. I don't even have a boyfriend or a cat."

"I have a picture of a man I'd like to show you."

"Okay."

I slipped Michael's photograph out of my file. The moment I came here for.

"I'm going to show you this picture, and I'd like you to say the first thing that comes to mind."

"All right."

I turned it over and slid it to her side of the table. She took a long look and immediately began nodding.

"Yep. That's him."

"That's the man you saw in the aisle that day?"

"Definitely."

"That's the man you saw shoot the customer, the woman?"

"Yes. Shot her three times. I'm certain it was him. You know one reason why I know for sure?

"No, why?"

"See those scars on his face? They match the ones I still have nightmares over, the man who saw me through the shelf."

"Did he see you, is that what you're saying?"

"I can only guess he did. He should have: he looked right at me."

"Okay. Did you see what the man did after he shot the woman?"

"Not really. He walked back out of the store, I guess."

"Were you frightened?"

"Only a little. It looked to me like he had come in just to shoot her and leave."

"Please describe how the man was dressed."

"He was dressed like a cop. But he wasn't a cop."

"Why wasn't he a cop?'

"Because cops wear badges. This guy wasn't wearing a badge. A real cop wouldn't be caught dead without his badge. I should know, my dad is a cop in Phoenix."

"No badge. You're sure?"

"He faced right at me. I took it all in."

"Can you tell me whether the man said anything?"

"He did. He looked at me and said, 'Hey, Peaches.' He called me 'Peaches.'"

"Does anyone else call you 'Peaches'?"

"Nope."

"Why would he call you 'Peaches'?"

"When I went to the aisle and looked at the woman, at first I wanted to help. But I saw the bullet holes in her head and knew I couldn't. There were cans of peaches on the floor behind her. I don't know how that happened. I had stocked those myself."

"So maybe he wasn't calling you Peaches, maybe he was saying peaches fell on the floor?"

"I don't know. He said, 'Hey, Peaches,' like you're calling someone that. He must've just made it up."

"Have you seen this man since the shooting?"

"No."

"Would you recognize him if you saw him again?"

"I guess."

I was running low on questions. My goal was to get her to reverse herself and say it wasn't Michael after all. But I didn't know how I was going to do that. So here's where I was: I had gone all the way to San Diego for this woman's statement. I was going to show her Michael's picture and have her confirm that the guy in the picture wasn't the guy who did the shooting. Instead, she confirmed the shooter was Michael! Shit: Note to Michael: We need to bury this memo. We need to bury all reference to this girl. She convicts you of Linda's murder.

I stopped reading and sat back in my chair. I was going to be convicted of Linda's murder. All that remained was the trial.

One more thing came to mind about Agnes. We had questioned the store management about the availability of video from aisle 10 where Agnes claimed to be. Like aisle 11, there was no video coverage of that aisle. It made me crazy to learn this but there was nothing that could be done now.

Imprisonment—and maybe worse—was inevitable for me.

I took a long look around my office.

Just when I was beginning to like this place.

29

Marcel came straight to my house after landing at Reagan. It was six-thirty at night, and we'd just started eating steaming plates of Verona's fettuccine Alfredo when the doorbell rang. I answered it myself so the others could keep enjoying.

Marcel came in without saying a word and sat down heavily on one of two wingback chairs in the living room. It was the room we never used; maybe that's why he chose it so that we wouldn't be interrupted.

He sat back and pinched his eyes between thumb and forefinger; then he shook his head.

"Michael, I'm sorry."

"For what? Problems in San Diego?"

"I talked to Agnes Streith. I showed her your photograph."

"You wanted her to say the shooter didn't resemble me at all. So what are you sorry about?"

"She identified you as the killer. I went over several different ways, but she wouldn't budge. She's certain the man she saw pull the trigger was you. In fact, she was in the aisle next door and says she watched you between shelves. She tells me you looked right at her and said, 'Peaches.'"

"Peaches?"

"That's right. Michael, I've heard you call other young women you didn't know 'Peaches.'"

"You have?"

"Don't you know it? Did your dad call girls by that name? You learned it somewhere."

I suddenly convulsed involuntarily. Marcel looked at me. "What is it?"

I shook my head. "Peaches. My younger sister who died when she was ten. We all called her Peaches."

"Oh my God. So it is something you might say."

"Hold on, Marcel. Whoever she saw, I don't know. But it wasn't me who killed Linda."

He sat back and waved. "I know that, Michael. Never in a thousand years would I believe you'd do something like that. The problem is, I'm not gonna be on your jury."

I froze in my chair. "You think it's going to come to that? Me on trial?"

"If the cops ever find out about her and hear her identify you, yes. She's a pretty together gal. Wouldn't surprise me if she's already called back here and talked to someone."

"Oh, my God. Did you show her my picture?"

"She said she recognized you by your scarring. The photograph confirmed it for her."

"Good God."

"Got any ideas, Michael?"

"It feels like a nightmare. I hope you're not waiting for me to confess or something, Marcel?"

"Come on, brother. You know how I am. Never in a million years."

"I know, I know."

"All right. I'm going home now. We can dig into this some more tomorrow." He stood to leave. Then he spread his hands in the "I don't get it," expression.

"Me neither," I said.

He went out the same way he'd come in. I heard the whine of his SUV starting up and saw the lights sweep across our living room when he turned to head left out in the street. Then it was quiet.

Just me and my thoughts. I was no longer hungry.

I was just scared. Scared from the top of my head to the bottom of my feet.

Agnes Streith was supposed to be the witness that excluded me from the list of possible suspects. She was the eyeball, the one person who'd seen the killer in action. She was supposed to see my picture, say, "Hell, no," and then let Marcel record her statement.

But it hadn't gone down like that. Agnes had fingered me as the perp, and no one had taken anyone's statement at all. I not only wasn't going to be exonerated by her, but I was also going to be convicted by her if anyone on the other side heard about her and took her statement.

What she had to say, coupled with the fact Linda died with my child in her belly, would be way more than enough to put me away for life —or worse. They could charge it out as a federal crime and seek the death penalty.

I could die for something I didn't do.

It was time to take some serious action, but I honestly didn't know what that might consist of. Pay her to move to Japan? Kidnap her and do away with her? Please. There were no options.

Except for prayer. I could pray the cops didn't ever hear from her.

So I decided to take the case to Annie, help her locate a suspect, and do everything I could to convict that person with investigation and logic. If I could do that, maybe I could take my findings to Boudreaux, and he'd realize he was on the wrong track in coming after me. Maybe he'd do a one-eighty and go after the real perp.

Maybe, maybe, maybe.

First, though, I needed a name.

I needed Annie.

30

We were living in Georgetown at the time Marcel went to San Diego. Four bedrooms, four baths. It was a beautiful home in Georgetown's West Village. We even had a carriage house in the back, adding another bedroom and bath. The money to buy the place came from the sale of my house in Evanston plus a fifteen-year mortgage. The price tag was outrageous, but it was worth every penny—three-point-five million. I shivered to think of the debt load.

Our bedroom was on the second floor, along with three others.

It was just after midnight when Annie came into our bedroom and sat down on my side of the bed. I'm a light sleeper; I immediately came awake and sat up. I turned on the light. She turned her face away from the light; her back was to me. She was huddled over, her arms wrapped around her mid-section, moaning and moving up and back, up and back. Verona's light came on, and she immediately sat up and reached across to touch Annie's back.

"What is it, honey?" she asked our teenager.

"Oh-oh-oh-oh. Michael, I feel bad."

"What is it? Your stomach feels bad?"

"Yes, yes, yes."

"Okay, have you been eating something that we didn't give you to eat?"

"Yes."

"What did you eat, honey?"

"Batteries. I thought it was food."

"How bad do you feel one-to-ten?"

"I don't know what that means, Michael."

"I mean does it feel terrible? Or just kind of terrible?"

"Terrible!"

"Do you want me to take you back to the hospital so they can look at you again?"

"Uh-huh."

"All right, Michael," said Verona, "I'll stay with the little guys. You take her to GWU Hospital."

Without another word I dressed while Verona sat beside Annie, her arm around her back, comforting her. Then she wrapped our bedspread around Annie and led the two of us out to my car. We loaded up and left Verona standing under the porch light, shifting from foot to foot as if she would run out and flag me down and ride in with us. But there were the kids. She made a roll-down your window mime when I got turned into the street to leave. I rolled down the glass.

"I'll call Gina. See you soon."

She would call the kids' nanny and then come to GWU in her car. I nodded and waved and gunned away. Annie was half-lying in the front seat, eyes closed, making gurgling sounds that were something less than human brought about by a terrible pain.

Fifteen minutes and we reached GWU Hospital. The entrance was located just south of Washington Circle on 23rd Street on the west side of the street. I stopped and called out for help. Within minutes a gurney was brought out, and the staff was wheeling her inside. I parked and followed.

GWU Hospital had a FastTrack system that guaranteed Annie would be seen almost immediately. We began in a curtained exam room with an ER doc, a young woman from Jamaica. FastTrack meant hospital admission was done at bedside, test results went ahead of non-emergent tests, and bed availability was reserved. It was all happening very fast, for which I was grateful as Annie was crying out with pain. One thing led to another and within about fifteen minutes Annie's GI doctor from the last time we were here, Dr. Gendum, had been summoned and was walking into the exam room. X-rays were done; it looked like small batteries had found their way into her stomach.

"She's swallowed six batteries," the head ER nurse said after the X-rays came back. "Has this happened before?"

"Yes. She swallowed quarters."

"What would make her swallow quarters?"

"Dr. Patent told us savants have a hard time telling food from other stuff. She's swallowed quarters before. Her chart should show that."

"Okay. We'll get all her chart together."

Dr. Gendum finished a quick appraisal of Annie.

"I'm going to need to scope her again, Mr. Gresham."

"Same thing as before?"

She scowled. "Maybe, maybe not. It looks like her bowel may have perforated this time."

"What's that mean?"

"It can be very serious. Batteries can be quite deadly. Depending on what I see she might very well need surgery to fix the rupture and extract the foreign objects."

Annie didn't appear to be listening. She was still moving almost involuntarily now, trying to get comfortable on the examination table.

"I need to call my girlfriend. What happens now?"

"I'll take her into the GI suite and scope her. Then I can tell you more."

"How long will that take?"

"Forty-five minutes. You can wait right down the hall."

"I know, I know, I've waited there before."

Four chairs, a love-seat, flatscreen TV going on mindlessly about a roller contraption guaranteed to take twelve pounds off your midsection in twelve days—exactly what I expected to find where I'd be waiting outside the endoscopy suite. Wearily I sat down on the love seat and reached for the top magazine on the table to my right. A magazine I'd never heard of about some GI disease I'd never heard of. I called home; the nanny told me Verona had already left. Then I closed my eyes and thought about Annie, realizing how much I loved my daughter and how frightened I was just then. I said a prayer for her and kept my eyes closed, wishing for a sign she was going to be okay. I'm not the kind of person who ever listens and looks for signs, but that night I had nothing else to hang onto but my faith. I remained there with my eyes closed, mind wandering, when maybe ten minutes later I came awake with someone touching my shoulder.

Verona had arrived. "Hey," she said, holding my chin in her hand and looking into my eyes. "Sleeping?"

"I guess. A little."

"Update, please."

"They found blood. They're worried she might need surgery."

Just then Dr. Gendum came looking for us.

"I need a consent signed. Annie's going to need a laparoscopic procedure. It's serious, but it's something that the surgeon says is necessary. I'll let you speak with him in ten minutes after he's finished with his preparations."

As she spoke, an elderly gentleman wearing greens and a lowered germ mask strode briskly into the waiting area. He introduced himself, told us he suspected Annie might have a bleed in her bowel and assured us he could fix her problem with a closed, laparoscopic procedure. I signed the consent, and both physicians left us alone.

"Kids okay?" I asked Verona.

She sat down beside me on the love-seat and took my hand in hers. "Kids are okay, but we're not."

My heart jumped. "We're not okay?"

"After you left with Annie, I received a call from my middle son's wife. His name is Sergey, and he's twenty-one years old. His wife is Katya. Anyway, long story short, he didn't want Katya to call me, but she insisted. My son is very sick, Michael."

"Oh, my God. What is it?"

"A glioblastoma on the brainstem. I'm not entirely sure what that means, but evidently, it's fatal in my son's case. There is no operation possible."

I turned to her and found her eyes filled with tears. I pulled her close to me, and she laid her head on my shoulder. I massaged her hand and muttered how sorry I was.

"What's the outlook?" I asked. I would regret this, but I couldn't help myself. I regretted it because it forced Verona to state a reality that she probably wasn't ready to acknowledge. Or maybe she was. She was always ahead of the curve with me.

"Katya says my son has about nine months to live. Maybe twelve, with radiation and chemo."

"Oh, my God."

"Yes. I'm very sorry, Michael." She lifted her head from my shoulder and looked off into the distance.

"What can we do to help?"

"You can't. But I can. I'm flying home to him. I need to help with him. Katya didn't ask for my help; I told them I was coming. Then I insisted my son come to the phone. He was in shock, and his voice sounded terrified although he was trying to cover it up. But you know how you can always tell with your kids, Michael. He wasn't fooling me."

"You're going to Russia? When?"

"Tomorrow night. I'm so, so sorry."

"You know I'd come with you if I could."

"But that's impossible. You have the kids, and you have your business. No, this is something I'll have to do on my own. But we can talk every day if we want."

"We will," I said, "We definitely will. We'll set a time to talk."

She slumped back against me, and I settled back against the loveseat. It was too much to begin to comprehend: Annie sick and in surgery; Verona headed back to Russia. I had to consciously slow my thoughts to maintain composure. Our children's illnesses couldn't have come at a worse time, either, with me trying to locate Linda Burrows' killer and disentangle myself from that mess.

Verona's breathing slowed, and within five minutes she had fallen asleep with her head on my chest. I sat there staring at meaningless TV images, wishing I'd turned the damn thing off. By craning my head hard left and moving my wrist, I could track the time on my watch. Twenty minutes in. I didn't have good feelings about the surgery just then. Then I was silently weeping and kicking myself for not doing a better job with Annie and her eating disorder. Didn't I owe her more of my time? More caregiving?

My crying caused Verona to lift her head. She reached up and touched my face.

"Oh, my darling Michael. What are we to do?"

"I've let her down!" I cried. "I failed her!"

"No, not at all. Sometimes we can help someone, and that's good. But sometimes we can't help them, and that always makes us feel guilty. That's you right now. But anyone in this hospital that understands these things would insist you're not at fault. The problem is way bigger than just you, Michael. And remember this, too, please: you didn't create Annie's problems. No one did. It's just how things are."

"Oh, Verona."

"I need you to remember these words while I'm away."

"You are coming back, correct?"

There was a pause as she gathered her thoughts.

"As much as I love you," she said, "how could I not? All else being equal, I mean. I have other children in Russia, too. I love our children, but I'm missing my own more than you know. Maybe I reached for the golden ring too late in life by following you here. Maybe I should have known how important my kids would be once I left them behind. I was blindsided, Michael."

My heart was tight in my chest. Her voice seemed disembodied as if the words weren't her own but belonged to someone else. Still, when I looked at her, I saw her tearstained face and her hands tight in my own, trying to hold onto me while feeling me slipping away. Or maybe it was me who felt her slipping away. I'll never know, except my sense of loss was growing by the moment, with each word she spoke.

"I can't let you go," I managed to say. "I'll do whatever I need to do to have you in my life."

"Will you come live in Russia?"

I knew that was coming. I also knew what my answer would be.

"Maybe, except for Annie. I need to set her up here so after I'm gone she'll have the resources to have great people caring for her. My chances of making money and contacts I would need to make that happen in Russia—that feels too chancy to me. I owe her more than taking a chance with her life to make my own happier. So no, I can't come to Russia. Not to live, anyway."

"So, we're stuck."

"Evidently."

"Maybe we should make a clean break of it, Michael. Do the adult thing."

I tossed my head back and drew a deep lungful of air.

"Would that make you feel better?" I whispered.

"I think it might. Otherwise, the pain drags on, the hope that won't die but that tears the soul apart. I don't want that for either of us."

"Oh," I said. I had no other words. What she was saying was logical but unacceptable just then.

"Just let me get through tonight with Annie, okay?" I asked. "We can talk after."

"I didn't even mean to bring it up. Our dear Annie comes first right now."

"Yes."

~

IT WAS another two hours until Annie's surgeon appeared. He was still wearing greens, his mask flapped open, sweat beaded on his forehead.

"Whew," he said, "that was intense. But I got everything patched."

"She's okay?" Verona and I said in tandem.

"She's in recovery. She's going to be just fine. But seriously, folks, you're going to need to take serious action to see that this doesn't happen again. You don't want to be bringing her in for surgery every month or two. I've seen her chart. This isn't her first time here."

"No. It's her second," I said. "That I know of."

"She doesn't know coins or batteries from food," said Verona. "When she's hungry, and we're not with her, she'll find coins or batteries or God knows what and eat them. Anyway, we don't know where they're coming from. Not that hiding all the coins is any answer anyway."

"I'd suggest professional help," the doctor said. "Maybe some in-patient treatment to get her beyond this. I'm sure there's that kind of help available."

"I'll follow up on that tomorrow," Verona said.

Which I realized, just then, wasn't going to happen. She was leaving tomorrow. She wouldn't be there to help me. A cold shaft of fear traveled up through my abdomen. I was going to be alone with the kids and whatever they needed would come to me. Why was this so scary? I found myself wondering.

Then it became crystal clear. Because I was looking at an indictment and I was looking at going to jail if Boudreaux came ahead after me. Then what would become of my children? Who would be there for them?

It was almost more than I could think about. So, for the rest of the time Annie would be in the hospital, I wouldn't think those thoughts.

Annie was discharged the next day at noon. Which was when the thoughts of failing my children took over like a wildfire in my mind. I couldn't stop thinking about it, about how vulnerable I had made them all because of my stupidity one night with Linda Burrows.

There weren't enough ways for me to kick myself.

31

Word of my future came the next day just before I was to take Verona to the airport. We had spent most of the day tracking down health care providers for Annie that might be able to address her food issues. We had made some calls and received some callbacks as we sat gathered around my desk in our home. Annie was upstairs in her room, resting on her bed with her computer propped on her lap. Dania was at school, and Mikey was at kindergarten. Their nanny would soon be picking them up, as I didn't want them riding the school bus. I didn't want that kind of discontinuity in their lives where I wouldn't know about their well-being while they were on a school bus. There was too much going on—many criminal lawyers I knew felt this same way. Seeing the horrible crimes you saw, you began to lose faith in systems of all kinds, and you began taking extra steps to secure your loved ones. So, no school buses. At least not back then.

My desk phone rang. I imagined it was a mental health facility getting back to me.

"Michael Gresham speaking."

"Michael, glad I got you. This is Niles Boudreaux."

"Hello, Niles. How are tricks?"

"I wouldn't know about tricks, but I do know about someone you're going to wish you hadn't found."

My heart fell. She had gone to him. It was all over.

"I don't know what you're talking about," I lied. "Who did I find?"

"Agnes Streith. Not only did I find her too, but she also called me. She's sitting right here with me in my office. She told me about the visit from your investigator. She told me about watching you gun down Linda Burrows. I thought you'd like to know."

"I don't—I don't—"

"Please don't even try. My staff has already had Agnes before the grand jury. I'm sitting here looking at your indictment. Do you want to come to court voluntarily in the morning or should I send the marshals out to pick you up?"

My head was spinning. My life was collapsing all around. First Annie, then Verona, and now a murder indictment? I reached across the desk and took Verona's hand in mine. Her forehead was wrinkled, and she was pleading with her eyes that I should tell her what was happening.

"I'll show up in court. When and where, Niles?"

"Tomorrow morning. Nine o'clock. Judge Frisson's courtroom."

"Okay. Do you suppose you could—"

"Email the indictment to you? I'm about to click SEND right now. Your email is still the same, correct?"

"Correct."

"Well, here we go. By the way, my list of witnesses will include Agnes here. She wants to tell the jury how she saw you shoot Linda twice. In the side of the head. Bad stuff, Michael. That was a federal agent you killed. We'll be asking the court for the death penalty. Have a good rest of the afternoon, Michael."

The line went dead.

By then I was gasping for air like a fish out of water.

"What?" said Verona. "You're white as a sheet!"

"I've just been indicted."

"For what?'

"Murder of Linda Burrows."

"Let me call the airport. My ticket is insured. I can't leave now."

"No, you need to go take care of your son. I'm an adult man, and I can pull myself through this. It's not the first time I've had some over-zealous prosecutor try to put me away."

"Over-zealous? You told me you had an affair with her?"

"I got her pregnant."

"You got her pregnant. The baby's DNA matched your own. So I'm sure they're trying to argue motive out of that. The motive is that I wouldn't find out. Or that your family wouldn't know. Or to protect your job. Any number of things."

"You have been listening to me," I said.

"Sure I have. No, I'm staying with you for now. I can fly over and see my son later on. You want to know the truth, Michael?"

Her hands were shaking. This thing she was about to say was irrevocable once it was out.

"What is it? What's the truth?"

"There's nothing I can do for Sergey. He's going to die, and there's nothing I can do. But you're not dead. You're going to be around for many years, and your kids are going to need you. That's become very important to me. Those little kids are as much mine right now as they are anyone else's. We've gotten very close. Especially the time we were living in Evanston and you were living here in D.C. I can't leave them now that you're in trouble."

My eyes glazed over. "You're sure about this?"

"Absolutely. I'll call my son, and we'll talk. In fact, we can do Face-Time. He can see his mom every day. And I can see him."

Now she had me going. "And you can hop on Aeroflot and go see him every month. Take a week there if you want."

"Exactly. So let me call and cancel my flight."

"Bless you, Verona. Thank you."

32

In a kind of an ironic twist, the U.S. District Court for the District of Columbia is housed in a building named the Prettyman Federal Courthouse. There was nothing pretty about that day when Marcel pulled up in front of the courthouse on Constitution Avenue and let me climb out. My appearance was set for nine a.m.; it was eight-fifty when I walked through the front doors of the courtroom. The place was packed with Assistant United States Attorneys—AUSAs. Because the U.S. Attorney's office in D.C. handles not only the prosecution of the U.S. Federal crimes that all U.S. Attorneys handle but also the D.C. local crimes like theft and burglary, the USAO staff is larger than any other USAO in the country. And I would've guessed that when I walked into that courtroom, I could count at least a dozen AUSAs just gathered around the prosecution table inside the bar.

Because I was an attorney, I could pass through the bar and grab one of the chairs just inside, which I did. I leaned back, straightened my tie, and tried to look like someone who wasn't scared half to death. Verona had offered to come for moral support, but I convinced her I'd be better without an audience. Same with Marcel. He was going to wait with his truck until I called his cell. It just felt better this way.

Scanning the attorneys at the front table, I studied each one to try to figure out who was going to prosecute me. I was pretty sure it wouldn't be Niles Boudreaux himself. U.S. Attorneys seldom if ever go to court and I didn't expect my case to be an exception.

But I was wrong. When he turned around in his chair, I got a look at his face. It was Niles Boudreaux. And sitting beside him was Antonia Xiang—this couldn't be true, she wouldn't allow it—but it was. Antonia, my old friend, was at her boss's side. Was she going to assist in his prosecution of me? Could this be happening? My strong interior began to crumble when I saw that even Antonia—who'd hired me at the USAO and had been my boss there—was now a member of the staff bent on sending me to my death. It made me very angry when I got myself calmed down. It made me angry and resolute that I wouldn't go down without a huge fight. Bring it on.

Then the judge entered the chamber and court was called to order by the clerk. Following that, we all retook our seats, and the judge asked the clerk to call the first case. It wasn't my case called first, though that surprised me since Boudreaux's time was precious and the judge concurred in that. So I could expect to be next.

Judge Honoré Frisson was of French extract, olive-skinned and straight black hair combed straight back and gelled. His sideburns were sharply trimmed, and the length of his hair was circumspect for a downtown jurist. Not too long, not too short; picture-perfect. He would've fit in well with a picture of the U.S. Supreme Court justices. Maybe there was a message there. Wasn't that always the case?

Anyway, Judge Frisson heard the presentation of the first case on a bail motion. He quickly made his findings and set bail and terms of pre-trial release. Then, sure enough, the clerk called United States of America v. Michael Gresham, and I stood and made my way to the lectern, where I was joined by Antonia, who evidently would be the lead prosecutor on my case. I wanted to turn to her and shout out, "How the hell could you!" but I didn't. I knew that somehow she had been forced into prosecuting a case she wanted no part of. I didn't know the details, but I did know Antonia. There was no way she'd take this role on voluntarily.

The judge intently recited the particulars: the shooting in June, the location, decedent's name, and so on. He asked me certain questions, and I gave one-word answers. All of these comments were on the record, of course, and were required by the Federal Rules of Criminal Procedure, including a recitation of my rights and responsibilities. He asked whether I had an attorney and I replied that I'd just received the indictment yesterday and hadn't had time to hire anyone yet, but I planned to. He asked me if I wanted forty-eight hours to hire an attorney and then return for the hearing. I told him no, that I was comfortable with representing myself in this preliminary stage. At that point, I was somewhat sure I wanted Joy to serve as my defense counsel, but she was back in Chicago on an old case she was still hooked on so I went it alone. The judge then opened the matter to the consideration of pre-trial release: bail. Antonia got to speak first.

"Your Honor, Michael Gresham used to work for me in the U.S. Attorney's office. I always thought him upright and honest. But now he's been charged with a grave crime, and I must present our office's thoughts on bail in this new light. Accordingly, I would request that no bail be set. The reason for this is that Mr. Gresham is a wealthy enough person that he could afford to get on an airplane this afternoon, fly anywhere in the world, and live out his life on the interest from his investments. Live very comfortably too; I happen to know. For this reason more than any other, we would ask the court to deny bail in this case. Thank you."

She ended abruptly without having said very much. She surprised me and gave me the emotional boost I needed just then. So I took my turn.

"Your Honor, I have no intention of fleeing to avoid trial. The underlying crime here has nothing to do with me, and I plan to prove that. For one thing, I have an ironclad alibi with photographs. For another, I've been privy to the investigation of this case by the FBI and the

MPD, and I am quite familiar with the high possibility there are more likely suspects in the case than me. People who had a real motive for murdering Linda Burrows. Judge, this is a case where a wife who was sleeping around with staff from the USAO's office was murdered probably by her husband, a man who, I will argue, got fed up with her cheating ways and shot her. Jealousy, anger, rage—probably all of these played a part in his acting on a genuine motive to kill his ex-wife. So no, I won't be fleeing, and yes, I'll be here when it's time to go to trial."

I also considered moving to have Antonia removed as a prosecutor based on her conflict of interest in the case. After all, she'd been my boss, had helped with the case at the same time I was working it, and I had previously represented her husband in a criminal case in Russia. Did these things add up to a conflict? Maybe not, but the argument could be made. But instead, I remained silent on the issue. For all I knew she was going to be in a position of passing me information from her side of the street if she still held the strong feelings for me that she'd felt when she hired me and previously when I'd saved her husband's life in Russia. That was probably wishful thinking, but I was willing to roll those dice any day. Time would tell. So I ended my argument without much more, and we submitted the bail request to the judge for a ruling.

"The court is inclined to allow bail in the amount of five million dollars. A signature bond will be sufficient, given the defendant's ties to the community."

A signature bond is a promise to return to court without the need to put forward any collateral. I was to be allowed to sign a document promising to pay that bail amount to the federal government if I failed to appear at a court hearing. He knew, of course, whatever amount of savings and investments I might have, it would take time to liquidate those holdings, and the court system could grab enough of my assets to make fleeing the country a very unattractive proposition unless you like dumpster-diving in Paris.

The judge continued. "As you know, the court can impose various pretrial conditions upon the accused. So here are your conditions of bail, Mr. Gresham, effective from this moment on: surrender all passports; surrender any firearms you may have in your home; abstain from drug/alcohol use; be confined to a set curfew; not associate with known felons; not loiter in certain areas and institutions of the federal judiciary, including the U.S. Attorney's office; be monitored by a GPS tracking device, and other specific conditions to follow."

"I understand, your Honor," I said.

"What about the government, Ms. Xiang? Any other items I should consider?"

Antonia didn't look up from her yellow tablet. "No, sir."

"One more thing, counsel, and defendant," said the judge. "There is a large media contingent waiting outside in the hall. I get it; this is a newsworthy case. But in particular, I'm ordering both sides to make no comments to the press that would tend to bias any potential juror in the case. Am I making myself clear?"

"Yes, your Honor," we responded together. For what it was worth. While the USAO might not comment, the FBI and police were always free to comment all they wanted. They would fry me in the papers and TV before it was all over while making it look like they were calmly and rationally just doing their job. I would be hacked to pieces before they finished with me before the trial ever began.

"Very well, this case is in recess."

Antonia and I turned and went our separate ways.

As for me, I couldn't get out of there fast enough. It is one thing to be inside a courtroom while you're defending someone. It is quite another, I was finding out, when that someone is you. As I walked the long walk up the aisle to the hallway doors, my pulse was racing, and I had broken a cold sweat under my suit. Then I pushed through the door and found myself staring into maybe twenty reporters and their camera crews, all of them waggling microphones at me and asking about my defense. I made my way through them, smiling my most friendly smile but not stopping to speak. It was all I could do not to cry out that the U.S. Attorney hated me and this was a personal grudge prosecution, but I kept wearing my sweet smile instead and then broke free and hurried toward the elevators.

That night, the U.S. Attorney's office distributed a press release stating that the evidence against me was overwhelming and they expected a quick verdict once a jury was sworn.

Nice, I thought and closed my eyes against the statement on the screen of my laptop.

It had begun.

33

Joy returned to the office the next day. She didn't know until I buzzed her into my office that I'd been indicted for the murder of Linda Burrows. There she sat, in a gray pin-striped suit, her mouth half-open in astonishment while she read the indictment. "No way!" she said when finished. "You couldn't kill someone! What a load of rubbish!"

"What can I say?" I replied with a forced smile. "Someone wants to put me away."

"Niles Boudreaux, from the looks of things. My God, Michael, what did you ever do to that guy?"

"What did I do? In my mind, without telling a soul, I had begun harboring thoughts that he might be the killer. Did he read my mind and decide to get rid of me? I don't know. But something riled him up —and I'm guessing it's something as simple as putting the heat on someone else so no one would be looking at him."

She sat forward and stirred the cream into her coffee. "Probably right. The simplest explanation is usually the correct one. So. What can I do to help?"

"Defend me."

She looked startled. "Seriously? You know I've never even appeared in criminal court, don't you?"

"Yes, I think we talked about that. But I meant what I said when we first met, and I paid you. I want you at the defense table."

"I was afraid this was coming. Might I also suggest that you hire an attorney who knows his or her way around the criminal courts? Someone to second-chair me?"

I shook my head. "I'm your man. I've been there way more than most attorneys still in practice. I'm your backup. I don't want us to look overloaded with lawyers. When we appear before the jury, I want you, and I want me at the table. No one else. The government will have an investigator or two and maybe three or more attorneys also at the table to help. It's going to look like an unfair fight going in, and that's how I want it."

"I like that thinking. It works for me," Joy said. "Wow. Here we go."

"Yes, here we go."

"What's our defense?"

I looked carefully at her. I wanted to see how she judged what I was going to tell her.

"Well, for one thing, we're going to put on trial the empty chair. The defendant who isn't there because the government arrested the wrong man. I'm thinking we create a case around at least two other men who had motive and opportunity to shoot Linda."

"You're thinking her ex-husband and Niles Boudreaux, right?"

"At least the two of them," I confirmed. "Maybe one or two others, as well."

"Don't make the dartboard too crowded with targets. Two should be enough to turn the jury's head elsewhere."

"You're right. So we'll put Harry Burrows and Niles Boudreaux on trial."

"Let's get me involved with the investigation. I can get up to speed in just a few hours. Then maybe we can meet with Marcel and with Annie."

"I like that."

"Michael, it sounds like the defense to use. But let me review the investigation first and see just how strong the cases are that we can make against Burrows and Boudreaux."

"Fine."

We broke up, and I refilled my coffee cup in the kitchen. Then I headed for Annie's office.

Her door was closed when I arrived, so I knocked and waited.

No response.

So I knocked again. Then I tried the knob. Locked. I returned to my office and dialed her on the intercom. She had caller ID, so she answered.

"Michael?"

"I need to talk to you, Annie. Please unlock your door."

"All right."

She hung up, and I headed off to her space again.

She opened her door and stood aside. I led us back to her desk, which was a roll-top shoved up against the wall. It was the desk she chose when she went with me to the office furniture store. It wasn't the desk I would've wanted, but Annie was her own boss. Who was I to argue? Even if it was useless as a work surface on which things might get done.

"I need to hear what kind of profile you have on the Linda Burrows case," I said.

"Your killer is male, between the ages of thirty and fifty, Caucasian. This man will be someone who possesses an advanced degree, probably a Juris Doctor. Married young, a fan of the Washington Redskins and the Washington Senators, and smokes Marlboros."

"Marlboros? Where's that coming from?"

"Read your file, Michael. A loose Marlboro was found at the scene."

"Wait. Was the Marlboro studied for DNA?"

"Nothing in the file reflects a DNA workup on the cigarette. Of the possible suspects known to you, do any of them smoke?"

"Unknown. We probably won't be able to nail that down, either. So that's a loose end."

"Okay."

"Let's take your identifiers one at a time, Annie. First, why do you think the killer is male?"

"I believe it's a crime of passion. There's the possibility that a wife or girlfriend of one of Linda's lovers might have killed out of anger, but that's much less doubtful than her husband or another lover doing the deed. From what I can find out, the jealousy quotient between men and women is eighty percent for women versus twenty percent for men."

"Isn't that upside-down?"

"It is. But I'm only talking about feelings. As far as acting violently on the feeling of jealousy, the figures reverse. For men, it's about seventy-five percent while for women it's low twenties."

"Figures. I would've guessed that men are much more likely to pick up a gun and shoot a lover than a woman would be."

"Women are much more likely to have a good cry and then call a lawyer. Their get-even might be less violent, but it's much more sophisticated and almost always results in a significant loss of net worth to the object of her love-gone-bad."

"So the odds are it's a man."

"Correct."

"Advanced college degree for our killer? Why a college degree? Why even a lawyer?"

"Because she was a lawyer. Lawyers are very concerned with appearances: they don't like to marry beneath their education level. So the odds are elevated that he was at the lawyer level or Ph.D. level, that sort of thing."

"That's how you see us? Lawyers in general?"

"That's how everyone sees you, Michael. Very superficial much of the time."

"Wow. My daughter."

"What does my being your daughter have to do with the truth?"

"You've got me there, Annie."

"So the chances are better that you're talking about a graduate degree-level male. But there's one compelling exception to this. I'm talking about the shooter who might be any age who has developed a fixation on someone. They may or may not be lovers. The victim may even die never knowing the shooter had any feelings toward him or her whatsoever—a case of being idolized from afar."

"You're talking about the kooks now."

"Kooks?"

"Yes," I said, "the people who aren't well-adjusted."

Annie turned away in her chair. "Yes. Maybe even people like me."

So. Emotionally, Annie was still a child. I plunged ahead to roadblock what she was thinking.

"No, no, no, I don't mean that. That's not what I'm saying at all. There's a huge difference between someone like you and someone who might kill out of jealousy."

She turned back around. "All right, Michael. Explain that huge difference, please. I'd like to hear your logic."

She was boring in on me with those big eyes. I felt like a bug under a pin.

"Let's just say your makeup—your character—tends never to cling to other people. Compare this to the sociopath who loves from afar, who idolizes. That person is nothing like you. That person can be needy, and grasping, and fixated. You're never fixated on people."

"Because I don't have much need for people?" she asked.

I shrugged. "Hey, I don't know how else I'd describe it, so yes. People are not at the top of your list."

"You know, Michael, you know a lot about me that I'll never know. I just don't think that way."

"I know. Savants are seldom—maybe never—aware of the feelings of other people. Hell, a lot of the time they aren't even aware of other people at all. That's you."

"Where were we?" she asked, apparently having lost interest in any more analysis by me.

"What about the love for local sports teams like the Redskins and Senators?"

She lightly brushed her hand through the air between us. "That's easy. Your killer is in a high-pressure job. Professional sports are his escape. He brings the same drama to supporting his local sports team that he brings to his work as a lawyer."

She never ceased to amaze me. You always got more than you bargained for with Annie.

"Do you have any names for me that I should be focused on?" I asked.

"I do. Niles Boudreaux is an obvious candidate. Law degree, married young but divorced, already experienced in the use of guns. He fits as well as anyone. The other would be one of the office lovers who might've developed a thing for Linda and shot her out of jealousy. That seems like a huge stretch, to me. No, I'm happier with Boudreaux as my suspect. But there is one other, too. Plus, she's pregnant. Maybe the kid is his, and maybe she threatens him with a sexual harassment complaint."

"Why not just have an abortion? What's wrong with that? All he has to do is pay for it."

"Aha," Annie said, showing us one of the very few smiles I'd ever seen from her. "I've done maybe a little more background than you. I've been on the Internet. Your Linda Burrows was Catholic, just like you. She wasn't about to have an abortion."

"Good find!"

Then her face was troubled again. "However, there is one more possible suspect."

"Who?" I asked for I had no idea from our obvious candidates.

"You, Michael. You had a motive to kill Linda."

My mouth fell open. I had no response, slick or genuine that I could think to make. Most investigators would have found me guilty just for my reaction.

"I—I—"

"Sure, you're going to deny, deny, deny. But let's look at the facts, Michael. We know you had an affair with Linda, however short-lived. We also know you impregnated her. The DNA reports are all over the file, and that's how I established the affair you'd had with her. But why would Michael shoot her? Read the file, Michael. She's Catholic, so no abortion. You wouldn't ask her to get an abortion, though. If—and it's a big if—the people on the jury believe your devotion to your faith. They may or may not. Look at the facts: you're living with a woman you're not married to. You don't attend church."

"I do confession."

"What record is there of that?"

She had me there. "None."

"Secondary motive by you: ruining your relationship with Verona. You couldn't have her finding out you'd cheated on her in Washington, D.C. while Verona was clear out in Evanston, Illinois watching your children. I mean, Michael, what kind of man stoops that low?"

That caused me to suck in my breath and hold it.

But I quickly recovered when I considered the source of the comment. Annie didn't judge people. The comment, "What kind of man stoops so low" was more a scientific inquiry than an assignment of guilt to me. I fought down the urge to take it the wrong way from what she meant. My guilt was working against me.

I told her, "What you're saying makes sense. Which makes my defense in my court case much more difficult."

"It's a toss-up between you and Boudreaux, Michael. I'm betting it's him. I wouldn't bet against you on this one."

"Well, thank you, Annie."

She tossed her head and brushed a comma of hair from her forehead. "You're welcome."

Good grief. Busted by my own kid—up to a point. I did not shoot my lover. Annie's analysis of me broke down at that point. Which also proved an earlier thesis of hers from a previous talk we'd had weeks before in which she said I wouldn't be the jealous type. She was right: I had been cheated on so many times that someone like Linda wouldn't have fazed me. It wouldn't even turn my head.

"One thing in your favor, Michael, I might add. You're an old man. You've probably been cheated on a good dozen times by now. You've become inured to it."

"Well, that's certainly a relief," I stammered. "Thank goodness for my history of cheating lovers."

"Yes, it helps to winnow you out," she said.

At which point, I stood up and stretched.

"Let's do this, Annie. I'd like you to go ahead and write up your rationale for Boudreaux. Pin it down why you think he might be the killer. Link the evidentiary items to him. Then we'll meet with Joy and go over all this again."

"Joy's going to defend you?'

"Yes."

"Then might I suggest, Michael, that you not strike up a romance with Joy? You don't need to confuse her feelings for your case with feelings she would develop for you. Keep your hands in your pockets, Michael."

"I'm headed back to my office, Annie. I'll certainly think that over."

I left her behind and heard the door locking behind me.

I couldn't get out of there fast enough.

34

Saturday following my initial appearance I drove down to the Foggy Bottom Grocery. I intended to locate Delores and speak to her again about the cop she saw leaving the store after the shooting. As I was entering the store, I was stopped by a uniformed police officer. He held out a photograph to me.

I looked it over.

"Ever seen this man?" The officer asked me.

It wasn't a bad photograph of me, the one the bar association had on file. A good likeness. Why the cop didn't connect the photograph to my face, I don't understand. Probably never will, except to say he was probably bored with his duty that day and not paying close attention. Whatever.

"No, I haven't seen him," I replied, and passed on into the store. Delores wasn't working any of the four cash registers. The lines were backed up, the place was jumping with Saturday shoppers, but no Delores. Making my way back inside the store, I decided to walk up aisle 11. I saw nothing unusual as I made my way along there.

At the rear of the store, I found the usual enclave of closed-off offices, employee dressing rooms, and break room. I made my way inside, checking out each one as I searched for Delores. But she was nowhere to be found. Cursing my luck, I exited that part of the store and headed back up front.

Which was when I heard a voice behind me, commanding me to stop.

"You in the white shirt! Stop right there, please, sir!"

I stopped and began to turn around. Using lots of force the cop grabbed my shoulder and spun me around, so I was again facing the front doors of the store. He told me to place my hands on top of my head, fingers interlaced. I complied. He then proceeded to pat me down.

"Driver's license, please."

I pulled my wallet out of my jacket pocket and opened it. I held it out to him, and he studied the license.

"Mr. Gresham, I just observed you trespassing in the back of the store."

"What?"

"I followed you from in front of the store all the way to the back. You then went inside an area plainly marked 'No Customers - Private.' Did someone tell you it was okay to go in there?"

"No, no one told me. I was looking for the bathrooms."

"You didn't see them on the north side of the store?"

"No, I didn't go over that way."

"But you were still trespassing."

"Let me show you another piece of ID, please. If you'll let me open my wallet?"

"Turn around and open your wallet."

Following his okay, I turned and opened my wallet to my U.S. Attorney ID. He read it over, compared the name to the name of my license, and pushed it away. "Nice," he said. "A federal prosecutor trespassing inside a neighborhood grocery. Please don't do this again where I'm on duty. Got me?"

"Yes, officer," I said as if I appreciated his guidance. I didn't, but my tone was gracious.

"Okay, you can go, Mr. Gresham."

"Hey, one question. Why were you following me?"

"Something about you just didn't look right. Then you walked directly over to the aisle where that woman was gunned down. That's when I decided to follow."

"What didn't look right?"

"Hard to say. Maybe I've seen you around the courthouse before."

"Am I being followed by anyone else?"

"What? Nobody's told me if you are. I was just doing my job in the store."

"Who told you to come here and show my photograph around?"

"My sergeant."

"What's his name?"

"Cantor Comiskey."

"Give me his phone number. Type it into my cell phone, please."

He did as asked. I completed the new contact with his sergeant's name and put my phone away.

"All right," I said, "thank you. And if you're ever at the U.S. Attorney's office look me up. I'll buy you a cup of coffee."

"I'd like that."

"And a donut."

"Funny man."

∽

I DIDN'T GET hold of Sergeant Comiskey until Monday morning. He came to the phone and gruffly answered, "Comiskey here. Who's calling?"

"My name is Michael Gresham. You ordered one of your officers to show my picture around at the Foggy Bottom Grocery on Saturday."

"So what if I did?"

"Well, before we talk about invasion of my privacy, why don't you tell me who ordered you to do that? Tell me, and I'll just let it drop."

"I don't have to tell you anything, Mr. Gresham. But you know what? I'm gonna be a gentleman because today's my birthday. We received the photograph and the request from the U.S. Attorney's office."

"What was the sender's name?"

"Antonia somebody."

"Antonia Xiang?"

"Yes, something Chinese."

"All right. You've been a great help, and I thank you."

"Goodbye, Mr. Gresham."

"Happy birthday, Sergeant."

"Whatever."

35

Weeks came and went while I bounced off the walls at the office and basically couldn't put two useful thoughts together. Why? Because I was scared. I hated to let fear stop me from trying new things or plunging ahead and doing hard things. But this time it had me whipped because I couldn't get my brain to come up with a strategy to make this whole terrible prosecution just dry up and blow away.

Instead, it kept coming on stronger and stronger. The government (Antonia) filed a lengthy list of witnesses it planned on calling at trial. They were good, reliable names, most of them CSI's M.E.'S, and FBI and MPD, which meant they were all professional witnesses. They had been to witness school—literally—and were capable of destroying the defendant whose counsel is asleep at the wheel and doesn't see the truck coming. Plus they were capable of killing you with a smile, so the jury came away thinking what nice witnesses the government had this time. These are the thoughts that persisted, kept me awake all night, and that I didn't know how to fight.

Agnes Streith's name was listed by Antonia Xiang in the government's witness list too. I cringed every time I saw that name. For the life of me, I could not imagine how she could be claiming I was the shooter. Joy was looking at ways of keeping her testimony out, primarily based on the prejudicial way Agnes had identified me through the one-person lineup they used. As a general rule, lineups are considered to be a "critical stage" in the criminal justice process, and the prosecution may not admit into evidence in-court identification of defendants based on out-of-court lineups or show-ups if they were obtained without the presence of defendant's counsel. This would be my case, so Joy was preparing a *motion in limine* to present before trial, which would prevent Agnes identifying me as the shooter based on seeing me in a photograph out-of-court when my lawyer wasn't present.

Compared to the government's case, my case was weak and more hope than substance. I was relying almost exclusively on Verona, who would show the jury the films and snaps of me at the Punch Brothers concert on June 24. She was my ticket to surviving this thing; she was the only path to a defense verdict.

There was one other bright spot, and that was Marcel. Just having him back with me was incredibly reassuring. We hadn't lost many cases since we teamed up; he had a way of finding trial-changing evidence in places where others had looked and seen nothing. He was very imaginative this way, very creative, which is precisely how defense lawyers and their investigators must be if they're going to win the impossible cases.

On the day of trial, Joy and I, with Marcel coming in thirty minutes, showed up for trial an hour before we were scheduled to begin. Judge Honoré Frisson had ordered us present to begin at eight o'clock to deal with any motions, problems, or needs before we began selecting a jury. As it turned out, the key pre-trial motion was one filed by the government. They wanted all polygraph test results barred from coming into evidence. They cited a long line of cases that make polygraph exams inadmissible. Joy tried to argue that the results in my case were the results of a test administered by the government and therefore the government should be bound by the test results and they should be allowed before the jury. Judge Frisson listened to all of this then made a quick ruling. The polygraph test would not be allowed into evidence. The polygraph exam couldn't even be mentioned before the jury. Round One to the government.

The *Federal Rules of Criminal Procedure* allowed the court, or the court and the attorneys, to choose a criminal jury. In most criminal cases jury selection in and of itself creates many motions and arguments by the lawyer that must be addressed by the court before jury selection can begin. These same rules also gave the government twenty peremptory challenges and the defense twenty peremptory challenges because the government was seeking the death penalty.

The death penalty in my case was sought because the killing of a government prosecutor—a member of the U.S. Attorney's office— was considered as serious a crime as there was. Antonia had filed what's known as a *3593 Notice*—a written pleading telling the court and the defense that the government would be seeking the death penalty. In all honesty, I couldn't—wouldn't—even think about this possibility. That's why I'd hired Joy—to let her think about such things.

When it was all said and done, the seating of the prospective jurors, the court's voir dire of the jurors, and the attorneys' submission of additional questions for the court to consider asking—all of this took three solid days to complete. We used all twenty peremptory challenges and, as usual with jury selection, we didn't have the jury we wanted; we had the jury that remained after all of the jurors we didn't want had been kicked off the jury panel.

We were allowed to go home or back to our offices an hour early on Wednesday. Once the jury selection was completed, the jury was sworn-in and admonished to avoid reading accounts of the case or trial, and not to discuss the case with anyone, and to notify the court if someone approached a juror in an attempt to influence them. There were other strictures, too, common to all juries whether state or federal. I was glad to be released early, even if it only meant we'd be going back to the office at four instead of five o'clock.

Ten minutes later, I had Joy and Marcel in my office, fresh coffee served, with my door closed and a directive to Tammy that she not bother us with phone calls.

Sitting and stirring my coffee, I noticed how quiet we all were.

"It's like a tomb in here," I said.

"We're worried about you, boss," said Marcel.

"What did you look into today?" Joy asked Marcel.

"I started my day at the scene of the crime."

"The Foggy Bottom Grocery," Joy said. Marcel nodded.

"Then I worked my way over to Linda's condo. I didn't go up to her floor because I didn't want the police—if they were outside her door —to know I was snooping around."

"I don't think they're at her condo," I said. "I mean, why would they be?"

Marcel shrugged. "Don't know. But I didn't go up. Sometimes, you know, they'll have an officer or two lurking around just to see who does show up. They'll take surreptitious photographs of you and then put them on the big screen back at the office and run ID software on your face. I didn't want that because I'm included in every law enforcement database in the world."

"Understand," Joy said. "What else did you do?"

"I spent several hours here in my office reviewing CCTV video taken by the store's interior and exterior cameras. I'm looking for anything that might suggest the killer was someone other than Michael. There were over eighteen cameras, meaning we're waist-deep in video that we can review. I'd been through it before, but my intuition was telling me to look again."

"Is there anything at all there?"

"There were many faces—shoppers—inside the store when the shooting occurred. Unfortunately, none of the cameras offer a view down aisle eleven."

"Unfortunately," I said. "But aren't they supposed to have video on every aisle at all times?"

"Their insurance policies require that," Marcel said. "But sometimes there's a slip-up, and they miss some area of the store. People get fired over stuff like this. I'm sure heads will roll here, too."

I took a swallow of my coffee and noticed my hand was shaking as the cup chattered when I returned it to its saucer.

"Nervous," I said weakly. "I need a drink."

"I thought you didn't drink," Marcel said.

"Very rarely—you know that," I replied.

"Well, don't do it now. We need your head to be very clear as we try to save your life," Marcel said, and I saw Joy nodding her agreement.

"It was just a stupid comment. Don't get all bent out of shape, okay?"

Marcel scowled in return, and it was only then I realized just how frightened he was, too. Which scared me even more.

36

Marcel stubbornly tried a re-visit to the Foggy Bottom Mall.

He parked in front of the market then jogged across the parking lot to the end store. "Phil's Friendly Pets," said the black and yellow sign along its roofline. Marcel walked inside.

At the cash register, he asked to see the manager. The youngish man at the register said he was the manager.

"You're Phil?"

"No, I'm Franco. There is no Phil. I mean there was when Phil owned it, but he died. He was my uncle."

"Oh, sorry to hear that."

"How can I help you? You're here about our ad?"

"Ad?"

"Free cats. We try to recycle used cats here. It's a public service. I love cats."

"No, I'm not here about a cat. Let me ask. I noticed that just over your door outside there's a TV camera. Does it work?"

"You mean is it just to scare off crooks or does it take pictures?"

"Exactly."

"No, it works. Very well, too. I've never been broken into."

"Was it working this past June twenty-fifth?"

"Far as I know," the young man said. He reached inside a Pet Taxi and pulled his hand out holding a white guinea pig. Ever so carefully he began clipping the animal's toenails.

"Have to clip them every couple of weeks. Otherwise, they get them caught in the wire, and they bleed. Can't have that, not for these little guys."

"Well, let me ask you this," Marcel continued. "If I paid you to allow me to review your CCTV video from June twenty-fifth would that work?"

"Can you see our video? Sure. It's stored by days on the hard drive. After six months the oldest month is erased. You're here just in time if you want June."

"I would love to see June."

"Hang on. Let me finish with this guy, and I'll take you up to my office."

Marcel stood smiling amiably and bided his time until the young man had finished with the guinea pig and replaced it in the Pet Taxi. "Follow me," he said with a smile.

They went to the side of the store and took an open stairway to the upstairs floor, which was a loft built up over the cash register area. A door and windows allowed employees to look down on the store. In particular, the cash registers could be monitored as workers operated them.

The young man bent to the single computer on the single desk and clicked the mouse. He clicked twice again and then stood back. "June two-five right on-screen. Have at it, mister."

Marcel thanked the young man and sat down at the desk. Satisfied he'd accommodated his visitor, the man went back down the stairs, leaving Marcel alone—oddly enough, considering the possible security breach—with his CCTV video.

Marcel clicked the video file and began watching the stream, date- and time-stamped. It started at 12:01 a.m. On June 24, 2017, and progressed through the minutes—then the hours—from there.

Nothing. So he rolled into June 25.

Now he could only keep his fingers crossed and watch images shift, take shape, and move away.

It was all he knew to do to help Michael Gresham at that point.

Three hours later, he had triple-timed through the video. While it did show a uniformed police officer coming from between two vehicles and entering the store, it didn't show the police officer's vehicle because the angle was too sharp to see beyond the nearer vehicle. He needed a more direct line of sight of the cop's vehicle.

It was time to visit "Koci's Nails" two doors down. If there were CCTV inside that place of business, the camera would have caught what Marcel was seeking. If, if, if.

Marcel thanked the young man, again resisted leaving with a free cat, and walked out onto the sidewalk, where he took a right and headed for Koci's.

He hit a brick wall at Koci's. The woman behind the counter insisted that the camera outside was only for show. "It doesn't work," she told Marcel. He looked at her askance. Deep down was the feeling she wasn't telling him the whole truth. But he had nothing to prove his suspicion. Moreover, he couldn't just go storming into their back office, commandeer their computer, and begin searching for video files. That was called trespassing and could lead to big trouble for him.

"I told the detectives the same thing. No video, sorry."

He backed off, almost sure the woman was lying to him.

"You say the detectives were here? I would be surprised if they weren't here."

"No video," she repeated and then turned away.

He pushed through the front door and stood beneath the camera mounted overhead.

A green light just above the lens indicated it was working.

There had to be a way.

37

Opening statements were given Thursday morning.

Antonia on behalf of the USA went first. As she launched into her talk, almost at the very start, I suddenly tightened up and expelled a stream of air as if I'd been stabbed. I passed Joy a quick note: "OMG!" I wrote, "Did you hear the date the government lawyer just gave the jury for the date Linda was killed? June 25? My exhibits are date-stamped June 24."

"Check the dates on the exhibits themselves," she wrote back. "The actual exhibit list has them dated June 25."

I opened my laptop and, with shaking hands, located our list of exhibits. I read the brief explanation of the video: "June 25, 2017," said the exhibit list. I clicked a file and brought up the exhibits themselves. I checked the date-stamps. Which was when the roof caved in, and I was hit by fear unlike I'd ever known before. "June 24, 2017," said every last date-stamp. Then I riffled through them again. All said the same thing: June 24.

"Exhibits are date-stamped June 24," my next note said to her. "She told the jury the crime occurred June twenty-fifth. If she's right, our video and photographs go right out the window."

I was stunned. I heard nothing further of Antonia's opening statement. In one sentence from her, my entire case evaporated. I had no defense for the date she was using. My only hope was that she'd misspoken, that Antonia's date was wrong. When Antonia finished, thanked the judge and jury, and then sat down, Joy asked the court for a ten-minute recess. A recess at that point in the trial wasn't common, but Judge Frisson allowed it.

We went into the hallway and located a vacant conference room.

We quickly took a seat. I looked across the table at my lawyer. Joy was having trouble making eye contact with me. The look on her face was one of desperation. Enough said.

Then she said, "Please tell me our exhibits are mislabeled. Please tell me the photographs and video are June twenty-fifth." She looked first at Marcel and then fixed me with her eyes. "Michael?"

I didn't know what to say. We'd received the indictment months ago and, as I pulled it out and read the dates of the allegations, I was again floored. Same thing with the exhibit list: June 25. They'd told us all along it was June 25 when the murder occurred. My team—Joy— had blown it.

Or had she? She said, remembering, "Your photographs and video never showed up in your file. I remember asking you for them. You never uploaded them, Michael."

That day swam into focus for me. She was right. I had been transported by her soft lips and glossy lipstick and had completely forgotten to move the photos from my phone to the network. It was all on me.

Then Joy pulled the exhibit list out of her folder and laid it on the table before her. She quickly read through it.

"Oh, no!" she suddenly cried, "Here it is. Our exhibit list says June twenty-fifth, but you're saying there's a date-stamp a day earlier?"

"Unfortunately for my freedom, that's what I'm saying. The list we filed says the twenty-fifth. The actual exhibits are date-stamped the twenty-fourth."

I was stunned. Marcel gave me a look of disbelief and looked away.

It was a terrible mistake, and it was about to send me to prison.

"My God," Marcel said, "come on everybody, let's get creative!"

My brain had stopped working. Too much stress, too much fear, and it had stopped functioning. I couldn't grab onto any aspect of the date problem and figure out how to overcome it or work around it.

Nor could Joy. "I don't know," she said. "Our defense just flew out the window. I don't know how to get creative, Marcel."

At just that moment, a deputy knocked on our door and announced, "Two minutes! Let's get back to our places!"

We folded up our files and put away our copies of exhibits and marched single-file back into the courtroom. "Try not to look glum when the jury comes back," Joy whispered over her shoulder. "I know I don't have to tell you that, Michael. But tell Marcel, too, please."

A minute later and we were seated at counsel table, the jury had been brought back in by the bailiff, and the Judge Honoré Frisson appeared out of his door and climbed up to his seat.

Then he looked down at Joy. "Counsel, is the defense ready to present its opening statement?"

Joy did the smart thing. She reserved her opening statement until the start of the defense case. Which would give her more time to adjust her opening comments to what we had instead of what we had thought we had.

Judge Frisson next told the government that it could call its first witness.

She stood and called to the stand John Ames.

Jack Ames stood up from her table and took the witness stand.

"State your name."

"John Ames. Everyone calls me Jack."

"What is your profession?"

"Special agent with the Federal Bureau of Investigation."

"You're an FBI agent?"

"Yes, ma'am. Fifteen years now."

"Where is your office?"

"Here in Washington. I work Washington, D.C. cases."

"Are you familiar with the case involving the murder of Linda Burrows?"

"I am. I was assigned by my SAIC to work that case from the first day it came into our office."

"Have you, in fact, worked that case?"

"I have."

"Tell us what you've done."

Ames leaned back and collected his thoughts. It was all for show, and I knew it. He knew exactly what he was going to say to slowly skewer me.

"On the day the case was assigned to me I drove over to the U.S. Attorney's office and met with the defendant, Michael Gresham."

"He was an assistant U.S. Attorney?"

"At that time, yes. He was assigned to investigating and prosecuting the Linda Burrows case in the U.S. Attorney's office. The case was very high profile, so having an assistant U.S. Attorney assigned to help us investigate was somewhat unusual. I'd seen it before, but it was rare."

"What did you do the day you first saw Michael Gresham?"

"We sat at his desk, introduced ourselves, and talked about the case. We talked about who Linda was, how and where she'd been murdered, and who we thought going in might have a motive to kill her."

"We've talked, and I know some of the people you and the defendant might've considered. But let me ask you this: did the name of Michael Gresham himself come up?"

"Of course not. He wasn't connected to her death in any way when we first met."

"When did he become connected, in your view?"

"Number one, when the DNA tests post-mortem revealed that Mr. Gresham had fathered the child Linda was carrying at her death, and, number two, when Agnes Streith came to us and said she'd witnessed the shooting and the person firing the gun was Michael Gresham himself."

"We'll connect up these matters later on, but for now, you knew none of this the first day you met with Mr. Gresham?"

"No, nobody knew these things."

"Did you and Mr. Gresham then proceed to investigate this case together?"

"Yes and no. I was allowed to add my partner Marty Longstreet to our list of investigators, and I mainly worked with him from then on."

"What did Marty bring to the team?"

"Marty became suspicious of the defendant way before any of the rest of us. I don't know if it was a personality conflict or what, but Marty seemed to see right through Michael Gresham and knew he was the killer way before the rest of us figured it out."

"Now let's talk about what else you and Marty did during your investigation into the death of Linda Burrows. Who did you interview?"

"First we joined with the defendant in his interview of Harry Burrows."

"That would be Linda's ex-husband?"

"Correct. Harry is a cop. First on the scene after Linda was shot. Gave her CPR. He was found by the next officers as he sat on the floor holding his ex-wife's hand. He told the officers he'd like to split open Niles Boudreaux's head for sleeping with his wife. But other than that, Harry appeared shattered by Linda's death."

I looked over to see the jury watching Niles Boudreaux. I smiled inwardly. Now we were getting somewhere.

"Who else did you talk to?"

"Oh, let's see. According to my notes, we talked to Edmund Rasmussen. Ed is the detective who headed up the case from Metro PD. He had interviewed several people himself, and he told us what all he had learned. It's all in my notes."

"Yes."

"We—Marty and I—also met with Michael Gresham at a restaurant and sort of what you might call an interview of Gresham. Marty didn't trust him, especially after he found out Gresham had gotten Linda pregnant. The upshot was, Gresham would submit to some further examination."

"Did he?"

"Yes."

They were skirting the polygraph exam I took. Polygraph exams weren't admissible in court. Worse for their side, I had passed mine. They didn't want those results in front of our jury. So they lightly glossed it over and moved away.

"I have just a few more questions. I believe you and Marty Longstreet accompanied Michael Gresham at Mr. Boudreaux's office when Mr. Gresham interviewed him, correct?"

"I don't remember who asked the most questions. It seems to me we all had questions for Mr. Boudreaux."

"Can you summarize his interview?"

"He said he also slept with Linda. He said Linda's husband, Harry, caught him and Linda together in a hotel room. Linda had been nude. He also said he was unmarried when all this happened."

"What else have you done?"

"There must be others we've talked to. I can't recall any right this minute."

"Judge," said Antonia, "the government passes the witness for direct-examination."

"Very well," said Judge Frisson. "Why don't we go for about thirty minutes more and then we'll take our mid-morning break. Everyone okay with that? Good. Proceed, counsel."

Joy took up her position at the lectern and flipped through her notes. Then she launched right in.

"Mr. Ames, isn't it true that Michael Gresham convinced you he was innocent of this murder?"

"Objection!" cried Antonia. "Seeks to violate the court's pre-trial order!"

"But the reference to the matter was raised by the government when she asked about additional questions they had for Michael Gresham."

The judge nodded. "They did open the door, but only a small crack. Not enough to overrule the court's previous order. Objection sustained. Please move along, counsel."

"Mr. Ames, did Mr. Boudreaux tell you how many times he slept with Linda Burrows?"

Good, she was going to parade this sad fact in front of the jury and grind it into their heads.

"Just the one time."

"Did you specifically ask Mr. Boudreaux how many times he had sex with Mr. Burrows' wife?"

"Not that I recall."

"So he could have had sex with her multiple times that you wouldn't know about?"

"Anything is possible."

"Agent Ames, did anyone of you ever ask Boudreaux whether he was being pressured by the White House while the murders were occurring?"

"No."

"Wouldn't that have been important to know?"

"I don't understand."

"Well, what if the president was pressuring Mr. Boudreaux to solve the case, that it was making the White House look bad because everyone knew Linda was promiscuous? Did you ask him whether he was getting that kind of pressure?"

"No."

"Would that kind of pressure be enough for Mr. Boudreaux to shoot Linda Burrows?"

"Objection! Calls for an opinion and analysis for someone's state of mind. The witness is unqualified for either."

"Sustained."

Joy came back another way. "Did Mr. Boudreaux ever tell you the president called him about the murders?"

"No."

"Did anyone of you ever ask him whether that was the case?"

"Not that I recall."

"Wouldn't it be important to know whether he was getting pressure, especially when you're looking for someone with motive?"

"I—I don't know."

"Did Mr. Boudreaux have a motive?"

"Objection! State of mind."

"Sustained. Counsel, you've about beat this horse to death."

"One last question. Did you ever interview any of the other police officers who responded to the shooting call?"

"We didn't, no. But Edmund Rasmussen did."

"Do you know the results of those interviews?"

"No suspicions were raised."

"Have you believed all along that Michael Gresham was the killer?"

"No."

"Who was your first choice for that honor?"

"Not Michael Gresham."

"Why not?"

"That's just not the way he is."

I could have jumped up and kissed the guy.

But I didn't.

Jack Ames winked at me on the way back to his seat at counsel table. No one else saw it but me.

For the first time that day, I felt the band around my chest loosen one click.

Now only eight more witnesses to make our way through. One of whom was going to say she saw me pull the trigger.

It always came back to that.

38

After the morning break, Antonia called to the witness stand two crime scene investigators from the Metro Police Department. They talked about the dead body, footprints in the blood (footprints were traced back to store employees and a cop), the search for fingerprints, the search for DNA, and all the other undertakings of their group.

Joy pretty much left them alone, except to ask the second witness, Suzanne Montoya, "Do you remember the name of the employees who left footprints in Linda's blood?"

"The detectives would probably know that."

"Did anyone follow up with them on the off-chance that one of them might have been the shooter?"

"I don't know. I'm just crime scene. We don't interview."

"Fair enough. Maybe one of the police officers will tell us about those interviews."

Antonia started to object to the assumption there were any such interviews but then thought better of it. It was a tiny thing, but I appreciated how Joy had made something out of nothing.

The Medical Examiner was up next. She described taking custody of the body at the scene. She talked about transporting it to the M.E.'s facility where the autopsy was performed. She said the bodies are kept in body bags in a large cooler. There are six autopsy tables in the autopsy room so all six of the forensic pathologists in the office can perform their work at one time if desired.

No headway was made with the M.E. At least none that I could see.

Judge Frisson: "Call your next witness."

Antonia said almost stridently, "The government calls Dr. James Spence."

He came lumbering in through the hallway doors, a hulk of a man whose massive hands made me wonder how they could handle the art and practice of the dissection of human tissue. He took the witness stand, crossed his legs, and tugged the knee of his pants, releasing the pressure from sitting.

Antonia began. "Would you state your name, please?"

"James, J-A-M-E-S, Spence, S-P-E-N-C-E."

"Where do you live, Mr. Spence?"

"I live in Washington, D.C."

"Your occupation is what?"

"I am a doctor of medicine."

"Dr. Spence, do you have a particular specialty?"

"I do. I am a pathologist, and within that specialty, I practice forensic pathology."

"Could you tell us what forensic pathology is?"

"I can. Pathology, the larger field, is one of the medical specialties, and it has two subcategories: anatomic pathology and clinical pathology. Anatomic pathology deals with the study of disease, that's really what the word means, from actual anatomic inspection. So it involves areas such as performing autopsies, looking at surgical specimens under a microscope, those sorts of things where there is an actual anatomic either naked eye or microscopic examination for the most part. Clinical pathology is the laboratory area, and clinical pathologists usually head a hospital laboratory and serve as a consultant to hospital physicians in ordering and interpretation of tests. Forensic pathology is a special area in pathology. The word forensic comes from the Latin word forum, which was the Roman courtroom. And the term is applied because forensic pathologists are often involved in clarifying medical or scientific questions that come up in the courtroom. Most pathologists work in a coroner's office or medical examiner's office and investigate sudden or unexpected death."

"Would you give the jury a brief review of your medical education?"

"I grew up in Maryland and went to Maryland public schools. My parents divorced, and my mother moved to Minnesota. I, of course, moved with her. There I went to college at Hamline University in St. Paul and University of Minnesota. After college, I went to medical school at the University of Minnesota Medical School from 1985 to 1989. Following that, I had a year as a rotating intern at Regents Hospital in St. Paul. Then I took three years of my five-year pathology training at that hospital in clinical and anatomic pathology. The fourth year I took a year of forensic pathology at the Hennepin County medical examiners office in Minneapolis. That's the office that covers Minneapolis and the surrounding suburban areas. Then following that I had one more year of clinical and anatomic pathology at Hennepin County Medical Center, that's the city-county medical center in Minneapolis. So I finished that training in 1995. By now my father, in Annapolis, Maryland, had become very ill and had no one to care for him and, frankly, no money to hire nursing care. I loved him very much, so I moved to Maryland, moved him in with me, hired nursing care, and went to practice in pathology in Washington, D.C."

"Are you board certified?"

"I am board certified in clinical, anatomic, and forensic pathology, all three areas."

"Do you currently work?"

"I serve on the staff of the Washington, D.C. Medical Examiner."

"What is the medical examiner?"

"The medical examiner heads the office. The office is charged with two major types of death investigations. Non-natural deaths, the accidents, suicides, and homicides that take place in a community. And then the sudden unexpected deaths, or deaths where there is not a doctor in attendance who might be in a position to sign a death certificate. Just by way of example, in the District, we have something in the range of 135 to 175 cases reported to us yearly. So investigating those cases, working with and supervising a team of doctors who work in the office and investigative personnel is basically what my career has become."

"Is performing autopsies one of the things that you do?"

"Yes, it is."

"I am going to refer you back to June of this year. Did you perform an autopsy on a woman named Linda Burrows?

"I did, yes."

"Tell me, that would have been on June twenty-eighth, is that correct?"

"That's right."

"This year?"

"Yes."

"What did you find on your initial exam of the body?"

"The body was well preserved; there was a great deal of powdered preservative that was on the body. There was an unremarkable degree of deterioration and, as I examined the body, I asked to have some X-rays taken. In examining the body, I noticed there was some seepage from the forehead."

"What portion of the head?"

"Excuse me?"

"What portion of the head was this?"

"It was showing on the forehead. Also, I felt with my fingers on the side of the head; I felt something firm in the left temple area, and about that time the X-rays came back."

"What did the X-rays reveal?"

"The X-rays showed a metal projectile in the side of the head area where I felt something."

At that point, Exhibits 31 and 32 were marked for identification.

Antonia then continued.

"Dr. Spence, I have handed you Exhibits 31 and 32. Can you identify those, please?"

"These appear to be the X-rays that were taken that day or reproductions of them, and they do show the projectile."

Antonia looked at the judge. "I offer Exhibit 31, Your Honor."

Joy responded she had no objection.

Judge Frisson nodded. "Exhibit 31 is received."

Antonia then added, "And 32."

"No objection."

THE COURT: "Exhibits 31 and 32 are received."

"Now Doctor, I have Exhibit 31 on the screen. Can you explain what we are looking at there?

"This is a front view of the head; it shows the bones of the skull. On the left side of the individual, is a bright white area, that is a projectile. It is lead, and as a result, it doesn't allow X-ray beams to go through it, so the film doesn't get exposed there, that's why it is white as opposed to being dark."

"I've drawn a circle around it, is that what you're talking about?"

"That's the item, yes."

"Was that a bullet?"

"Yes, it was."

"So that would have been located in the front left?"

"Right in the left temple area."

"Now I have put Exhibit 32 on the screen. Please describe."

"And that is a side view of the left temple area. Again you can see the same intense white object which is again the bullet."

"How many bullet wounds did you find?"

"Three bullet wounds were found in the head. One in the forehead, two on the left temple."

"Did you remove the bullet?"

"Yes, I did."

"What did do you with the bullet?"

"I gave it to an FBI agent, Mr. Jack Ames."

Exhibit 30 was marked for identification.

"Doctor, I have handed you what has been marked Exhibit 30, can you identify that, please?"

"That is a picture of the bullet that has the sequential number I used on my cases at that time, and of the scale that I used. So this is a photograph of that projectile."

The photograph was admitted into evidence without objection.

"Doctor, when the X-rays were reviewed, is that the first time that you were aware that there was a bullet in the skull?"

"Well, I guess so. I felt something there; I didn't know what it was. I waited for the X-rays before I concluded that it was a bullet, I think."

"Were there any FBI agents present at that time?"

"There were two."

"Do you remember who they were?"

"Jack Ames and Marty Longstreet."

"Did you discuss with them your findings and measurements specifically regarding the bullet entry wounds on the left side of the head?"

"I did. I told them that based on the angle of entry, the shooter was standing to the right of the woman when the two shots were fired into the side of the head."

"He—or she—would have been standing to her right? So he would have been facing the grocery shelves she was facing as she was lying on the floor?"

"Let me see if I understand your question. She was facing grocery shelves?"

"Yes. Coming up the aisle from the cash registers, she was found lying on her right side, the crown of her head angled toward the shelves on your left as you approach her."

"Yes, that would be congruent with my findings as to the angle of entry of the bullets with the shooter on her right side."

"So the shooter's face was exposed to the same shelving?"

"Objection! Speculation!"

The judge nodded and then shrugged. "Probably so, but I'm going to allow it. It sounds foundational to me. Objection overruled."

"Please answer. The shooter's face was looking toward the shelving when he shot her twice more?"

"Yes, that would be correct. I have no way of knowing what he was looking at of course, except to say that at one point he looked where he was aiming his gun at her head."

"Now, if an employee at the store, a shelf stocker were standing in the adjacent aisle 10 and looking between the shelves, she would have had a view of the shooter's face?"

"Objection!"

"Sustained. Speculation."

Now I saw what Antonia had been building toward: she was establishing that her witness Agnes Streith would have had a head-on view of the shooter's face. While the objection was sustained, the image had been planted in the jury's mind. How clever of Antonia to do that.

Antonia moved on. "What was your conclusion as to the cause of death?"

"It was my conclusion that the cause of death was a gunshot wound to the head."

"From your examination of the body, can you give us an opinion as to how far away the gun would have been from the forehead when the bullet was fired?"

"In a general way, I can."

"What is your opinion?"

"It was very close. There was black gunshot residue that surrounded the perforation that was in the front of the head. That only travels a short distance from the gun barrel and was very intensely deposited, so I would say the weapon was very, very close, maybe touching the skin or just a very short distance. To know the specific distance you would have to test with that weapon and similar ammunition, but we are talking just a very short distance from the skin surface."

"What about the two bullets in the side of the head?"

"No gunshot residue found there. The gunshots were probably the killer standing above her, executing her in case the forehead gunshot hadn't done its job."

"Anything else remarkable about the body?"

"Yes, the victim was pregnant. The fetus didn't survive, of course. I would place its age at about fifteen weeks."

"Were samples taken of the fetus?"

"They were."

"For what purpose?"

"DNA matching."

"Thank you, that's all I have, Your Honor."

Judge Frisson, "Counsel for the defense, you may cross-examine."

"No questions," said Joy, which surprised me to a degree, but there's a rule among trial lawyers, and that is that if the witness can't help your case going in, leave them the hell alone. Joy apparently chose to do just that. As I sat there, I tried to conceive of what questions I might have had if I had been trying the case and honestly could come up with none, not on the spot. So she got a gold star from me.

We then took the noon break. When we returned, we would hear from store employees.

39

Marcel caught up to us coming out of the courtroom. He placed his arm around my back and began speaking confidentially into my ear as we moved toward the elevators.

"I think I'm onto something. I won't know until later."

"Good, good. What is it?"

"Don't get your hopes up, because I haven't seen it yet. But I'm after more video."

"Excellent," Joy said, as she'd obviously heard him from on my left. "Keep up the good work, Marcel. But please don't mention these things in public places again."

Chagrined, Marcel pulled away from me. He shook his head and gave me a dour look. "I know," I said, "but she's the boss, not me. We'll listen to her."

"I've got a call to make. Talk later," Marcel said and broke into a lope for the stairwell. The door opened, and he disappeared. Joy looked at me. Her eyes held a look of annoyance.

"What?" I said. "He can be effusive, Joy."

"He's got a big mouth," she retorted.

"Not at all. You just happen to have very acute hearing. That's all. I could hardly hear the man with all the noise around us."

"Whatever," she said and began punching the elevator call button repeatedly. Other people, ahead of us, had already punched the same button but that didn't faze her. She was in a hurry to get me alone and go over what we'd heard so far. I was ready, too. I was anxious, is more accurate.

We walked into the Bindoor Indian Palace for lunch and decided on the buffet. Following Joy through the line, I became aware that she was very likely vegetarian. Not yours truly, however, as I piled my plate high with tandoori chicken. A woman took our drink orders after we had settled into a table at the very front of the restaurant and returned minutes later with two iced teas. Joy launched into a bolus of curried vegetables and I, unexpectedly ravenous, began putting the chicken away in my belly. After several minutes of this, Joy patted her linen napkin to her lips and took a swallow of tea.

"Excellent curry," she said. "You doing okay?"

"You mean besides the fact it looks like I'm headed to prison? Or worse?"

"You need to calm down, Michael. The key to their case is a supposed eyewitness. If we can cast doubt on her testimony, then their entire case has doubt. That's called a reasonable doubt and juries by law must turn defendants loose if there's a reasonable doubt."

"And how are we going to go about establishing reasonable doubt?" I asked.

"The medical examiner set up the eyewitness by establishing how she would have been looking head-on at him when he fired the two temple rounds into Linda. That was very effective testimony."

"For which you had no cross-examination," I said. I sounded whiny but it was my life we were talking about, and I did think she could have done something with the doctor to discredit his testimony insofar as he was speculating about the positioning of the shooter, the body, and so forth. I didn't understand why Joy hadn't done that and I felt let-down. Change that gold star to no star.

At just that moment, I realized I was feeling very sick. I quickly excused myself and headed for the men's room. There was no time to spare once I was inside: I ran into a stall and began vomiting up my lunch, my feelings, and the terrible weight I'd been carrying around. Retching went on for several minutes, with brief periods of quiet in between bouts. Then it would begin again. A man came up behind me and asked, "Need me to call someone?"

"No," I said between heaves, "I don't think anyone can fix what's wrong with me."

"Good luck, buddy."

There was nothing to do but surrender to the bug or whatever had taken over my innards. Then it came to me what Marcel had said. He was onto something, something having to do with additional video?

Wasn't that what he'd said?

40

I almost didn't recognize Delores Cheney when she took the witness stand. Someone had done a complete makeover—the whole nine yards: blush, eyeshadow, hair, nails, lipstick. She didn't begin to resemble the friendly, honest cashier at the Foggy Bottom Grocery that I had come to know. Her testimony, however, hadn't changed a whit. The man she saw leaving after the shooting was wearing a police uniform. Dark, bushy sideburns and eyebrows, sunglasses, and a gun. It was much the same. Her utility to the government's case was merely to set the stage for its next witness, Agnes Streith.

On cross-examination, Joy asked Delores: "Did the policeman you saw leaving the store look like the man sitting beside me?"

She was pointing at me. Did he look like me?

"No. He didn't look anything like the man beside you."

"No sideburns, no eyeglasses, unremarkable hair, and eyebrows?"

"Yes. Your client is very—sorry—plain. The man I saw was dramatic, overdone, you know?"

"I think I do. Thank you, Ms. Cheney."

The witness was excused.

In her most solemn voice, Antonia then said very confidently, "The government calls to the stand Agnes Streith."

The moment I had been resignedly waiting for. I was about to get my ass handed to me.

She was much younger than I'd expected. She was wearing navy slacks, a white shirt, a sleeveless sweater top with a red stripe, and her hair was up and looked very businesslike. She walked haltingly down the aisle, unsure in her gait, making me want to reach out and steady her in spite of myself. I could only imagine the jury felt the same protectiveness toward her.

Antonia wasted no time with her star witness after preliminaries:

"Tell us what you saw that day."

"I saw the man sitting at the table next to you. He was standing over the woman on the floor and shot her twice in the head."

"The witnesses have established three shots were fired. Did you see the first shot?"

"No, but I heard it. That's what made me peek between the shelves."

"Tell us about that."

"I was stocking baby food on aisle ten. I'd just put up a jar of Gerber's applesauce when I heard the first gunshot. So I lowered my head and looked between the shelves. The man at the table beside you was facing right at me. He shot his gun two times. He shot the woman in the head twice."

"How do you know it was the man at the next table?"

"The scars. The man I saw had the scars on his face just like the man at the table. It was terrible; he was so scary."

"Are you aware the government witness just before you said the man looked nothing like Mr. Gresham?"

"It was the man next to you."

"You're sure of that?"

"Yes."

"And there was no bronze face, nothing like that?"

"No. Just the scars."

"What did you do after the gunshots?"

"At first I just collapsed on the floor and started to cry. But I made sure I wasn't making any noise. I didn't want him coming around the end cap and shooting me too."

"Then what happened?"

"Then I ran into the break room. There's a bathroom there everyone uses. I ran inside and puked my guts out. My hands were shaking, I was drooling, and then I had the runs. I was in there a long time."

"Did any police talk to you that day?"

"No. I took off my apron when I was done in the bathroom and threw it in soiled linens. Then I took off my tie and folded it into my rear pocket. Next thing I knew, I had walked out of the store and was headed for my car."

"Did anyone try to stop you?"

"No."

"Did anyone ask you any questions?"

"No."

"Where did you go?"

"I was renting a room in a three-bedroom house. I went there and made popcorn and watched TV all afternoon. Popcorn was all I could keep down."

"What happened the next day?"

"I don't know. I never went back there."

"Why not?"

"Because I know what happens to witnesses who identify the killer."

"What's that?"

"The killer gets out of prison and comes looking for them. Then they kill you. Then there's a made-for-TV movie about you, but you don't care because you're dead."

Her worldview seemed pretty accurate to me. No one in the court-room could blame her for fleeing the scene. The looks on many jurors' faces said they might have done the same thing under the circumstances.

Antonia next took her star witness back through the shooting again, only this time accessing her feelings as she stepped through the moment-by-moment playback to let the jury feel the witnesses' feel-ings. It was an old prosecution ploy, but it never failed to hook another fence-sitting juror or two. Nicely done, I thought when she'd finished and taken her seat.

Next up was Joy, who stepped up the podium with great ease and confidence as if she were about to dismantle the witnesses. The jury was ready for a show-down.

The clash began.

And ended almost abruptly.

The witness wouldn't budge from anything she'd said before. The skilled cross-examiner tries to pry some daylight between the witness's direct exam certainty and her less-than certainty on cross-examination. Except it didn't work here. Agnes Streith knew what she had seen, and she wasn't about to let go of that for anyone or anything.

At last, Joy crept back to our table, bent low and asked me whether I had any other questions for the witness.

"You're done?" I hissed at her.

"What else should I ask? There's no video on aisle ten, and I have no way of hurting her testimony. So what else do you want me to ask?" She was waiting. It was awkward, with the judge impatiently staring down at us and the jury wondering what was going on.

I was flabbergasted. Joy had run out of questions to pursue. Now she was asking me what came next? I kicked myself. I had told her I would back her up at trial and now she was asking me to do that, asking me for a roadmap to a winning cross-examination. I no more had a map than a June bug. We were all over the place, erratic, and got nowhere with Agnes. The more Joy had persisted, the more comfortable and vigorous the witness had become. Which only sucked the air right out of our moment of extracting the real truth and showing the jury where the government was wrong.

But the government wasn't wrong when it was all over. They had an eyewitness who saw me shoot Linda Burrows twice and looked me in the eye.

"Peaches," he said to me, Agnes said when asked. "I'll never eat peaches again."

I doubted I would either, once I was introduced into the federal penitentiary's general population.

I stared straight ahead when Joy took her seat beside me.

She leaned against me. "You didn't help!" she whispered.

I only stared and hoped the jury didn't hear the cross-examiner's critique of her client.

There had been enough damage done without my counsel accusing me too.

41

After calling Agnes Streith as its last witness, the government rested on that high note.

Agnes had been firm, sure, and unyielding. Joy hadn't gotten any help from her at all and, in fact, had only further driven home the young woman's testimony.

Since the government had rested, it was Joy's time to present and argue a Motion for Judgment of Acquittal, what used to be known as the Motion for Directed Verdict. She presented a written Points and Authorities to the judge and Antonia and then launched into her argument regarding why the court should find me not-guilty at that point and acquit me. These motions almost never bear fruit and are primarily interposed because the rules allow it. The motion is not a predicate for making the same motion at the close of the case or before submission to the jury and is not a predicate for making the motion following a jury verdict. But still, Joy made the motion.

"Your Honor," she began, "the defendant, Michael Gresham, should be acquitted by the court at this point in the trial. There is no evidence linking Mr. Gresham to this crime except for the so-called eyewitness testimony of a self-proclaimed witness who left the scene without speaking to the police and who never did meet with the investigators and offer her version of what happened. Moreover, her description contradicts what the witness Delores Cheney gave the jury. Additionally, Ms. Streith moved out of state and tried to hide. At that point, she had seen the shooter once for maybe five seconds, maybe less, and never saw him again. She also testified she had never seen him before or since, except sitting at the defense table.

"Eyewitness testimony is inherently unreliable, as study after study has shown and as the court is aware. What may be one eyewitness's culprit is another eyewitness's saint."

Joy then went on to make three other arguments, none of them compelling, and I didn't blame Judge Frisson one iota when he summarily denied the motion even without asking the government if it would like to be heard on the motion. I'd never seen a judge do that before and it was probably improper, but it sent a resounding denial shooting up my spine when I realized just how guilty the court believed I was. The defense case—my case—was going to have to be incredibly compelling if I were to leave this courtroom without wearing manacles and a waist chain.

We then took a long lunch break and returned at 1:30 to begin putting on our defense case.

First up, Joy called to the stand Harry Burrows.

Harry came into court wearing khaki pants and a button-down shirt. No tie, no police uniform, nothing meant to sway the jury. He was very relaxed as he was sworn in and took his seat. Trained by the police as a professional witness, he even smiled briefly at the jury and nodded at counsel.

Then Joy launched right in.

"State your name."

"Harry S. Burrows."

"Mr. Burrows, what is your business, occupation, or profession?"

"Police officer. D.C. Metro Police Department."

"When did you begin working as a police officer?"

"After police academy training."

"I mean, what date?"

"August first, 1998."

"You have worked for MPD ever since?"

"I have."

"What are your duties as a police officer?"

"Patrol. I made detective but didn't like all the paperwork. So I went back to patrol."

"What is your rank?"

"Sergeant."

"Were you married to Linda Burrows?"

"I was."

"You were divorced?"

"We were. We were getting back together when she died."

"That would have been June 25, 2017, that she was murdered?"

"Yes. At the Foggy Bottom Grocery."

"Were you at that location that day?"

"I was. I received a radio message directing all cars to the grocery store. We were advised there had been a shooting, one civilian was down, and the shooter might still be on the premises."

"What did you do when you got there?"

"Drew my weapon and entered the store."

"Describe what happened next."

Harry then went on to tell the jury his story, including finding his ex-wife dead on aisle 11 of the store. He was heartbroken but tried CPR. Then he collapsed on the floor. He was in shock and still hadn't fully recovered. He was required to see a police psychologist and was still seeing him.

"Have you investigated your ex-wife's murder at any time since?"

"Not really."

"Are you aware of your ex-wife's romantic encounters with any staff at the U.S. Attorney's office?"

"That's a hard question to answer. I guess before she was murdered I was aware in a general sense. I didn't want to know names or hotels or any details, so I never forced her to tell me that stuff. But then since her death, I've been forced by circumstances to dig into what was going on."

"What was going on?"

A wounded look creased his forehead and made his eyes glisten. But he managed to say, in a halting voice, "Linda was sleeping with a male staff member at the USAO."

"USAO?"

"United States Attorney's Office."

"She was working there?"

"Yes, she was an assistant U.S. Attorney. AUSA they call them."

"So it wasn't until after her death that you became aware of the frequency of her encounters with the man?"

"That's right."

"Did you ever catch your ex-wife with another man?"

"Yes."

"Tell us his name."

"Niles Boudreaux."

"The U.S. Attorney?"

"Yes."

"Please tell the jury about that."

"My wife slept with Niles. The office staff knew that. Everybody knew it. I'm thinking Niles got jealous and murdered her. He lost his mind."

"Do you have any evidence of that?"

"I have my suspicions but don't know."

"Give us your suspicion," Joy said.

"Objection!" cried Antonia. "Calls for speculation!"

"Sustained. Move on, counsel."

"Tell us about your ex-wife and Niles Boudreaux."

"I caught them together in a hotel room. Linda was nude."

A gasp and wide eyes from the jury. We had scored a point.

"Where was that?"

"I caught them together at the Hyatt Hotel because I followed them there. I played like I was room service and Boudreaux opened the door, and I walked in. My wife was in the shower. Boudreaux was wearing a silk robe and drinking scotch straight out of a bottle on the table."

"What happened next?"

"Boudreaux tried to make a joke. I wasn't laughing. I even considered shooting both of them right then and there myself. Then she came sashaying into the room, nude. I turned around when I heard her voice, and she saw me. Her knees buckled, and she almost fainted on the spot."

"What happened next?"

"I told Boudreaux to get dressed and leave."

"What did he say?"

"Nothing. He was already throwing his stuff in his athletic bag and heading out."

"What about Linda?"

"Linda attacked me with her fists. She said she didn't love me. She begged me not to hurt Boudreaux."

"Were you going to hurt him?"

"Hell no. Neither one is worth me going to jail. I just left. She went back to work. I know because I called her office later and got her on the phone."

"What was said?"

"I asked her if she wanted to talk. She said there was nothing to say to me."

"Harry, how did it make you feel when you saw your ex-wife and Niles Boudreaux together?"

"I felt stunned. I felt like shooting him."

"What about her? Did you feel like shooting her?"

"Never. I loved my wife. She had this horrible thing about Niles Boudreaux. I hated him, but I still loved her. I would give both my legs to have her back right now."

Joy paused and appeared to be paging through her notes. In truth, she was allowing the witness's words to sink in with the jury. Then she slowly began again.

"You've told us about Boudreaux. Which was one lover. Were there more?"

"I asked the detectives, and I talked to the FBI agents working the case. They said there might be more."

"How did that make you feel?"

"Seriously? How do you think I felt?"

Judge Frisson frowned down at the witness. He was about to instruct Burrows to answer the question when Burrows re-phrased his answer: "It made me feel awful."

"Did you get angry?"

"Not at first. At first, I just drank too much. But that never helps. Then I got mad."

"Did you want to harm those who'd used your ex-wife?"

"Yes."

"Did you want to harm your ex-wife?"

"Never."

"Did you harm your ex-wife?"

"No, I did not."

"Why not?"

"Because I loved Linda. I adored her. I thought her behavior was the behavior of someone mentally ill. I only wanted her to see a counselor and get help."

"Isn't it true you hit Linda with your fist on at least one occasion, injuring her so terribly that she required medical treatment?"

It was a matter of public record. He had to answer truthfully now.

"Yes, I hit her once. Never did it again. I was ashamed and hated myself for it. I took a class in anger management."

Joy nodded and studied the witness. Then she was ready for the question we all were awaiting.

"Did you shoot her?"

"I did not."

"Do you know who shot her?"

"Not really. I mean I've heard what the witnesses were going to say, but I haven't been in the courtroom the whole time. I'll be the last to know."

At that point, the jury was physically leaning away from the witness, a sign that he was disliked. Joy had opened the possibility that Harry Burrows had murdered his ex-wife. But now she recognized the danger of continuing to pursue and hammer Harry as a possible shooter because juries don't like to see witnesses get harassed and their antipathy can quickly turn toward caring for the witness being bludgeoned in court. She backed away, having made her point.

She had managed to add Niles Boudreaux into the mix. Where that would go, I don't think I had any idea. But at least his name was fixed in the jury's mind as a not-so-attractive public official as he'd tried to come across when the trial began, and he introduced himself before turning the case over to Antonia. I wondered if the beating he had just taken would affect his chances for re-election. But of course, it wouldn't.

So, she ended her questions and turned the witness over for cross-examination.

Antonia, taking her time to walk up to the lectern to have her turn, arrived there without notes or notepad and only looked at Harry and said, "I'm so sorry for your loss. No questions, Your Honor."

At that point, Harry hurried from the courtroom, pulling a wad of tissues from his shirt pocket as he went and dabbed his eyes.

So there was that.

And I was no closer to leaving as a free man than before Harry had joined us in the courtroom.

WE TOOK a break and Joy used the time to amend her witness list to add Niles Boudreaux as a defense witness. She presented the motion to amend to Judge Frisson. Antonia Xiang fought long and hard against the amendment, calling Joy an opportunist, but Judge Frisson had heard enough from Harry Burrows to have his head turned. He, too, wanted to hear from Boudreaux.

Boudreaux was called by Antonia, and he said he would come to court without a subpoena. So, that afternoon he was sworn in and sat down in the hot seat at the front of the courtroom. For just a moment he removed his rimless spectacles and looked around with an almost bewildered look on his face. But he caught himself and resumed smiling at everyone again, and I could see the facade he always wore, but now I knew just how thin it was.

Joy wasted no time getting to the crux of what she wanted to ask the U.S. Attorney.

"Mr. Boudreaux, did you shoot Linda Burrows?"

An incredulous look came over his face. His eyes widened and he somehow even made them sparkle as if laughing on the inside.

"Good heavens! You don't mince words, do you?"

Judge Frisson wasn't impressed. "The witness will answer the question."

"No," said Boudreaux answering whether he had shot Linda.

"We've learned from her husband that he walked in on you and Linda at the Hyatt Hotel here in Washington. Do you remember that?"

"I do. Not my proudest moment."

"What's that mean?"

"I mean it happened only once, and I've been ashamed ever since. I've carried that guilt and still carry it around."

"So you had sexual relations with Linda at the Hyatt?"

"Yes."

"Did the two of you have a falling out after that?"

"There was nothing to fall out about. Our meetup was a one-time thing."

"Did she threaten you after you had sexual relations with her?"

The U.S. Attorney couldn't suppress a smile.

"Do you mean immediately after? Or some other time?"

"Either one."

"No, she didn't threaten me."

"Did she ever tell you she might file sexual harassment charges against you?"

"No, why on earth would she do that? We were two consenting adults. Nothing illegal about any of that. Nobody pressured anybody. Let me say this. Was it a smart thing for me to engage in? Definitely not. Did she regret it later? Probably. Did anyone threaten anyone? Definitely not. Were there hard feelings after? Not that I was aware of."

"Did you speak to Linda Burrows' ex-husband after he caught you in the hotel with her?"

"Yes, Harry came to my office to confront me. I told him I was sorry. I told him I didn't know he was still hoping to patch things up."

"Did you do or say anything in an attempt to arouse anger in him at his wife?"

"I'm afraid I don't follow that."

Joy nodded slowly and looked at her notes.

Then, "Did you try to make him angry enough to shoot her?"

"Why would you ask me something like that? Do I seem like that kind of person to you?"

"Mr. Boudreaux, you are instructed to answer the question, sir," said the judge.

"Did I try to make him angry enough to shoot her? No."

"Did you ever want to have her silenced?"

"No."

"Were you at the scene of Linda's murder the day it happened?"

"No. I don't visit crime scenes. I have staff and law enforcement personnel for that."

Joy turned and came to me at counsel table. "Anything else?" she whispered to me.

I shook my head. I thought she'd done a fair job and I knew she wasn't going to get any smoking-gun admission out of a legal professional like Boudreaux. Time to let it go before the jury started getting antsy.

She returned to the lectern to say, "Defense has no other questions."

"Counsel, does the government have questions?" Judge Frisson asked Antonia.

"No questions."

"The witness is excused."

We then took our lunch break and caught a taxi back to our office. I stared out the car window, thinking. I knew our case was virtually over as I wasn't going to testify. That much Joy had made clear to me. I wholeheartedly agreed. It could only go wrong for me if I testified, given that I had gotten Linda pregnant and would just remind the jury what a louse I was for it. No matter what I said, they would only come away hating me a little more. As I said, I knew we were finished with our case.

I also knew I was going to be convicted. That jury was going to find me guilty.

There was nothing I could do to prevent it.

CLOSING arguments heavily favored the prosecution. Joy, for her part, tried to cover all the bases but her lack of experience with criminal juries showed up at this point. She discussed reasonable doubt and how it existed in this case for all of about five minutes then went onto something else. Reasonable doubt is what criminal cases are all about. It should have been discussed regarding the testimony of all prosecution witnesses. But it wasn't, and there was nothing I could do about it.

After the lawyers had finished their closing arguments, the judge read the jury instructions, which all but put the jury into a coma.

Then the case was turned over to them, and they departed the court-room, headed to the jury room and the beginning of searching for a verdict.

Which, I guessed, wouldn't take all that long.

42

Desperate for a break in the case, Marcel returned to the nail parlor in the Foggy Bottom Mall. He had felt the woman behind the counter was lying to him before. It was time to try again.

Marcel encountered toxic chemicals hanging in the air of Koci's Nails, waiting to poison the unwitting. He hurried inside anyway; there was work to do, and the store maybe, just maybe, was withholding the video Marcel needed to save his boss.

The woman at the cash register was extremely bored with him before he even spoke. He figured she remembered him. He was right.

"Not you again," she said and yawned.

"Please," he began with her, "I desperately need some help."

She didn't ask how she could help; but neither did she look away.

"Outside, over your door. The camera mounted there for security. I'm here to pay you lots of money to review the video I'm certain it's recording."

She only looked at him with no change in her expression.

"Look, I need a pedicure. My toenails are out of control. Can you help me with that?"

Suddenly the woman smiled. "Of course. Take a seat in Chair One, please."

He did as directed and, when the woman indicated he should remove shoes and socks, he quickly slipped them off and tucked the socks inside the shoes before dropping them on the floor. While he did, the woman was busy flooding the foot bath with water and repeatedly testing it with her hand. Satisfied that the water temperature was perfect, she motioned for him to place his feet in the tub. Marcel complied and—he had to admit—his feet felt better than they had all day. For just a moment he was borne away by a lightness in his spirit that calmed him and made him want to linger.

He snapped himself out of that and looked down at the top of the woman's head as she violently attacked his feet with a scrub brush.

"Too long," she said, "too long."

"What's too long?' he asked.

"Come in sooner next time. Feet deserve better than this."

He couldn't argue with her. Ever since turning fifty he had found dealing with his toenails to be more and more a long-distance effort anyway. Maybe she had something here.

"Let me ask you," he began, reinvigorated with purpose, "Could you use a lot of money?"

She laughed. "Everyone needs money. But no video."

"I'm going to pay you five-thousand-dollars to let me review your video."

"Five thousand dollars? Are you serious?'

"Dead serious. I need to view your video from June twenty-fifth of this year. Can you help me do that?"

She looked up. "Very expensive."

"How much?"

"Ten-thousand-dollars."

"To view the video? You want me to pay you ten-thousand-dollars?"

"Sure thing."

"Okay. I can do that. When can I view?"

"We finish here first. Then we go look."

"Okay."

"Turn on back massage, please," she said and pointed to a keypad hanging off the arm of his chair. "Do you want leg massage too?"

TEN MINUTES LATER, they had adjourned to the sparse back office/break room just behind the only partition in the business place. Marcel saw a cold Mr. Coffee—no red lights; a silver radio with its speakers detached and placed strategically to pump music into the business area; a half-dozen wrought iron chairs with cracked red padding: proof that the Sixties weren't over yet; and a computer, a PC, ancient and fitted with the old, huge monitor in grayscale.

"Please," the woman told him, and he had a seat at the computer desk. "Now you pay me the money."

He was ready. He had guessed she would demand he cough up double his first offer. He pulled a roll of hundred-dollar-bills from his pocket. Counting off ten-thousand dollars, he saw her watching his every addition to the stack she was about to receive. He then passed it to her.

She pocketed the ten grand.

"You view now. I'll be back."

She left him alone, with their computer. Setting aside his mounting anger that she had been blatantly lying to him before, he began his review. He clicked and sought out the hard-drive folder he knew he would find. Sure enough, there were dozens of video files, arranged by date. June, 24 was two mouse-clicks away, and a third click had him viewing the video for that day beginning at 12:01 a.m.

Nothing on June, 24. So he moved to June, 25.

He wasted no time, setting the playback to 4x. Within just a very few minutes the video had made it to mid-morning, where he went into 2x speed. Suddenly he blew by images of a man—distant, across the parking lot from Koci's Nails—exiting an SUV of some make. The man was wearing a police uniform. Marcel froze the video. The vehicle was almost certainly not a police vehicle. It looked to be his personal ride.

He hit rewind and stepped through the video at 1x speed. The man in the police uniform exited the vehicle, patted his weapon in its holster —an amateur move, thought Marcel—and headed into the Foggy Bottom Grocery. Marcel let the tape play on. Not five minutes later, the man exited the store, walking much faster now, turning into the parking slot for his SUV and climbing inside.

Marcel froze the view of the SUV. It was parked maybe 150 feet from the store camera. Too far to make out the license number. He patted the pocket of his shirt, pulled out a thumb drive, and copied the video file onto his thumb drive. Then he restored the computer to the state in which it had been turned over to him. He dropped the thumb drive back into his pocket and went back to the front of the store.

"Listen," he said to the same woman, who by now was busy at work on another's feet. "I copied the video I needed onto my thumb drive. Do I have your permission to do that?"

"You paid ten-thousand-dollars. Copy what you need, please."

"Fair enough," Marcel said, and he walked on out of Koci's Nails.

Once he was back at the office, Marcel treated the video with enhancement software but was still unable to improve the details much at all.

He pushed ahead. Without pausing even to eat, Marcel tried everything he could think of to visualize the license number of the vehicle.

But to no avail. Not only couldn't the license plate be read, but neither could the make or model of the SUV the uniformed man drove.

Then it occurred to him. He went online and typed in "FBI Crime Lab."

Thirty seconds later he was placing a call to the Operational Projects Unit, Photographic Operations Program, FBI Crime Lab, Quantico, Virginia.

It was thirty-six miles from where he sat.

43

The jury was still out.

After two days of sitting idly around the courthouse while the jury deliberated, I was startled out of my dream state by the bailiff. He unlocked the courtroom doors from the inside, stuck his head out, saw me sitting alone on a bench, and announced, "We've got a verdict!"

Joy took a taxi from the office back to the courthouse, and together we entered the courtroom. Antonia and Jack Ames were already in place at the prosecution table. The court personnel was already in place as well: court reporter, two bailiffs, two armed deputies, court clerk, and, coming and going, the judge's secretary from his chambers. When we entered, she scooted off to alert the judge. We were ready to go.

Judge Frisson, black robe flowing, strode into the courtroom and ascended to his perch above us all. "Are the parties ready?"

"Ready."

"Ready."

"Very well, the court is back in session. Case number 17-02921, *United States of America versus Michael Gresham*. Mr. Bailiff, please bring the jury back in."

It was all I could do not to faint while we awaited the jury. Minutes later the jury trooped in. Every one of them avoided making eye contact with me, though I was trying. It did not look good.

Without wasting another second, the judge asked, "Mr. Foreman, do you have a verdict?"

The foreman arose. "We do, Your Honor."

"Please hand the verdict to the clerk."

The signed verdict was given over to the clerk of the court, who checked that it was signed and then brought it to Judge Frisson. She passed it up to him, and he unfolded the verdict. He read it and pursed his lips. Then he appeared to read it again.

"Ladies and gentlemen, is this your verdict?"

The jury nodded its assent.

"Very well. The clerk will read the verdict for the record." He handed the document back to the clerk of the court. She stood and read:

"We, the jury in the above-entitled case, being first sworn and duly empaneled, do find the defendant, Michael Gresham, guilty of murder in the first degree."

A murmur rippled across the crowd of court addicts and media. Standing as the verdict was read, I could feel my knees buckling, and I dropped down, falling sideways into my chair. My head was swimming, and my heart was pounding. Beads of cold sweat appeared on my forehead. I was blinking non-stop as if that might somehow make the scene before me clear up and make it sensible again.

But blinking wasn't what it was going to take.

"Very well," said Judge Frisson. "The defendant is remanded to the custody of the U.S. Marshal for transport to the D.C. Jail. He will be held there until sentencing on a date to be determined by the clerk once the pre-sentence investigation concludes. Is that all? Counsel?"

"We would like to make a motion for acquittal at this time, Your Honor," said Joy.

The judge gave her the fisheye. "On what grounds? Do you have something new for the court since the last time you offered the motion?"

I could see her treading water, analyzing her reply with light speed. Then she answered.

"No. It would be the same argument."

Judge Frisson nodded. "The motion for acquittal is denied. Court stands in recess."

The gavel came down, and everyone stood. Everyone, except me.

I needed assistance. All strength had left my body. In the next few moments, I felt arms seizing my arms and gently lifting me up and out of my chair.

"Please try walking, Mr. Gresham," said a voice from behind me, a voice I didn't recognize.

"Where—where am I going?"

"Mr. Gresham, you're going to jail."

44

"I'm furious at you, Michael," came the thirteen-year-old voice over the phone.

I was standing in the hallway outside the general population area of the D.C. Jail. A wall phone bank was in use one end to the other. I was on the far right; the old handset jammed hard against my ear so I could hear above the rancor and undying din of hell. I asked her to repeat herself.

"I said I'm furious at you, Michael."

"I'm so, so sorry, Annie. I wouldn't have left without saying goodbye to you for anything if it had been up to me."

"Who was it up to, Michael? Don't you move around of your own volition?"

"Not this time. This time a judge sent me here to prison."

"And why was that? Were you found guilty on the Linda Burrows case?"

"I'm sorry to report, I was."

"Sick, Michael. That's just sick. Not that you're not a strong man, but you just don't have what it takes to murder someone. Sorry, judge, a wrong person this time."

I couldn't help but smile. At least someone thought I didn't have what it took to pull the trigger. It was more than refreshing to be analyzed and described by my child, it was endearing, too.

"What does post-conviction relief look like, Michael? I'm sure you've discussed it with Joy Heavens?"

"Not yet. We're going to be filing a motion for a new trial and some other motions I haven't been told about yet. She's spending all of her days on it."

"She should. She lost what I would have called a slam-dunk case."

"Slam-dunk? Did you know there was an eyewitness to the murder? Did you know she said it was me who pulled the trigger three times? Do you remember telling me that I was a prime suspect, Annie?"

"I did know about the eyewitness. I've seen the news and read the *Post* online. But it seems to me there was minimal effort made to reconstruct the day of the shooting and your alibi once you realized your concert memorabilia was irrelevant. When it became apparent the date of the offense was the twenty-fifth instead of the twenty-fourth you should have put everyone in the office to work on reconstruction. That wasn't done, was it?"

"We did what we could, Annie. There just wasn't that much to go on."

"So says you. I wish you'd asked me to help, Michael. I know I could have been some use. But it's too late now."

I sighed. There was dead air time between us.

Annie, I had to admit, was increasingly harder to talk to. It was because she was becoming more comfortable with her new family and that seemed to be having the effect of causing her to be more verbal and—along with that—more disputatious. She loved to argue with me lately. I had no problem with it, in the end, because she was flourishing. It was all any parent could've hoped for her.

"Do you want to talk to Verona again?"

"No, just give everyone hugs and tell them we're figuring out how to spring me loose."

"I don't give hugs, Michael. But I'll relay the message to Verona."

"Fair enough. Good talking to you, Annie."

"Call anytime," Annie replied and hung up.

Call anytime? Did she think I was able to call anytime? I placed the receiver back in its cradle and stood there with my head lowered. This can't be happening, I thought. Then I turned, and the deputy waiting behind me escorted me back to the general population area. The door buzzed and clicked, and he pushed it open.

I walked inside, and my heart plummeted.

TV, weightlifting, dominoes or chess, endless prattle about your innocence and lack of guilt: take your pick.

45

Joy came to visit me two days after the verdict. I was now in a single-cell with a cell-mate named The Wanderer, a short dark man whose eyes reminded me of Charlie Manson's. He was all electric in his looks and gestures; more than anything else I knew not to turn my back on him. Which made sleep impossible. The last thing I wanted was to wake up in the middle of the night to some deviancy being practiced by my cellie. Especially those that might include the nonconsensual use of my body.

Anyway, I was lying on my back in my bunk trying to decide whether the floaters in my eyes were getting worse or whether the ceiling—I could reach up and touch it from the top bunk—was growing spots.

"Gresham on deck!" a guard yelped from just outside the cell I shared with The Wanderer. As quickly as I could, I jumped from my bunk down onto the floor and backed up to the slot in our bars with my wrists crossed behind me. Handcuffs swiftly encircled my flesh, and I turned to be escorted out of the cell.

It was good to be out and practicing that thing all free men get to do, that thing called walking. You don't walk inside a cell. You step, and you're there. You step twice, and you're right up in someone's grill.

So there we were, clumping down the hall—me in my flip-flops and white socks. At the first door, the lock buzzed and the guard pulled on the handle. We swept through and continued our journey through two more locks and buzzes, and two left turns until, at last, we were outside of a room marked Attorney Conference Room 12. The guard pushed open the door. He placed his back against the door, removed my handcuffs, and pushed me inside. He allowed the door to close behind me. He would be outside. I knew that drill.

Joy stood and held out her hand.

"Michael," she said. I noticed she left off the perfunctory, "how are you?" We all knew how I was.

"Hey, Joy," I managed to say.

We settled around the table, and she snapped open her black patent leather briefcase. A little over the top, I thought, but hey, who put me in charge of female attorney style?

She pulled out a yellow pad and looked across the table at me.

"So, where are we?" I asked.

"Here's the deal. Motions for new trial may be filed up to three years after the verdict. However—and this is huge—if the motion is based on newly-discovered evidence it must be filed within fourteen days of the verdict. We still have twelve days to find a showstopper and prepare and file our motion."

"How are we fixed for showstoppers? Has Marcel been able to locate any new evidence?"

She gave me a steady look. "New evidence of what?"

Oh, Dear Jesus, I thought, I am so screwed!

"Well, you know, new evidence of something that will get me the hell out of here!"

"Michael, you're raising your voice. No need to do that with me. I'm only trying to help."

"Sorry, my patience is exhausted."

She leveled her yellow BIC pen at me. "Don't forget, you're the one who talked me into defending you, Michael. I told you I'd never handled a criminal case before. You're the one who made it sound like my civil trial skills would easily transfer to criminal defense duties. I've never quite followed your thinking on that, and lately, I wish I hadn't agreed to help. I feel so, so helpless! I have no idea what I'm doing and don't know which way to turn. Verona hates me; Marcel hates me, your daughter Annie calls me at the office and asks me what I'm doing today to get you released. She calls every day with that question."

"Annie's calling you?"

"Yes. The one who hangs up on me when she's finished talking. No good-byes, or laters, or anything. Just bam! Hangs up!"

"Well, we have to let Annie be Annie."

"I've brought along a motion to withdraw as your counsel, Michael. The trial is over, I did what I said I would do, and now I want out. You paid me a lot of money, but that was for the trial, not for post-conviction relief or for appeal. I've acted honestly and honorably toward you; there's not much else you could ask of me. Will you oppose my motion? Or can I inform the court you've read my motion and you agree to it?"

The shock was coursing through my body. My brain went electric, and I could feel synapses firing that hadn't fired in many generations of my forebears: these were fight-or-flight synapses, the ones that fire when a wild animal suddenly accosts you in the jungle. I imagined I looked just then like The Wanderer.

"You're quitting?" I managed.

"Withdrawing. I have nothing else to offer you. I'm going back to civil law, Michael. Don't hate me, please."

"Hell, I don't hate you. I think it's a good choice for you."

Then I was reclaiming my usual calm.

"You do?"

"Civil law is where you've spent your life. Go for it and never look back. We'll try to refer all civil cases that come to our office."

Long pause. Then, "You mean I won't be with your firm?"

Was she kidding? After withdrawing from my defense, she thought there might be a chance I'd still want her around? When had the world suddenly started spinning in the opposite direction and where the hell had I been?

"No, Joy, you won't be with my firm. Do you have something for me to sign?"

"Yes, just sign the motion at the bottom confirming you've read and reviewed and consent."

I took up her pen and scribbled my name where indicated. Then I was done.

Without another word—there was nothing left to say—I stood and approached the door. Which I suddenly place-kicked. My big toe on my place-kicking foot snapped, and a hot pain shot up my ankle and ran up the back of my leg where the big nerves work. I fell onto my backside, and my feet rolled up and over my head. I was an upended beetle.

A trip to the infirmary and a roll of white tape around my toes later, I was returned to my cell.

"Don't do that again, Gresham," the guard advised me. "Only crazy people in flip-flops kick steel doors."

"Lesson learned," I said and entered my cell where The Wanderer was lying asleep on my top bunk. We had no pillows; his mouth had drooled onto my mattress. The entire scene was disgusting and so depressing that I sank down onto his bed and shut my eyes. I wanted to cry, but one thing you learn in your first twenty-four is there is no crying in prison. If you cry you die. You'll never be left alone again. Simple rule, like most prison rules.

That night, after the second meal of the day, I paid twenty dollars to use a smuggled cell phone from four cells down. The owner said I had bought just two minutes of airtime. Each minute after that was another twenty bucks, take it or leave it. I took it.

Arnie's number was committed to memory. While his medications changed every ninety days or so, his office phone number never did change. I knew I would catch him still in his office, the first home of the world-class litigator. He answered on the second ring.

"Arnie? Michael. I'm in jail."

"Where?"

"D.C. Jail."

"I'm on my way."

The phone was passed back to its owner hand-over-hand outside the bars.

"Hey!" I shouted. "Is there a refund? I only talked five seconds."

"Fuck you, Gresham! I'll refund your ass, boy!"

But I slept gloriously that night, taking care to avoid The Wanderer's drool spot.

Arnie was on the way.

46

Situated beside a small, spouting pond in Quantico, Virginia was the FBI Laboratory. Marcel had made an appointment. Now he pulled up to the building on the street side and pulled into Visitor's Parking. Getting an "in" with the FBI had required the help of a lawyer inside the U.S. Attorney's office.

That lawyer was none other than Antonia Xiang, the long-ago friend of Michael Gresham's who had just prosecuted him. Antonia had agreed in the first instance to prosecute her friend for one reason and one reason only: as the prosecutor she held all power over the case. And it was she who would ultimately decide—if Michael were convicted—on whether the government would be seeking the death penalty. Antonia had purposely taken on the case to ensure that never happened: her friend would never be exposed to the possibility of death being imposed because Antonia had refrained from making the death penalty an issue in the case.

But Michael didn't recognize this. All along he had felt betrayed by Antonia. With her working beside him, Michael had saved Antonia's husband—the abandoned CIA agent—from the firing squad in Moscow. Now she was returning the good deed. The entire dynamic was that simple—supported by the fact that both she and Rusty loved Michael.

So when Marcel approached Antonia for help in getting the video enhanced, the video he had lifted from the nail palace, he had done with a plea to her that justice required she join him in a request to the FBI that the video help was given. It required a law enforcement officer to convince the FBI to take on a criminal case, and it was in Antonia's name—and by the inherent power in her work as a U.S. Attorney—that the request was made. Assistant U.S. Attorney's from D.C. made such requests every day of the week. Antonia's application for video analysis slid right in without resistance from the crime lab.

"Just enhance the video and tell me what you can about the police officer and his SUV in the video."

The photographic analyst indicated he understood what she wanted and he began computerized-enhancement of the video that next morning. Marcel—at Antonia's request as well—joined the analyst and her team as the video underwent FBI scrutiny. In the end, some key facts became known to the FBI and Marcel and, indirectly, to Antonia.

First, the SUV was, in fact, a Toyota Highlander. Next, the license plate was easily readable once enhancement techniques were applied. It was a simple matter to then trace the registered owner of the vehicle. His name astonished Antonia; not so much Marcel.

The owner of the vehicle was Niles Boudreaux. But who was dressed as a police officer and driving the Toyota?

The FBI's help didn't end there. At one moment in the video, as the same "police officer" was leaving the Foggy Bottom Grocery and returning to the Toyota, his left hand became prominently displayed. Enhancement revealed that he was wearing on that hand a college class ring from Niles' law school, Harvard University. Embedded in the ring was a Harvard crimson shield emblazoned with the Harvard motto: "Veritas," Latin for "Truth."

Marcel and Antonia met at a small coffee shop north of the Capitol that night. He presented the FBI's findings to her.

"The Toyota is registered to Niles Boudreaux," Marcel began by way of summary, "and the class ring is a Harvard class ring from the same school where Boudreaux attended law school."

"And that's Boudreaux wearing the police uniform?"

"Facial recognition software couldn't get a clear enough read to make an identification positively. But it did reveal one other thing."

"Which is?"

"The phony cop isn't wearing a shield on his uniform. There's no badge."

"No cop would ever be caught dead without his shield," Antonia added. "The guy's wearing a total disguise."

"I guess that if you were to execute a search warrant on Boudreaux's house, you would find a police uniform and no badge."

"Sorry, can't do that. No search warrants on the U.S. Attorney."

"Why not?"

Antonia slowly turned her coffee cup in its saucer. "Why? One, because I think the class ring and the Toyota license plate give us enough to work with. And two, because Boudreaux is smarter than all of us. He wouldn't hang onto a uniform he'd worn to a murder. He's way down the road on that, Marcel. So, if we executed a search warrant, we would be generating evidence for his defense: his lawyer could point to the fact we'd searched his house and could find no evidence of the murder of Linda Burrows. That's a setup, and I don't want to do it. That makes it just that much easier for him to defend himself."

"Good thinking," Marcel said after letting her words set in. "We don't need to create evidence for the little bastard. So," he said, indicating to the waitress that he'd like a refill on his iced drink, "where does that leave us?"

She shook her head and held eye contact with Marcel.

"It leaves us where I've put the wrong guy in jail. Marcel, we now have twenty-four hours for Michael to file a motion for a new trial. Tomorrow is the fourteenth day since his conviction. It's got to be done, or Michael will forever lose the opportunity to bring this new evidence to the attention of the court. Will Joy be filing?"

"Joy's off the case. Michael's brother, Arnie, has flown in to help. He's waiting at the hotel right now for me to bring him the results of the video enhancement. What can I tell him about your position on the case as the prosecutor?"

She drew a deep breath. She knew, from the moment she agreed to the meeting that night with Marcel, that it would come to this time. She was on the spot to make a decision. Her friendship with Michael demanded it; however, her role as a justice-seeking prosecutor demanded it tenfold: prosecutors aren't supposed to send the wrong people to prison. And when they do they must clean up after themselves, make it right, do whatever justice required.

She exhaled slowly.

"Tell Arnie the government will join in the motion for a new trial."

"And then?"

"And then I'm going to indict Niles Boudreaux on one count of murder and in the same hour I'm going to dismiss the case against Michael with prejudice."

Marcel sat back. He didn't gloat, didn't smile, but inside he was exulting.

He had done it.

47

Arnie was itching terribly in court two weeks later. He thought it might be a new med they had him on. Or, on the other hand, it might be plain old nerves. Because sitting beside him at the defense table was me, his brother, Michael, all decked out in my favorite pinstriped suit provided by Verona from my closet, and the new, hastily starched and pressed button-down white shirt and foulard tie Arnie had picked out for me to wear.

Judge Frisson was running late. I glanced over at the table beside us. Antonia Xiang was sitting there alone—FBI Special Agent Jack Ames was not inside the room. It occurred to me that Ames and Longstreet were probably not all that pleased with the development of the video evidence on a case they had helped put together against me without scouring the retail outlets around the Foggy Bottom Mall and reviewing all video. Antonia would later tell me that as we waited for the judge that day, the two FBI agents were even then trying to explain to the Internal Affairs investigator just why they hadn't done so. Ames was forced to give up his partner, Marty Longstreet, and Marty was prepared to take one for the team. Longstreet told the IA man that he had thought the Metro

Police through Ronald Holt were performing the door-to-door review of all video evidence. But, in the end, it was Longstreet who hadn't followed up with Holt to ensure the video reviews were completed.

"We're not perfect," Longstreet offered his supervisor by way of explanation.

The supervisor—a cold, company man who'd worked Internal Affairs at the FBI for a dozen years and had heard every conceivable excuse from the very bright agents at the FBI—wasn't impressed with Longstreet's, "We're not perfect."

He set aside his investigative file and slowly released its cover before replying to Longstreet, who sat across from him at his desk in the District. Then he spoke.

"Yes, we are."

That was all he said, "Yes, we are perfect."

Then he added, "The American people deserve no less."

Longstreet was suspended with half-pay for ninety days.

JUDGE FRISSON MADE short shrift of the motion for a new trial—granted without comment—and of course, Frisson could only order that the case be dismissed with prejudice once Antonia had placed on the record her reasons for dismissing.

A day later, I was led out of the cell I shared with The Wanderer and taken to the Discharge officers. They returned my clothing and personal effects. They ignored me as I walked out the doors that led outside, to the parking area.

There, in his Ram truck, waited Marcel. As I approached, he leaned over and threw open the passenger door.

"Hop in, counselor," he said with one of the rare smiles I'd ever seen on my best friend's face. "Let's blow this popcorn stand."

I settled into the passenger's seat and fastened my seat belt.

He nodded with approval at the click.

"Don't want to get stopped by the cops for not wearing a seat belt now, do we pard?"

I smiled and avoided looking back at the D.C. Jail.

"Never again," I whispered as the tears of relief washed over my eyes.

He reached across and punched my shoulder.

"How about we go see your family?"

"How about?" I said and closed my eyes as we pulled out of the lot.

48

The president had no alternative except to fire Niles Boudreaux after his indictment for murder. A new U.S. Attorney was appointed from out of the ranks of the existing office staff—but it wasn't Antonia who got the job. In fact, the new U.S. Attorney transferred her to the team prosecuting local misdemeanors—a huge demotion—within a half-hour of taking the oath of office as the chief law enforcement officer for the District of Columbia. Without a word to anyone, she removed her few personal items from the building.

Then she drove straight to my new offices.

I was waiting when she came in.

"They transferred me to misdemeanors," she said, striding confidently into my office and taking a seat without being asked.

Misdemeanor prosecutions. I knew exactly what that meant.

She looked around. "Where's my office?"

"Let's not jump the gun," I said. "The USAO fits you very nicely. You were born to prosecute."

"Horseshit. Where's my office?"

Her look was fixed on her face. She wasn't going back.

"Up to you," I said, "choose one. Tell Tammy what furniture you want."

"You mean am I a French Provincial girl? A little bird told me there's an empty office already furnished with it. That works for me."

Just then Annie strode in and she took the seat beside Antonia without acknowledging either one of us.

"Marcel told me what you did," I said to Annie. "Thank God for you."

"It was nothing, Michael. I just knew there had to be video from the other stores."

"Really? In all of your days as a criminal profiler, what led you to believe there was more video?"

My daughter crossed one leg over the other and loudly popped her bubble gum.

"Get with it, Michael. This is America. You can't go outside without some video camera, someplace, recording your every move. All I did was remind Marcel that he should go look."

"Well, you saved your dad. All my thanks, Daughter."

She blew a bubble with her Dubble Bubble.

"What did Verona tell you about bubble gum?" I asked her out-of-the-blue, always the dad looking out for his kids. Especially those who eat coins and quarters.

"Please, Michael, I'm way down the road on the ingestion of foreign objects."

I shook my head. "Not good enough. What did she tell you?"

She looked just then like every teenager ever forced to recite a rule she didn't wholly ascribe to.

"She told me not to swallow it."

"All right. Good on you."

"Well, Michael," Antonia said, "Marcel's waiting downstairs with your car. Verona's with him."

"Then let's not hesitate," I said.

"Where are we going?" Annie asked.

I smiled at her; it was the happiest smile I'd enjoyed in months. "We're going to the H. Carl Moultrie Courthouse. We have an appointment with Judge Honoré Frisson at noon straight up."

"God, Michael, you're not in trouble again?" Annie asked.

"No, honey, not that kind of trouble, anyway."

"Well, what kind?" Annie persisted.

"The marrying kind," Antonia said. "The marrying kind."

Annie's expression changed. She might even have smiled, but it was hard to tell. "She finally said yes?"

I shrugged. "What can I say? Even the mangiest dog has his day."

I didn't bother turning out the lights when we left my office.

I'd be back. Yes, there would be ten days in Maui first and a week in Moscow while Marcel watched our kids.

But I'd be back. After that, who could say? Deep inside me was the nagging feeling that I hadn't finished being a prosecutor yet.

But this was no time to think about that.

I had a marriage ceremony to attend.

EPILOGUE

Sergey died two weeks after we reached Russia. It was a peaceful passing but Verona was shattered and who wouldn't be? Sergey was twenty-one when he passed, leaving Katya, his wife, who was very pregnant. Verona and I funded a trust for the newborn that would give him a start in life. We did the same for Katya. She planned to bring the baby to us for a visit when he turned one.

When we returned to the states we learned Antonia had been re-hired at the U.S. Attorney's Office, a development she explained to me in a long, hand-written letter she left sealed on my desk. In it, she revealed that the new U.S. Attorney of D.C. had called her into his office with fresh news about my case. It seemed that Niles Boudreaux had confessed to murdering Linda Burrows in return for the USAO taking the death penalty off the table. And there was another thing, something that had puzzled me all the way through. Agnes Streith had been arrested and charged with perjury. Boudreaux, in his confession, admitted to bribing the young woman to commit perjury and say it was me who she'd seen pump two more bullets into Linda. I was present at her sentencing when she broke down and admitted it was her boyfriend, a biker, who had stopped my car while posing as a cop and shot me. The shot was meant to kill me, and the gun he left behind was intended to prove I was Linda's killer. Boudreaux admitted to the police he had hidden the weapon in a locker at the bus station. It was simple, then, for the boyfriend to plant the gun in my dead hand.

Except I didn't die.

Boudreaux' sentencing is next week. I have been asked by the court to attend the sentencing and make my recommendation. Boudreaux should hope a nor'easter blows up before then and sends me and my boat to the bottom of the Potomac River.

Annie surprised us by ingesting plasticware that came with a dinner delivery while we were gone. The surgeon removed a plastic knife, fork, and spoon from her stomach. Yet another surgery. Her psychiatrist was called in. She recommended that we place Annie in a setting where there would be eyes on her 24/7. Verona and I are still discussing this. What other choice do we have? We're looking into what's out there. So far, it isn't much.

As for me, I'm now teaching Criminal Procedure at Georgetown Law. The practice of law has lost its luster for me, and I avoid the office whenever possible. Feeling the heat through the gates of hell will do that to a person.

BELIEVE IT OR NOT, I'm thinking of writing a book. Maybe one about a World War Two spy. She'll depart the Russian Front and infiltrate the Nazi hordes threatening to overrun her beloved Russia. She will have to be strong-willed and capable of setting aside normal human reactions--such as staying on even though her lover has cheated on her. She would thus transcend her humanness for the greater good. She will also have to be beautiful, highly educated, and in love with me. And I with her.

Her name will be Verona.

THE END

ALSO BY JOHN ELLSWORTH

THADDEUS MURFEE PREQUEL

A Young Lawyer's Story

THADDEUS MURFEE SERIES

The Defendants

Beyond a Reasonable Death

Attorney at Large

Chase, the Bad Baby

Defending Turquoise

The Mental Case

Unspeakable Prayers

The Girl Who Wrote The New York Times Bestseller

The Trial Lawyer (A Small Death)

The Near Death Experience

Flagstaff Station

SISTERS IN LAW SERIES

Frat Party: Sisters In Law

Hellfire: Sisters In Law

MICHAEL GRESHAM PREQUEL

Lies She Never Told Me

MICHAEL GRESHAM SERIES

The Lawyer

Secrets Girls Keep

The Law Partners

Carlos the Ant

Sakharov the Bear

Annie's Verdict

Dead Lawyer on Aisle 11

30 Days of Justis

The Fifth Justice

PSYCHOLOGICAL THRILLERS

The Empty Place at the Table

ABOUT THE AUTHOR

For thirty years John defended criminal clients across the United States. He defended cases ranging from shoplifting to First Degree Murder to RICO to Tax Evasion, and has gone to jury trial on hundreds. His first book, *The Defendants*, was published in January, 2014. John is presently at work on his 25th thriller.

Reception to John's books has been phenomenal; more than 2,000,000 have been downloaded in 60 months. All are Amazon bestsellers. He is an Amazon All-Star every month and is a *U.S.A Today* bestseller.

John Ellsworth lives in Arizona in the mountains and in California on the beach. He has three dogs that ignore him but worship his wife, and bark day and night until another home must be abandoned in yet another move.

johnellsworthbooks.com
johnellsworthbooks@gmail.com

CPSIA information can be obtained
at www.ICGtesting.com
Printed in the USA
LVHW022015071019
633407LV00001B/47/P